My Enemy's Enemy

Barrie Hyde

Pearce Publishing

𝒫𝒫

To the family

and Nev

Thanks for your support

Also by Barrie Hyde

A Higher Authority

The Organisation

The Organisation works closely with NATO, but they're not part of the CIA, MI6 or indeed any national security agency. They are however funded legitimately through government sources from around the world, but nobody would admit to it.

Surveillance is part of their work, tracking and interviewing terrorists, working in political hotspots, dealing with the Mafia, drug barons, business despots, in fact anyone with a track record of not playing it straight. Their job is to take these people out by fair means or foul, but quietly.

Chapter 1

For six months I'd either been drunk or stoned, often both. I was a complete mess, a lost soul with no direction or purpose. Sitting on the deck of a scruffy houseboat just outside Amsterdam I gazed into the void that had become my life. Replaying the scene for the twentieth time since waking I vaguely wondered how often I'd done that since it happened. I neither knew nor cared.

It was early spring and although the sun shone weakly ice could be seen on the rails above the deck. I became vaguely aware of someone walking along the tow path.

'I believe they call you Jonathan.'

I turned my head and half nodded.

'Caroline,' I said, feeling a little startled as I looked at her. She'd become a close friend at one point. *What the hell is she doing here?* I thought, *I really don't need her platitudes or sympathy.*

'Can I come aboard?'

She was smiling and looked so pretty, wearing a duffel coat, scarf and bobble hat.

'Yeah, why not,' I said sighing.

She climbed up and gave me a hug.

I held her tight and closed my eyes.

'I'm so sorry,' she whispered, 'You don't deserve this.'

Pulling away she looked at me, 'My God you're in a real state. When did you last wash?'

'The facilities aren't too good here.'

We sat down and holding my hand she said, 'What are we going to do with you?' I could see the concern in her eyes.

'I don't know and if I'm honest, I don't care.'

'I do,' replied Caroline, 'You helped me when I was down, now it's my turn.'

I shook my head.

We sat quietly for a few moments, 'How are the kids?' I asked.

'They're fine thanks, it was Jake's birthday last week, we had fifteen over for a party, total mayhem. Jamie's becoming quite the little man; he bosses his older brother around all the time.'

'That's nice,' I said half smiling for the first time in months, 'I told you things would work out.'

'And they will for you,' she said squeezing my arm. 'There's a lot of people rooting for you Jonathan.'

'Why are you here?'

'Since we last spoke I've been doing a fair amount of work for The Organisation. Not full time and nothing of any great significance. Courier work mainly, meeting and transporting people, organising hotels, accommodation, that sort of thing. They pay well, and they're good people.'

I looked at her, 'You know they are,' she said, 'they look after their own.'

I put my head in my hands, 'They didn't look after Zan, Frank or John and God knows who else.'

'I know how you feel, and Mark knows, he told me everything.'

'Is he your boss now?'

'No, I report into the UK Head of Operations, but Mark came to see me and explained what had happened. He desperately wants you back, but he says you won't talk to him.'

'What's the point?' I said standing up and walking across to the side of the boat, 'I've nothing to give, I can't do it anymore, I'm sorry.'

Caroline followed and put her arm around me.

'He needs you Jonathan.'

'Why? I'm just a liability.'

She looked at me, I could tell she had something to say, it was as if she didn't quite know how to phrase it.

Hesitating she spoke, 'The girl I knew as Josephina, you call her Caterina, she's in trouble.'

'What's happened?'

'After the shooting she recovered well, to the point where she was fit enough to go back into the field. She was assigned a role in Zambola, it's a small country in Central Africa, an old French colony, I'd never heard of it,' she paused.

'Go on.'

'She's disappeared Jonathan, there's no trace of her.'

'Oh bloody hell,' I said, 'And you say they look after their own, do they hell.'

'We've got to find her Jonathan, I don't know her as well as you, but I do know she's a thoroughly decent person who needs help from her friends.'

'So why are you telling me this?'

'Mark wants you to go out there.'

'No' I screamed, 'I told you, I can't do it anymore, why me?'

'Because you know and care for her, because you speak French, because maybe you'll try just that bit harder than others, because it's personal.'

I stared at her shaking my head. 'So what do you propose I do?' I asked with more than a hint of sarcasm.

'You join a Christian Missionary that has a base in the capital Kanina.'

'What was Caterina doing there?' I thought of the gorgeous Latino from Argentina. She had one of the sharpest minds I'd ever come across and an incredible sense of humour. I could feel myself getting sucked in, and I hated it.

'The Chinese are investing heavily, rebuilding the economy after a dreadful civil war that destroyed the infrastructure. She got a job with The National Mining Company setting up computer systems for them.'

'Yes, but why was she there?'

'To find out what the Chinese are up to.'

'Maybe they should have googled it.' I said drily, 'They're investing billions right across Africa.'

'You need to speak to Mark, he'll give you the inside track.'

'I don't need to speak to anyone,' I replied angrily. 'The Organisation have fucked up again and they want me to dig them out.'

'This isn't The Organisation' replied Caroline with just a touch of irritation, 'This is Caterina, I thought she was your friend.'

'Yes she is my friend, a very good friend, and I care for her deeply. For your information, I saved her life once.'

'Oh does that mean you can't help her again?'

I could feel the anger subsiding.

'Don't be so pompous Jonathan, she needs your help, what would Zan have said?'

'That's below the belt.'

'Well, maybe it needs to be, to knock a bit of sense into you.'

We glared at each other.

'Jonathan, I know you've been hurt, but there comes a point when you have to start living again and your friend needs help.'

I looked upwards and breathed out slowly.

'Look' she said, 'Come back to the hotel, clean yourself up and let me buy you a meal. It can't do any harm to talk.'

'And I suppose The Organisation will have a nice set of new clothes waiting for me,' I replied acerbically.

'Is that such a bad thing?' she took me by the hand, 'Come on, remember the dead but life is for the living. Help Caterina, please.'

I shook my head slowly, 'Let's go and eat,' I said in a resigned manner.

Chapter 2

The simple fact was that the love of my life, my fiancé had been blown away by a couple of thugs and I'd been left with nothing. To make matters worse, she told me as she died that she wasn't the person I thought.

Zan had been my colleague, friend and lover working for an operation known as The Organisation. Sponsored by governments from around the world, its aim, to sort out the bad guys when governments couldn't get at them legitimately. We'd been together on an operation finding out how a company had grown at lightening speed. Having discovered it was a cover for drug running and money laundering we disappeared, but they found us, and killed her.

As she lay dying she told me that she was involved with the Chinese Triads. She'd joined The Organisation to find out what their intentions were towards her own people. She was quite simply a double agent and I'd fallen for her hook, line and sinker.

I tried to hate her because she hadn't been straight. But I couldn't, despite everything I knew she loved me, and I loved her. We'd planned to leave the Organisation and spend the rest of our days together. I believe she thought that by getting out her treachery would never be discovered and we could live happily ever after. A single bullet put paid to that.

****

We climbed down from the boat and made our way along the tow path. Conversation was polite but stilted. I was limping slightly having been shot when Zan was killed. Only I lived, and she didn't.

'How is your foot?' asked Caroline.

'The foot's OK, it's my brain that's buggered.'

Caroline held my hand again and as we approached the main road she hailed a taxi.

'Marriot please.'

'Niet de toeristische route' I continued using my best Amsterdam accent, 'I told him not to take the tourist route.'

'You speak Dutch?'

'Not fluently but I've been here a few months, it's inevitable.'

'How many languages is that?'

'God knows, ten or eleven.'

'What a wonderful gift.'

'For all the good it's done me.'

'It may just save Caterina.'

I nodded saying nothing.

We went straight up to a bedroom on the fifth floor of the hotel. As I walked in I said sadly, 'I haven't seen one of these since I was with Zan.'

Caroline looked at me, I could see pity in her eyes and I hated her for it.

'Go and shower' she said, 'I'll organise some clean clothes.'

As she left I sat on the bed feeling a little confused. I'd vowed never to get involved with The Organisation again. Yet I knew, no matter how hard I argued, I'd be going to Africa soon, I couldn't let Caterina down.

Here I was, in a decent hotel, such a contrast to the squalor I'd endured in recent months. I felt as if a veil was being lifted, I had purpose again, but I resented it. Maybe I was turning the corner, I knew I could never forget Zan, but at least this gave me a sense of direction. I felt though it was all happening too quickly and I wasn't ready to go back into the world. Sadly I knew I had no choice.

I stripped and showered. As I dried off I heard movement in the bedroom.

'There's a change of clothes on the bed together with a shaver. I'll wait for you in the lobby.'

'Thanks Caroline.'

It's amazing how a good hot shower, a shave and clean clothes can make you feel. I'd been wearing the same jeans for months and hadn't washed much. I must have stunk and felt rather embarrassed. God knows what Caroline thought.

I'd been in a black hole, but now I had a chance to re-enter the human race. I can't say I felt like my old self, I felt hollow, but at least I felt as if I was escaping a void and could start moving forward. It would be a long road and whether I could ever really find myself again I had no idea, but I had a goal to aim for. I had to find Caterina, she was my friend.

I caught the lift down to the lobby and as the doors opened I saw Caroline sitting at a table talking to someone with his back to me. The silver grey hair was a give-away. It was Mark, my mentor and trainer from The Organisation. My initial impulse was to walk straight out of the hotel and resume life on the boat. I felt anger welling up. *'Christ,'* I thought, *'I can't be the only person who could do this job, I'm not that indispensable.'*

As I looked across Mark turned round and stood. He held out his hand without moving, just looking at me. I walked across, I couldn't be bothered to play silly buggers and as I approached he grabbed me and held tight.

'Jonathan, I can't tell you how good it is to see you.'

'You look almost like the Dean I knew and loved.' Caroline said grinning. Dean had been the name I was using when I met her.

We changed identities for every mission to avoid contagion. Even Jonathan wasn't my real name. Sadly it wasn't foolproof as Zan and I discovered to her cost.

'You need a haircut though', she continued pouring coffee from a cafetiere.

'Quite the Mother hen,' I replied taking a cup and sitting next to her.

'You didn't come to see me this morning,' I said to Mark.

'I thought you might have thrown me overboard.'

I looked at him, 'I've been a bit of a pain in recent months, I apologise.'

Mark lifted his hand, 'Not necessary, you had good reason, correction, you have good reason, I realise it's not the sort of thing you can walk away from.'

I sipped my coffee, it tasted good, so different to the instant crap I'd been drinking recently.

'Tell me about Caterina,' I said looking at Mark.

'Let's have lunch first, I know a superb Indonesian close by, we can talk later.'

We walked up Hoofstraat past some upmarket shops with trams and single decker buses thundering past. Considering how long I'd been in Amsterdam I'd seen little of the city. I'd spent most of the time sitting on the boat wallowing in self-pity. Looking at the street teaming with life made me feel better in myself. It probably sounds strange but I felt as if I'd been released from a prison sentence. Caroline was the catalyst I needed to shake me out of my lethargy. I took her by the hand.

'Thanks for coming to get me.'

She squeezed my fingers and that said it all. I realised I was going to be OK, now there was hope.

As we walked into the packed restaurant the pungent scent of Indonesian spices hit me. The darkened room lit by candlelight had misted Georgian windows creating a wonderful ambience.

With deep red carpets and padded Victorian chairs to match it somehow reminded me of Dickens and The Old Curiosity Shop. The colours were such a vivid contrast to the black and white life I'd been leading recently. As I'd been snacking on garbage for months the aromas and the warmth made me feel extremely hungry.

A waiter came across and Mark gave a name. Our coats were taken and we were ushered to a table. As we sat down he said, 'May I suggest the Rijsttafel? It's about fifteen dishes of truly exotic food.'

'Sounds great,' I replied, Caroline nodded.

'And to drink?'

'Water will be fine' I said, 'I'm going to dry out for a while, I'll be quite honest, I've been hitting it pretty hard recently and if I'm coming back to work I need to straighten out a little.'

'Music to my ears' said Mark. Caroline beamed, I felt very secure in the company of good people.

The food arrived quickly and was superb. We had all sorts of amazing dishes, chicken satay, tender spicy beef, pork stew, fried rice, deep fried banana, and lots of vegetable side dishes cooked in a variety of eastern spices which somehow blended together. I probably ate twice as much as the other two put together but I was hungry.

Conversation was light, we talked mainly about Mark's experiences in the far east as a young man and Caroline's family, keeping well away from The Organisation. I thought back to an Italian restaurant Zan and I had eaten at in Sydney, Australia just a week before she was killed. We'd spoken to the owner about travelling to Fiji. It transpired he had links with the Ndrangheta, an Italian organisation similar to the Mafia. We had just been responsible for an operation severely wounding them. They had tentacles which spread across the world and the word was put out that they were looking for an Italian speaking

Englishmen travelling with a Chinese girl. The owner fed the information back and they traced us to an idyllic paradise island. Because of our stupidity she was now dead. If only we'd gone to an Indonesian that night, or at least, kept our mouths shut…

'Are you OK?' asked Caroline.

'Yeah I'm fine' I said, 'Sorry my mind was wandering a little, I'm not used to such fine cuisine and company, I can't tell you how good it is to see you guys.'

May I suggest we go back to the hotel,' said Mark. 'We can talk more openly in my room and bring you up to speed with events.'

By now it was late afternoon, cold, raining and beginning to go dark. I felt an odd sense of belonging as we walked together along the sodden street. I had a sense of vocation and wanted more than anything to help find Caterina.

'What a difference a few hours can make,' I thought. I knew that I had needed to drop out for a period of time to find a way forward. I also knew that I was far from over Zan. I doubted I ever would be, but at least I was on the road to recovery.

Chapter 3

Mark ushered us to a suite in the hotel and we sat down around a small dining room table.

'Okay,' he said, 'the situation is this, Caterina had been working at The National Mining Company in Zambola for about four months. It was state run, been bust a couple of times and managed by fraudsters and con men. We know millions have been transferred into offshore bank accounts by directors of the company working with previous presidents of the country.

About eighteen months ago there was yet another coup, but this time the new president, Michelle Kasenga was a bit different. He'd been educated in the west, firstly at the École Nationale Supérieure des Mines de Saint-Étienne in France where he trained as a mining engineer and then Harvard Business School. He's fluent in French and English together with half a dozen Niger Congo languages.

'He's ahead of me then.' I said smiling ruefully.

'Yes but you do speak Mandarin Chinese as well as French, and this is where you could be a valuable asset.'

'Go on.'

'He's not a saint by any means, his Father, Laurent Kasenga was a ruthless dictator of the country back in the 1970s. He killed thousands of people from other tribes, ethnic cleansing at its worse. Amnesty International said in a report that entire Muslim communities were forced to flee, and thousands of Muslim civilians who didn't manage to escape were killed by government militia.

At the same time millions were siphoned across to banks in France and Switzerland. That's what paid for Michelle's education. Laurent was assassinated in 1982 and Michelle was brought up by his Mother and cohorts in France.'

'I don't remember hearing any of this,' I said.

'The French swept it under the carpet. The monies from the mining company were channelled back into France and too profitable for anyone to worry about the niceties of tribal warfare.'

'That's obscene' gasped Caroline.

'The world never gets any better,' replied Mark, 'Look at Syria, Iraq, Afghanistan and Zimbabwe to name but a few.'

'So how did Michelle gain control of the country?' I asked.

'His Mother is the power behind the throne. She was very much in control when Laurent was the leader. The puppet master, but she needed a stooge as a front because a woman would never gain power in such a society. After his death, she plotted for twenty five years to regain control. Her stooge this time was going to be Michelle. However he has her genes, cunning and intelligence. As an educated man well versed in western culture he was able to use his Mothers power base and money to take control of the army. Don't get me wrong his Mother is still very much part of the throne but Michelle is his own man. However only factions of the army came across to him and a bloody civil war ensued. Michelle eventually gained control but by then the country was in ruin. Rather than use his own money to rebuild the economy he courted the Chinese. They're investing millions in the infrastructure together with manpower and equipment.'

'What's in it for them?' I asked.

'51% of The National Mining Company and all its profits, the land is rich in diamonds, gold and oil.'

'So why does The Organisation have to get involved?'

'The Chinese are gradually taking control of Africa. Nearly all major projects are being developed by them. Within ten years they will manage at least 60% of African resources. The question is, then what? Why are they investing so much in the continent? Why not invest in the infrastructure of their own economy? Think about it, vast swathes of China are still peasant communities living life well below the poverty line and no further advanced than many of the countries they are investing in. It doesn't make sense. It's estimated eight hundred Chinese corporations are doing business in Africa with one million Chinese people living there.

We have all of fifty people spread across the continent trying to make sense of it, plus seventy five living and working in China. We're barely scratching the surface.'

'So Caterina was one of the fifty?'

Mark nodded and went on.

'The Chinese Ministry of Foreign Affairs tell us that China and Africa are making, and I quote, "Joint efforts to maintain the lawful rights of developing countries and push forward the creation of a new, fair, just political and economic order in the world".

'What does that mean?' asked Caroline.

'What indeed?' replied Mark, 'It's hogwash in my opinion. To put it into perspective, in 1980 trade between Africa and China was worth about one billion US dollars, now it's nearer 200 billion. Over one third of Chinese oil supplies come from Africa, so that's an obvious contributory factor. Africa also exports to China cotton, cocoa, coffee and fish. But, and it's a big but much of the work is done by the Chinese themselves, so in many areas jobs are being lost rather than economies enhanced.

There's a large peacekeeping Chinese military presence on the continent, again using their own people rather than training the local populace. And they provide arms at knock down prices. They've also flooded the continent with cheap Chinese consumer products. This has had the effect of accelerating the decline in industrialisation. Africa's textile industry alone lost 750,000 jobs over the last decade as a direct result.

In Senegal domestic peanut processing factories face the threat of being driven out of business as Chinese exporters buy up the crop to ship home. Beijing's money comes with its own strings: it must be spent on Chinese goods or Chinese-built infrastructure. And Chinese firms often source their supplies and workers from back home. In Ghana, tensions flared into violence when police and residents attacked Chinese gold miners, claiming they were driving locals out of the industry. Many Chinese were brutally beaten and some two hundred were deported.

They've also been supporting all sorts of disgusting regime such as Syria, Zimbabwe, and Sudan.'

Mark paused, 'In other words, it's a complete mess. At best they are twenty first century colonists, at worst they could create an economic and strategic strangle hold firstly across Africa and then what? That's what we've been trying to find out.'

'Jesus,' was all I could say.

For a second we sat and looked at each other, I felt a little stunned being back in operational mode and was having a difficulty taking it all in.

Caroline broke the silence, 'What was Caterina's role in this?'

'Very much a watching brief. Officially she was helping to build and implement a new computer system at The National Mining Company. They needed specialist expertise which could only come from Silicon Valley in California. In their normal pragmatic manner, the Chinese outsourced the development to Joteque Systems, a US company and that's where we were able to get involved. Caterina applied for a job and with her expertise was a sure fire bet to secure the role.'

21

'Did she find anything?' I asked.

Mark grimaced, 'Not really, getting close to the Chinese was proving difficult. They kept themselves to themselves, rarely socialising with Westerners. Business meeting were precise and to the point. They didn't like US interference and resented the fact they had to use American expertise. She built a bit of a relationship with one girl, a Chinese Catholic which is at best unusual. There's about twelve million Catholics in China, but out of 1.4 billion that's less than 1% of the population. Many of the bishops are state appointed without the approval of the Vatican. However, Caterina was able to build up a little rapport with the girl and even took her to a local Catholic church service. It was soon after that she disappeared.'

'When was that?'

'Just over a week ago.'

'What do we know?'

'Truthfully, nothing. The US company is threatening to pull out unless they get some news of her but the government authorities are claiming to know nothing. The Chinese are just washing their hands of the whole business.'

'Did she not have a tracker?' I asked. This was a Sat Nav system developed by The Organisation and built into a watch.

'She did, but we're not getting a signal.'

'Okay,' I said, 'So what's the plan?'

'We donate quite generously to The Christian Missionary Society – it's a non ecumenical church based in Oklahoma, established in 1872. Their aim quite simply is to spread the word across third world countries. Unlike other groups, they are quite happy to work with all Christian faiths be they Roman Catholic, Anglican, Presbyterian etc. By adopting this approach they have been successful in establishing missionary bases across Africa, the Indian sub continent, and South America. They have a programme to place graduates into missions around the world for a short period of time to help teach local kids, not just about Christianity but a rounded education programme.'

Mark paused and took a sip of water. It was pretty obvious what was coming next.

'What we'd like to do Jonathan is to place you in the mission in the capital Kanina as a language teacher and see what, if anything you can find out about Caterina's disappearance. Try and find the Chinese girl she befriended. Talk to the missionaries, the kids, their parents, anyone who may throw some light on where Caterina is being held. There are not many people in Africa who speak Mandarin, I'm sure you can use that to your advantage. It's a long shot but if I'm honest, it's the best we can do.'

'Does The Christian Missionary Society know of us?' I asked. It was amazing how quickly I had slipped back into my role.

''Let's just say some of their senior officers are very helpful when we need operational help.'

'Just one more question, I thought the Chinese contributed to The Organisation.'

'They did until about five months ago, and I'll be quite honest it's created a lot of upset. But there's been a power struggle over the past couple of years and the latest incumbents of the Central Politburo are not so keen on working with the capitalist economies of the world, and that includes Russia. So they've isolated themselves.'

'When do you want me to go?'

'Yesterday would be good,' Mark smiled, 'There's a direct flight at 23.30 from Paris tomorrow to Kinshasa. From there you can get a connection to Kanina.'

'Let's do it' I said.

Caroline stood up, walked across and put her arms around me.

'Thanks, it's good to have you back.'

Mark shook me by the hand again, 'I'll have the usual documentation delivered here tomorrow morning. Keep me in touch every step of the way; I'll be your communication officer.'

'You're coming down in the world' I joked.

Mark smiled, 'Oh no, when it comes to our own, the most senior of senior people roll up their sleeves, trust me on that one.'

He checked out of the hotel soon after. His job was done, he'd got me back on board and was heading back to headquarters in Geneva. Caroline and I went back to my room where a medium sized suitcase lay open on the bed. As usual, The Organisation had been their usual efficient selves and packed the clothes I would require for a trip to the tropics.

'They won't fit' I said, 'I've lost weight recently.'

'Well, you'll just have to put it back on again' replied Caroline, 'A few more lunches like today and they'll be too tight!'

I went over and held her hands, 'Caroline, you've given me my life back, how can I thank you?

'Oh Jonathan' she said and squeezed me tight.

This was the first time I'd been near a woman since Zan and I was suddenly aroused, what's more, she didn't pull away. We kissed, I felt alive and wanted her desperately, but I was confused and full of guilt for Zan. After a few moments I pulled away.

'Caroline,' I said, 'I can't offer you anything, I like you so much and I don't want to hurt you, but I'm not ready for a relationship yet.'

She kissed me again and whispered, 'Let's worry about relationships another day.'

I threw the suitcase on the floor and for the first time in many a month put the guilt behind me.

Several hours later I was awoken from a deep satisfying sleep by Caroline shaking me.

'I'm hungry' she said.

'Me to' I replied grabbing her, 'But not for food.'

The following morning there was a knock on the door. Caroline grinned as I rolled my eyes.

'Who is it?' I shouted.

'Hi Jonathan, I've got a package from Mark.'

'Hang on' I said as Caroline ran into the bathroom. Seconds later she threw a bath robe at me. Suitably attired I opened the door. A middle aged small man stood smiling and handed me a thick envelope.

'Safe journey' he said, and turned to go.

'Thanks,' I replied as he headed back down the corridor raising his hand in acknowledgement.

'He had a lot to say for himself' I said as Caroline reappeared from the bathroom. 'Is that the sort of thing you do? Knock on strange men's bedroom doors.'

'Well I knocked on yours,' she replied laughing as she pulled at my bathrobe.

'I thought you were hungry' I said.

'Not anymore' she responded, pushing me onto the bed.

Later that morning while Caroline was dozing I opened the envelope and looked at the travel itinerary.

'Bloody hell'. I said.

'What's the matter?'

'They've booked me on the 12.30 flight to Paris. It's nearly eleven now.'

'That's stupid you're not flying out till 11.30 tonight.'

She grabbed the itinerary and took a mobile from her bag.

'Hi Stefanie,' she said, 'You've booked Thomas Simpson on the 12.30 Amsterdam to Paris Charles de Gaulle. Can you put him on a later flight please?'

She looked at me and winked.

'18.50 or 20.30, what time do they land?, best make it the 18.50, and book me on the 19.30 to Heathrow, thanks my love, Bye.'

'Trying to get rid of me early huh,' I quipped.

'Not at all, but the later one doesn't arrive until quarter to ten which is cutting things a bit fine.'

'Such efficiency, but what are we going to do till 18.50?' I asked trying to sound as innocent as possible.

'Well, you can buy me lunch for a starter and then have a hair cut.'

'Yes but before that, I think we better make love.'

Chapter 4

Later that afternoon I checked all the contents of the envelope. There was a British passport in the name of Thomas Edward Simpson with my picture, one thousand US dollars in various denominations including about fifty single dollar bills. These would be useful for tips and purchases in Africa. I also found a couple of credit cards, a smart phone and a watch. We called the phone the 'O' phone and I knew it would be connected to the 'O'cloud, the Organisation's supposed impenetrable communication system. The watch would have a tracker built into it. I remembered it wasn't foolproof, I'd been tied up once before and couldn't access the knob to activate the system.

A note told me where to find my brief and alias on the 'O' Cloud, as usual, the attention to detail was exemplary.

After lunch and a haircut the hotel salon we got a taxi back to the houseboat to pick up my meagre belongings. The Organisation had given me a fresh alias after Zan's murder which I'd been using for the past few months.

'Better not leave the passport lying around' I said to Caroline, 'I think we need to lose that phase of my life.'

As we walked along the tow path someone shouted in Dutch.

'Hey Eric man, what have you done to yourself?'

A bearded long haired hippie in his early sixties and well overweight stood on board grinning at me.

'Jan hi, this is a friend of mine, Caroline.' I answered in English knowing that he spoke the language almost as fluently as me.

'I think I'd get my haircut for a beautiful lady like this' he said laughing, 'Where have you been hiding her?'

'It's a long story' I replied, 'but I'm leaving you mate.'

'I'd leave me for her, when are you going?'

'Now, I've just come back to get my things and then I'm away, Caroline and I have some rather urgent business to sort out.'

Jan wasn't the sort to ask too many questions so he just nodded sagely. It took all of five minutes to pack what was mine in a small rucksack and as I was leaving he gave me a bear hug.

'Hey man, you look after yourself, and that lovely lady.'

'You too, and thanks for being here for me over the last few months, I couldn't have made it without you.'

He looked at me quizzically, 'I never asked, but I know you took a hell of a beating. I hope you've found a way forward.'

'So do I, next time I'm in Amsterdam, I'll look you up.'

'I'll be here.' He paused 'Hey Caroline, you look after him, he's a good guy.'

With that we climbed down from the boat and I walked away from six months of hell.

'What's his story?' she asked.

'In that society you don't ask questions, if someone wants to talk, they tell you, Jan never bothered, All I know is that he's lived on the boat for the past thirty years and he scrapes a living by renting beds to travellers.'

I threw the rucksack into a bin. 'I won't be needing that, but I'm a bit loathed to dump the passport. I think I'd better burn it.'

'Give it to me' said Caroline, 'I can shred it when I get home.'

'I'm not the only one who's found a way forward,' I said thinking back to the girl I'd met less than a year before. She seemed like a lost soul at the time, broken marriage, two young kids and little money, 'Now you seem to have total control.'

She smiled and squeezed my hand, 'It's all down to you,' and with that she kissed me tenderly on the cheek. I hailed a taxi and we sat quietly on the way to the airport, content to be in each others company without forced conversation.

We checked in for our respective flights and sat at a coffee bar waiting to be called.

'Penny for them?,' she asked.

'I don't know,' I responded, 'I like you Caroline, I like you so much, I always did, but before, I had Zan and I very deliberately suppressed my feelings for you. I suppose in a way now I feel guilt, as if I'm betraying her for you. But it's stupid and I'm not and I want to see you again if I'm honest and yet my heads spinning, I've spent so many months wallowing in self pity and yet you've made me feel alive again. I'm confused, and I'm sorry if I've hurt you.'

She looked at me and smiled, taking my hand again she said, 'You've not hurt me you numpkin. Remember last year? I was on my own with two kids and no work. I couldn't pay the mortgage and I was totally up a gum tree. By getting me involved with The Organisation you gave me a whole new life, and hope. I like you Jonathan, I like you a lot, but I don't know if anything can come of us as a relationship. Give it time and we'll see what happens. I'm not in a hurry, are you?'

I smiled and shook my head. Looking at the monitor, I could see my flight had been called. It seemed an appropriate time to leave. I got up and felt a little embarrassed, not quite knowing what to do next. I grabbed her and we kissed passionately.

'I'll keep in touch on the 'O' phone' I said.

'Look after yourself.' We kissed again and I headed off towards the pier to catch the flight to Paris.

I sat on the plane drinking coffee. It's funny looking back, for months I'd been knocking back up to a bottle of brandy a day, smoking weed and dropping the odd tab of cocaine. Now I felt completely sober and didn't have the slightest urge to try anything stronger. I felt alive and had purpose in my life. Although I was concerned for Caterina I felt excited for what lay ahead. I picked up the 'O' phone opened it with iris recognition and read about my cover for the mission:

Thomas Edward Simpson or Tom as he liked to be called had graduated from Balliol College Oxford the previous year, the same college as I attended. I thought this could be a bit close to reality but then realised his alias had been deliberately based on my own background. Probably due to the speed the thing had been set up and to keep mistakes I could make in the future to a minimum. The main difference being that Tom was awarded a 2:1 in Modern Languages where as I'd got a first in Italian. I smiled at my own conceit. He'd become a graduate trainee with a major oil company and due to disillusionment with the commercial world decided to take a year out and teach kids in Africa. His Father was a merchant banker and he'd gone to a small public school in Bath. The brief told me about his school grades, likes and dislikes, family and the fact he was a practising Catholic. Unlike me, who'd failed in that department. However, having been a chorister as a kid I was well versed in the faith. I was to report to Father Steve McAvoy at The Christian Missionary Society in Kanina the following day.

We touched down at Paris Charles de Gaulle airport just over an hour after take off by which time I'd had enough of learning about Tom Simpson. I turned the 'O' phone off and walked through a myriad of corridors connecting international flights. Looking up at the monitor I could see the flight to Kinshasa was delayed by forty five minutes. I swore silently and prayed it wouldn't be delayed further. I then thought, 'Why worry, am I in a hurry?' I decided I was, Caterina needed help so I had an excuse to feel pissed off with the airline's lack of efficiency.

Eventually, the flight was called and I was astonished at the number of people boarding. The plane was packed and I found myself sitting in a window seat with quite a dapper looking African in his mid thirties next to me. He was smartly dressed wearing a sharp suit, shirt and tie. I smiled and he spoke in French.

'What takes you to Kinshasa?'

I replied in the same language, 'I graduated last year from university and I'm now taking a sabbatical to teach at The Christian Missionary Society school in Kanina.'

'Mon Dieu' was the response as the man's eyes rolled back, 'That's bandit country, why there?'

'I just wanted to do something useful with my life before I'm too old.' I was warming to this conversation as it gave me a good opportunity to test my brief.

'What do you do?' I asked.

'I work for the Banque Congolaise in the International department, setting up credit lines for companies, that sort of thing.'

'I thought most of the funding came from the Chinese these days.'

'You're well informed,' he eyed me suspiciously.

'I read the newspapers.'

'Well you're not far wrong, but we've been in Paris keeping old alliances alive, we're never too sure how long the Chinese are going to stay.'

I don't know what it was, but this man was a bit too glib for me. The line *smooth operator* comes to mind when I think of him. He had all the answers. For example, I said to him:

'I'd have thought an international banker would be flying first class.'

'Normally I would, but my boss got the last seat on the plane, so I'm here with you. Shall we get a drink?'

He had a nasty habit of changing the subject whenever it came to detail. I tried to dig for information on Zambola but his answers told me little. It became obvious that he knew less about the country than me. I decided I could trust him as far as the seat on the other side of the aisle. He was a total show off, telling me all about his achievements in business and with women. With the training in banking that The Organisation had given me I could see that in reality he was little more than a clerk and I realised quickly that he was probably a courier and nothing more. He was a great talker and asked little which was disappointing as I really wanted to test out my alias. As the drinks were complimentary he ordered two miniatures of Scotch at a time and very regularly so after about an hour and a half he was totally pissed and almost comatose. That suited me so I settled down as best I could and dozed for several hours.

Fortunately, the flight only took about eight hours so by the time my drunken friend had woken from his slumber we had breakfast and it was almost time to get off. He insisted I took his card, Jacob Mazanwa, International Vice President. *Titles come cheap*, I thought.

As we stepped down from the plane I felt the warmth of Africa hit me. It was only about 7.30 in the morning but the temperature had already climbed to the mid twenties centigrade and there was a pleasant level of humidity. A darn sight more agreeable than freezing on an Amsterdam houseboat, I mused. Looking around there was no sign of my banker friend, he'd obviously used a few dollars to help speed his entry into the country.

The airport looked dishevelled, still using the infrastructure built by the Belgians during the colonial era back in the 50s, A bus of a similar vintage took us to the run down two story terminal building and I followed the international transfer signs to the waiting area where an old TV screen gave me the news I was half expecting. The flight to Kanina was delayed by four hours.

I sighed and looked around. Hard plastic seats surrounded me and a small kiosk stood at the far end of the room. I walked across, more for something to do rather than having any intention of buying. Stale looking jambons and croissants were on offer along with coffee, bottled beer and water. No refrigeration could be seen and the thought of a curled up sandwich and warm beer turned my stomach.

Dozens of people, mainly men were dotted around the transit lounge, some sitting, others standing, several asleep lying across three seater airport chairs I was the only white and must have stuck out like a sore thumb. Sitting down, I pulled out my 'O' phone and was rather surprised that I had a signal. I re-read my brief and by then was becoming more than comfortable with Tom Simpson.

I thought long and hard about how I was going to find Caterina. I didn't have much to go on but the Chinese girl who attended church seemed like an obvious starting point. With luck, the missionaries would give me some direction. I stood gazing at the desolate airport through a large dirty window. Being in the international departure lounge there was little else to do as there was nowhere to go. A couple of old planes stood motionless on the tarmac, one was being refuelled but apart from that the place looked deserted.

I picked up a local newspaper lying on a seat - *The Congo Indèpendent*. It had all the platitudes to the government you'd expect together with stories of rape, corruption and a fine coverage of the European sports scene. Obviously football was big here and there were in depth articles about the week's European Cup matches.

Chapter 5

After what seemed like an eternity, the flight was called and dozens of people rose as one. They stood in line waiting for the ticket inspection and at the last moment I followed, joining the remnants of the queue. We were shepherded onto another bus and taken to an old Boeing 727. I wondered if this would pass any flight tests outside of Africa and questioned its ability to take off. *In for a penny*, I thought as I ascended the steps.

The stench was revolting. Cleanliness and Air Zambola didn't go hand in hand and once again I questioned the air worthiness of the plane. For a second time I'd been given a window seat and a middle aged man wearing a scruffy suit came and sat by the aisle leaving a gap between us.

Once on board, the air crew seemed surprisingly efficient and less than an hour later we touched down in Kanina. This is where the frustrations began. The queue through immigration stretched for an eternity and a silly little man ran up and down shouting 'Ne pas utiliser les mobiles' – Do not use mobiles.

I surreptitiously turned mine on, just to be bloody minded, but there was no signal. I smiled at the ridiculousness of it all.

I thought about the situation I was in, a few months ago I would have been climbing up the walls, pushing to move things along, now I actually felt quite relaxed, I was in no hurry and what's more, I couldn't do much to change the situation. Caterina would have to wait, it wasn't a case of callousness, just reality.

After an hour and forty five minutes I walked over the painted white line and stood at the kiosk where a vicious looking man in his early thirties glared at me.

34

'Purpose of visit?' he snarled in French.

'Teacher at The Christian Mission.'

'We don't need English teachers' he replied sarcastically.

'What about Mandarin Chinese?' I responded politely, eye balling him. He stamped my passport and threw it back at me.

'*Welcome to Zambola*' I thought.

I walked out into the main concourse where there was the usual throb of humanity shouting and waving name plates.

'Taxi, vous voulez un taxi?'

I looked around and there was a greasy looking man with teeth missing smiling at me.

'How much to The Christian Mission in Kanina?' I asked in French.

'One hundred dollars US.'

'Va te faire' I responded – 'Fuck off', and started to walk. I had a thing about taxi drivers the world over.

'Non non non Monsieur, eighty dollars.'

'Forty' I said continuing to walk.

'Sixty.'

We agreed on fifty and I followed him to an old Renault Megane which had seen much better days. I climbed in the back and he locked the doors as we set off.

'Pour la protection,' he said, as we sped away from the airport complex at break neck speed. The journey into town took nearly an hour and the squalor was as bad as anything I had ever seen. Shanty town followed shanty town with kids begging on the streets in front of squalid bars and ramshackle shops. I saw what looked like large families living in shacks made from mud, corrugated iron and rubbish. The refuse was piled everywhere obviously creating disease and death. The smell of pit latrines permeated into the taxi making me want to heave. Life was obviously cheap here and death just an everyday event.

Having been bumped and tossed on the decrepit and dilapidated roads, we approached the town centre. The infrastructure looked a little better, with a real feeling of France, patisseries and boulangeries adorned the streets. There were French road signs, markets, a gendarmerie and a very smart Hotel de Ville which stood in the main square. There was also plenty of fresh food on sale in the market with crowds of people bartering for their purchases, such a contrast to what I had seen just a few miles away.

The driver pulled up on a side road which looked straight out of the left bank of Paris. Buildings with art décor façades, Gothic architecture and a church with a large bell tower dominated the street. Money had obviously been spent recently on the infrastructure. No doubt paid for by the Chinese using Chinese workers and equipment. The driver pointed at two big heavy doors to the side of the church where several beggars sat, including a couple of young children, their eyes devoid of life.

A small sign had been erected above the doors - The Christian Missionary Society. I walked past the beggars and a couple of them grabbed me by the leg, I pulled away and pressed a big old fashioned white door bell. The door was opened almost immediately by an elderly black lady dressed in a long flowing blue and white robe. I didn't think she was a nun, this was obviously some sort of uniform.

'Bonjour' I said 'Je m'appelle Tom Simpson. Je suis ici pour voir Father Steve McAvoy.'

'Entrez Monsieur' her French spoken with an obvious African intonation.

I followed her into a hall, it was dark and musty with a wide staircase rising up from the centre. Corridors peeled off on either side and several doors could be seen together with heavy baroque furniture. There was a real feeling of peace here, such a contrast to the squalor I had recently driven through.

'Un instant s'il vous plait' she said turning and walking down the corridor. Knocking on a door, she opened it and disappeared into a room. Several moments later a tall overweight white man appeared. He had flowing grey hair and his demeanour gave him an instant air of authority. He was in his late sixties and wore a black cassock with a white dog collar.

'Hi Tom,' he said shaking my hand. 'I'm Father Steve, come and have tea, I'm sure you can use some after your journey'.

He was one of those people you liked instantly, with a twinkle in his eye you could see kindness exuding from every pore.

'You're obviously American' I said.

'Colorado' he boomed, 'but I haven't seen the place for over forty years. Spent most of my life in Africa, trying to help the poor people left here after the great colonials pulled out. That's where I picked up these ancient and quaint traditions like tea in the afternoon. You Europeans left many cultural niceties, it's a pity you couldn't have left a decent education system.'

'Sorry,' I responded not being quite sure what to say.

Father Steve guffawed, 'I'm not blaming you personally, take a seat.'

He ushered me into his office, or library I should really say. Every wall was covered in books. Scanning them quickly I could see there were works on Christianity, Judaism, Islam, together with many other faiths and religions These were mixed up with Harry Potter, John Steinbeck, Stephen King and Dan Brown.

'Eclectic mix' I said.

'They keep my mind alert,' he replied, 'TVs not up to much, and the locals' conversation leaves a lot to be desired.'

I sat in front of a huge desk covered in paper. I guessed he was the sort of man who could lay his hands on any document buried deep in the clutter.

'So you're here to teach languages I gather.'

'Happy to do so, are there any you would like me to focus on?'

'What have you got in mind?'

'French, English and Mandarin Chinese.'

He looked me straight in the eye, 'Bright boy.'

'A gift I'd like to share with others less fortunate.'

'In return for what?'

It was as if his eyes were now penetrating deep into my soul. He was no fool and I pondered how much I should tell him. My mind went into overdrive, '*Is he on our side, Should I take him into my confidence, Is he a stooge for the regime?*'

I then thought, '*He knows the territory, he understands the politics, he'll know we support his society and finally, where the hell else do I start?*' With that, I answered his question.

'I'm looking for a friend who's disappeared.'

'And you think that because your organisation throws a few dollars at the Mission we should be at your beck and call?'

'I'd have thought you would want to help a fellow Catholic who's in trouble.'

He glared at me for a second but at that point the tea arrived breaking the tension. The old lady pushed through the door holding a tray and placed it on a side table. She poured from a pewter pot into two bone china cups and after Father Steve shuffled a few papers out of the way she put a milk jug and sugar bowl on his desk. She then ceremoniously handed me a cup and finally with a flourish put two slices of Battenberg cake in front of me.

'Tuck in' said Father Steve helping himself to some cake as she left the room.

'Would you help her if she was in trouble?' I asked.

'Unnecessary,' came the simple response.

I took a sip of tea and Father Steve chewed on his cake staring at me. I felt as if I was at the OK Corral, the young gun slinger facing up to the wise old prospector.

'Trying to keep the so called authorities on side here is a nightmare' he said, 'They hate Christianity and all it stands for. Although Kasenga our illustrious leader was educated in France and brought up a Catholic he and his Mother are too politically shrewd to admit that. To the locals he practices Yoruba a traditional African religion. That's a whole different debate and I could spend several hours bringing you up to speed. Suffice to say it holds that all human beings possess what is known as "Àyànmô" that is destiny or fate and they're expected to eventually become one in spirit with Olódùmarè, the divine creator and source of all energy. Furthermore, the thoughts and actions of each person in Ayé, the physical realm interact with all other living things, including the Earth itself.'

'I can see where Avatar got its ideas from' I said.

He nodded sagely and poured some milk into his cup. I sat waiting to see where this was going. He took a sip and went on.

'If I'm seen helping America or any of its cohorts the mission here is finished, and I can't allow that. We do too much good work. Not just selling religion but children's education, health and sex education, and believe me with the spread of Aids that is a crucial one. Farming, there's no point in giving people food, that's just false hope and false promise. We have to teach them how to grow the food. There's also no point in just handing over a tractor. Communities need to learn how to use and share them. The trouble is the great charities give away all sorts of farming equipment and before long it's either stolen or wrecked by ineptitude and greed. These people have to begin to appreciate the value of this stuff. It's an impossible conundrum, but at least by being in situ we can help control the forces of evil and give people the two things they need – hope and education.'

'So what do you propose?' I asked.

'I propose nothing, as far as I'm concerned for the next few months you are here to teach kids foreign languages. What you do beyond that is down to you. As for your friend, I can't and won't help. I'm sorry.'

'Where the hell do I start?' I asked feeling exasperated.

'Oh I can talk in generalities' he replied grinning, 'and happy to do so. Firstly there's La Maison, the expat bar, it's hardly what you'd expect from Empire days, but you'll meet the few Westerners who live and work here.'

'What about the Chinese?'

'Difficult one, they live in their own communes and are rarely seen outside. Nearly everything is imported from China and they are totally self sufficient. That is one of the big bug bears, they don't really contribute to the local economies.'

I thought of the Chinese girl Caterina had befriended.

'There is a small Christian community In China, do any of them go to Church locally'

'You're well informed, and funnily enough a Chinese lady has been coming to my Church in recent weeks.' He went silent for a few moments. 'She came with a Spanish girl, but last weeks she was on her own.' He paused again and I could almost hear the cogs turning in his brain, 'The Spanish girl, is she your friend?'

I nodded and he lowered his head, as if in prayer. He suddenly looked ashen, the shock of realising that he knew the girl who'd disappeared weighed heavily on him.

'Oh my dear Lord' he said in a resigned tone, 'Now it's personal.' He shook his head and sighed, 'I will make discreet enquiries, but I promise you they will be discreet. As I said, the Mission comes before us all.'

'Thank you, I can't tell you how much I appreciate that. Perhaps I can join you at a service tomorrow?'

'The girl comes to the eleven o'clock Mass, but tread carefully. If she's lost one western friend she'll be extremely wary.'

I nodded, 'How secure is the present government?'

'Good question, and if I'm honest it's a bit like asking how long is a piece of string. There's always rumours, the Muslims have a hard time of it and too many people disappear no matter what their religion is. The army aren't happy as they're only paid spasmodically. It's a powder keg waiting to go off. I keep hearing that there will be an uprising, but nothing ever comes of it. I really don't know.'

He sat looking pensive for a couple of seconds.

'I'll ask Yvette to take you to your room, head down to La Maison tonight, the food's half decent and it'll give you a chance to meet a few people. Yvette will sort out breakfast tomorrow morning and I'll take you up to the missionary school on Monday. We'll be rising early I'm afraid, lessons start at 7am.'

'I'll have to get use it,' I said, 'thanks for your help.'

'I haven't given you any and won't give you any.' With that he stood up, winked and shook me by the hand.

'Good luck my friend.'

He heaved his bulk from behind the desk and shuffled out of the room shouting for Yvette. She appeared almost immediately and took me upstairs, pointing out a bathroom and handing me a front door key. The bedroom was precisely what I expected, small, bare floor boards, a rickety wooden bed with a thin mattress and a crucifix above it. There was a small desk at the bottom of the bed together with a single wooden wardrobe circa 1930.

Feeling tired, I lay on the bed. By now it was nearly six in the evening and with broken sleep on the flight from Paris I was

41

bushed. I set my alarm for 7.30 on the 'O' phone and dropped off immediately.

Chapter 6

I woke with a jolt, shaking. I'd had my usual dream about Zan, I was pushing her to one side to stop the bullet. Lying there I felt tired and deflated. I missed her, I missed her like hell and could not escape the feeling of loss.

Eventually I pulled myself together and went to the bathroom. A big old fashioned bath dominated the room together with a dated shower, basin and toilet. Pulling the heavy chain reminded me of my Grandparents place in Tuscany, no concerns for mod cons here, as long as the utilities were functional. Everything was spotlessly clean and a heady aroma of ammonia clung to the air. I splashed my face which freshened me up but did nothing for my mood.

As I went down the stairs Yvette appeared. I asked for directions to La Maison. She told me to walk up the road and turn right at the junction. By now darkness had fallen and there were no street lights. The beggars grabbed at me again as I walked using the muted glow coming from the buildings. Not that there was much, most of them were in darkness and those with light had closed their shutters and curtains.

It felt very eerie walking in near darkness and I half expected to be jumped on at any moment. I could feel eyes staring hidden in the gloom and felt very relieved when I turned the corner onto the main street. At least there was some light here but the street was deserted. It stank of sewerage and felt very creepy. Shops were boarded and no traffic could either be seen or heard. After fifty yards I saw a rusted steel plated sign on a doorway with 'La Maison' engraved on it. A dim light could be seen through a small window towards the top of the door. I tried pushing but it was locked. Finding a door bell I pressed it and a hatch opened.

'Oui,' I heard a half whisper.

'I've come for a meal' I said in French, not really sure whether I was at the right place.

'Entrez Monsieur.'

I walked in and a small young black man wearing a white jacket and black bow tie smiled at me, 'The restaurant is upstairs'.

The smell of floor polish hit me and I noticed the varnished wooden stairs had a lustre that could only come from regular cleaning. Seedy velvet wallpaper was peeling from the walls and as I opened a door at the top I stood looking incredulously at the scene.

I felt as if I had been transported to a small Parisian restaurant. It was however hot and sweaty with no obvious air conditioning. About twenty dark wooden tables and chairs were dotted around the room and in the dimmed light I could see what looked like a well stocked bar. Soft muzak could be heard and several people sat at the tables eating. Shabby chic came to mind, not what I expected in the middle of Africa. Two middle aged men stood by the bar drinking beer and they both smiled as I took in the scene.

'You must be new judging by your reaction' said one in French as he proffered his hand. 'I'm Jacques, don't worry it has the same effect on everybody.'

'Bonjour, I'm Tom, it does seem incongruous, I feel as if I should be in Montmartre.' They beamed and I noticed that apart from the waiter and the barman everybody was white. The other man introduced himself as Henri.

'American?' asked Jacques.

'English' they scowled and then burst out laughing.

'We're all friends here' said Henri. 'What brings you to Zambola?'

I explained about my work at the mission and they nodded in unison, looking at each other knowingly. *'What do they know?'* I wondered.

'Beer?' asked Henri.

'Thanks'. I replied. Although I'd vowed to stay away from alcohol for a while I could see that asking for a coke wasn't going to endear me to these two. I needed to get to know the territory quickly and felt they could be a mine of information. The barman opened a bottle, poured the beer into a glass and handed it to me.

'Sante' I said, it was cold and tasted good, 'Delicious'.

'Local brew, we taught them well,' said Jacques grinning, 'We're about to eat, would you like to join us?'

We sat at a table and a waiter handed each of us a laminated menu that had seen better days. I hoped the food wasn't of the same standard.

Jacques waved him away, 'I know the menu better than him,' he said laughing.

They ordered steak, I went for chicken, fries and a salad. I wasn't really that hungry and still felt tired after my journey. However this was too good an opportunity to find out about the country and culture so I wasn't going to blow it by going to bed.

'Red or white wine?' asked Jacques, 'You'll find the local plonk perfectly acceptable. *'So much for my liver,'* I thought, 'Red would be good, many thanks.'

A carafe was put in front of us and Jacques poured. We toasted each other again.

'This is very good,' I remarked somewhat surprised.

'Without wanting to repeat myself' said Jacques clearly delighted at my comment, 'We taught them well.'

'So what do you two do?' I asked.

'I'm third generation African' said Henri, 'We have a farm about thirty kilometres from here, mainly cattle with some crops. Come out and have a look at it some time.'

'I'd love to thanks, what about you?' I said turning to Jacques.

'I've been here for over twenty years, done a bit of mining, some farming, I ran a hotel for a while, now I earn a few centimes exporting stones.'

'Diamonds?'

'Yes that sort of thing, anything I can lay my hands on really.'

'Henri also owns this place,' said Jacques.

'Now you're not supposed to say anything until he's eaten,' Henri faked annoyance, 'That way I find out what people really think of it.'

'Well if the food's as good as the beer and the wine I'll be very happy.'

Henri smiled and slapped me on the back, 'Good man.'

'So what languages will you be teaching?' Jacques asked.

This seemed like a good opportunity to find out their thoughts on local politics.

'French, English and Mandarin Chinese.'

Henri almost choked on his wine, 'Sorry' he said, 'I know you mean well but the Chinese are no friends of this country.'

'Not quite true' said Jacques, 'there are quite a few of the local politicians who are very friendly towards them.'

'Yes and we know why, contributions to their political funding, it makes all the difference.'

'Bribes' I said.

'That's not what we call it here' replied Henri, 'Sadly the Chinese are taking everything out and putting nothing back in, apart from filling Kasenga's bank account and those of his cohorts'

'Steady' warned Jacques, 'You never know who may be listening.'

'I don't give a damn,' responded Henri draining his wine glass and immediately filling it again.

'The trouble is that everyone's pussy footing around the Chinese while they are taking all our natural resources and using their own people to do it. They even import their own food. It's a sick joke. Teaching the kids Chinese won't help our people, they'll never get the chance to use it.'

'Do you ever get to meet them?' I inquired.

'No, they have their own bars, restaurants even cinemas. The only thing they use our people for is brothels.'

'I thought they were investing in the infrastructure.'

'Oh my naïve little English friend, they built a few roads and the UN has made the City centre look pretty, but people are still starving, corruption is out of control and the place is totally fucked.'

'Henri' said Jacques sternly, 'Enough, this is not the time or the place.'

Henri looked at him blankly and drank some more wine, I realised he was well pissed.

The food arrived giving Henri a little time to cool off. As we were eating Jacques continued the conversation.

'It's difficult' he said, 'We thought that when the Chinese arrived they'd create some stability, sadly that's not the case. They live in a parallel universe, it's as if the rest of us don't exist.'

'But I thought they worked with French companies over here, surely they contribute to the local economy.' I deliberately said French rather than American as I didn't want to accentuate my knowledge.

Henri piped up again, 'The French do nothing, they've watched the slow degradation of this country ever since they pulled out in the fifties and done nothing to help. The Americans work with the Chinese and take as much of the Yuan as they can. As long as they can convert it into the mighty dollar they keep their mouths shut.'

'What do the Americans do?' I asked trying to sound as innocent as possible.

'Good question, replied Henri, 'Whenever they come to the restaurant they're always extremely vague. I know some of them are into computers and others have mining expertise. Why the Chinese need Americans God only knows, fate makes strange bedfellows.'

'I'd have thought Americans would love this bar,' I said trying to glean more information while sounding naive.

'Well you tell me' Henri went on, 'You speak their language. I've no idea how many of them are over here but if we see more than one group a week I'm surprised. And they don't want to mix, not like you. They sit at a table in the corner and talk in low whispers.'

'Very un American,' I quipped, the two of them guffawed.

By now we had finished eating, the meal was good and I told Henri so.

'Thanks he said airily, it's not always easy getting supplies but we manage. Now my little English friend you must try some of the local cognac as a night cap.'

At that point I knew it was time to go. We'd drunk two bottles of wine with the meal and I really didn't want to get into a drinking session, especially as I was hoping to bump into the Chinese girl at Church the following morning.

'Guys, I've had a long day, would you mind if I excused myself, I'm knackered.'

'I'll run you back to the Church' said Jacques.

'Don't be silly, I can walk'

Jacques looked at me sternly, 'Tom, you never walk around Kanina by yourself after dark. It's tantamount to suicide. Trust me.' I reached for my pocket but Henri waved his hand.

'Tonight you are my guest, welcome to Zambola.'

'Thank you.'

We shook hands and I followed Jacques down the stairs where a Toyota Land Cruiser was parked outside. I noticed him handing something to a young lad who ran off immediately.

'Parking fee' he said grinning, 'Or to put it another way, insurance. That's how it works here.'

'I have a lot to learn' I said as we drove around the corner.

'One other thing, never walk round with more than fifty US dollars and a credit card. A mugger will be happy with that and hopefully leave you alive. Good luck Englishman,' we pulled up outside the church and shook hands, 'No doubt we'll see each other again soon.

Chapter 7

The sound of church bells pounding in my head woke me at about 7.30. I felt relieved I'd stayed off the brandy the night before. The thought of loud bells combined with a hangover was too much to bear. With a clear blue sky I could see it was going to be a hot day so I unpacked a short sleeved shirt. I was going to put on shorts but decided on a more formal approach as I was going to a church service. I put on some lightweight trousers and headed downstairs.

'Bonjour Monsieur.' I was getting used to Yvette appearing from nowhere.

'Breakfast is waiting for you in the dining room,' she said opening a door. A large dining table had a place set for one. A couple of croissants together with a small baguette, a miniature jam jar, fruit and coffee were laid out.

'Est-ce bon pour vous?'

'Oui merci.'

She smiled and left the room closing the door behind her. The coffee was good, but the croissant tasted strange, probably baked without butter. Given that my recent diet had consisted of little more than bread and cheese I wasn't too bothered and after a second cup of coffee I got up to go for a walk.

Outside the warmth of the sun hit me. Although early I could feel the humidity starting to rise. I'd read that Kanina was coming out of the official rainy season but that wet weather could persist for several months, I had a feeling today could be one of those days.

I headed back up to the main street where the market was in full swing. Sunday didn't seem to slow down trading and I watched several people bartering for eggs and live hens. Row upon row of market traders beckoned me to buy all kinds of fresh vegetables, speaking in the Niger Congo languages that Mark had mentioned, Strolling down the road I could see that I was somewhat of an attraction being the only white face in the vicinity. People kept coming up and touching me, not in an aggressive manner, I smiled, they smiled back and then backed away.

As I walked further down the road I could see the port in front of me with dozens of fishing and trading boats tied up to the jetties. The area was a hive of activity with people shouting and screaming at each other buying and selling whatever produce that had been transported from further up the river. I watched fish being unloaded and taken to a large building towards the end of the quay. I realised this was a fish market and dozens of people were streaming out, many on bikes laden with fresh produce. Given that it was only nine o'clock I could see these people had been up for hours. I assumed the produce went to shops, hotels and restaurants. Or maybe corrupt politicians and the Chinese fraternity.

What struck me was that although this was a poor country nobody in the capital appeared to be starving. They seemed happy and full of vitality. Such a contrast to the villages on the way in from the airport. I headed back to the church passing the usual array of banks and offices. There was even a small museum, although it was difficult to see when it would be open.

I got back to the mission at about ten and with time to kill I rang my Mum. She knew little of what had happened in recent months and I hadn't seen her for nearly a year. I felt a pang of guilt, but there was no way I could have faced my parents in the state I'd been. My brother knew a little more and it was he who had taken me to Amsterdam. He'd been a drop out all his life but his heart was in the right place. He'd introduced me to Jan stayed on the boat for a couple of weeks and then drifted off. I knew he'd reappear one day, that was the sort of relationship we had. We weren't close, but we were always there for each other.

Mum was in fine form and delighted to hear that I was going to Mass. She'd been a devout Catholic all her life, apart from marrying my Father who was failed Church of England. In that respect I'd inherited his genes but my Mother always hoped that I would find her faith. We chatted about her life, the Women's Institute, the flower committee at the church and her latest past time, selling junk on eBay. Quite the entrepreneur she'd made several hundred pounds getting rid of rubbish stored in the loft. At twenty to eleven I cut her short, as she didn't want me to miss Mass she fully understood.

I walked into the church and was amazed on two fronts. Firstly, the beauty of the architecture and secondly the number of people attending the service. The pews were full, extra chairs had been put out and people were standing at the back. I dipped my fingers in the holy water font by the door, crossed myself and stood with those at the back, feeling somewhat humble, a failed catholic surrounded by a sea of hope.

The congregation appeared to be mostly local with the odd white face dotted around. I looked for the Chinese girl but couldn't pick her out. The organ music rose to a crescendo and the congregation stood for the first hymn. A man standing next to me shared his hymnal singing with great gusto. Father Steve entered somewhat theatrically waiving the incense and wearing the traditional white garment used by Catholic clergy tied with a cord. He was followed by a choir of about fifteen girls and boys aged between eight and fourteen, all dressed in cassocks and surpluses. I remembered the doctrine taught to us by Sister Mary at Sunday School, 'The visual imagery of the smoke and the smell remind us of the transcendence of the Mass which links heaven with earth, and allow us to enter into the presence of God'. The words were imprinted on my brain.

It struck me as rather strange to be standing in an environment which felt so comfortable when I was so far from home. After the greeting and the Act of Penitence I lost interest and my mind wandered. I fumbled my way through the Nicene Creed and the Apostles Creed while looking for the Chinese girl but she was nowhere to be seen. Following prayers and hymns Father Steve stood to deliver the homily. I tried to focus on what he had to say but his strange mix of French, Latin, English and some local language made his discourse at best offbeat but in truth boring. His French accent was spectacularly awful and I assumed similar of his African dialect. I expected a much better presentation style from the big man and was somewhat surprised. However, the congregation sat and stood quietly as if they were taking in every word. I rather think they were like me, just waiting for him to finish.

I went up for the communion, more to be seen as one of the people rather than being the odd one out and finally after more prayers and hymns the service came to an end. I'd positioned myself close to the door so that I could get out quickly and watch the congregation leave.

Father Steve was waiting outside shaking everyone by the hand bidding them farewell. He called me over.

'Tom, let me introduce you to some of our flock.' He turned to those standing near him and announced in French, 'Monsieurs est Madames, this is Tom who is going to be teaching at the Mission School for the next few months.'

I was welcomed by all and sundry as I shook hands. Amazingly Father Steve seemed to know everyone but the names went in one ear and out of the other. Some of the congregation were teachers and children from the school, others were parents. I lost track of the number I shook hands with, they all wished me well and thanked me for coming to help the people and country.

Father Steve shouted across to me, 'Tom, I think you are the only person here who can talk to this lady in her own language.'

I turned and a Chinese girl stood smiling, looking somewhat embarrassed. She wasn't very pretty, probably in her late twenties, dumpy and wearing glasses.

'Shēntǐ hǎo ma?' I said 'Hello how are you'

She looked genuinely pleased that I spoke in Mandarin.

'Hěn hǎo, xièxie.' She responded, 'Fine thank you.'

'Qǐngwèn nǐjiào shěnme míng? ' – 'May I please ask, what is your name?'. The Chinese are so formal and I felt it important to keep that level of formality, especially for a first meeting.

'Fei Yen' she responded, 'I've not met many Westerners who speak Chinese,' she continued.

'That's why I'm here, so that I can help the local children learn your language.'

'Well it's very nice to meet you,' she said and started to move away.

I realised that if I didn't do something in the next few seconds I wouldn't see her until the service next week and I didn't want to leave it that long. The thought of Caterina languishing in jail spurred me on.

'This is very forward of me, I said, 'but I don't get much chance to speak Chinese. I would really like to talk to someone to sharpen up my skills a little. Is it possible we could meet for tea one day? Perhaps you could bring a friend?' I thought this may soften the impact a little.

'That would be nice,' she replied fumbling in her bag. 'Here is my card, we could meet on Tuesday after work.'

'Being new to the country I'm not sure where.'

'Nor me, I rarely go into town apart from the church.'

'I'll find somewhere and phone you.'

'Lovely', she said smiling and with that gave a little wave, turned and walked down the street. Father Steve said nothing and we continued shaking people's hands until the church emptied.

'Okay?' he asked.

'Yes' I said, 'I can't thank you enough'

'Didn't do anything, just introduced you to my flock,' with that he half winked again. I began to realise this man was a valuable asset, I had to keep him onside.

'Join me for dinner tonight' he said, 'It'll only be something simple, chicken and vegetables. It's the norm on a Sunday, you'd be very welcome.'

'That would be lovely' I responded.

'I'll see you just after eight, straight after the evening service.' With that he disappeared into the church.

I went back to my room and emailed Mark.

'First contact with the Chinese girl, meeting her again on Tuesday, Father Steve is being very helpful, also met two expats last night.'

The response was almost immediate, 'Excellent, keep up the good work.'

I rang Caroline and updated her. She sounded stressed, one of the kids was screaming in the background while the other was hassling her for cake.

'I think I better leave you to it,' I said.

'Thanks, phone me later in the week, evenings are best, after the kids have gone to bed.'

For the first time since meeting Caroline on the boat in Amsterdam I had time to reflect. I lay on my bed and for no real reason a feeling of guilt enveloped me. Guilt for getting on with life, guilt for spending time with Caroline, for finding a way forward, for finding a level of contentment. Quite simply the loss of Zan hit me again forcibly. For the first time since her murder I'd spent a couple of days not really thinking about her. I'd been pre occupied but now the loss was again too much to bare. I curled into a ball and held my feet tight, something I'd done so many times in recent months. The difference was, I couldn't cry anymore, there was rage, there was anger, but no tears. I dozed and Fei Yen was stood in front of me. Suddenly she was Zan, smiling as only Zan smiled. She kissed me and then I saw the terror in her eyes as she was shot. Once again she lay dying in my arms.

I woke to hear the sound of someone knocking. Stumbling to my feet I opened the door. Father Steve was standing outside looking somewhat concerned.

'Are you okay?' he asked.

'Yeah, sorry, I dozed off.'

'Yvette told me you were screaming, is there anything I can do?'

'Sorry, must have had a bad dream, I'm fine. Many apologies, I don't want to trouble anyone.'

'There's some tea downstairs, help yourself' He looked at me quizzically, 'See you later' with that he shuffled off down the corridor.

I was hot and covered in sweat so I went to wash my face in cold water to cool off. I suddenly felt a bit scared. I thought I could handle myself and get on with the job in hand. Now I wasn't so sure. My hands were shaking. I just sat on the bed trying to make sense of it all. I couldn't, but I knew I had to find a focus. I couldn't dwell on the past, no matter how much it hurt I had to move on.

'Caterina' I thought. 'I have to focus on Caterina. She needs me, and in a strange way, I need her. By trying to find her I may just find a way forward.' I resolved to focus on the now and what I had to do.

I went downstairs and Yvette appeared.

'Monsieur there is tea in the dining room.'

'I'm sorry if I scared you.'

'No problem'. She smiled for the first time since I arrived, 'Have some tea, it'll make you feel better.' I think she began to realize that I was human with all the frailties that came with such an affliction. I wasn't just an arrogant white man throwing his largess around to help the sad little people in Africa in order to salve his conscience.

The tea refreshed me and a slice of cake was good enough for lunch. I pondered what I should do for the rest of the day. I found myself in a stalemate position and didn't like it. I knew the longer it took to find Caterina the less likelihood there was of her being alive, but for the time being there was little I could do. Looking out of the window I could see the sky had gone extremely dark, there was no point in going out, very soon the heavens would open and I'd get soaked.

I opened the door and called for Yvette. Within seconds she appeared.

'Do you have any maps and books on Zambola at the mission?' I asked.

'Oui Monsieur, un moment.'

She returned a few minutes later balancing half a dozen books and a couple of maps in front of her. She put them on the table and then cleared away the tea things.

'Will there be anything else Monsieur?'

'Yes, could you show me on the map where the mission school is?'

She looked at me blankly, 'Non Monsieur, but perhaps Father Steve?'

'Not a problem, 'I'll see him at dinner.' I realised she probably didn't even know how to read a map.

I spread it out on the table. The date of publication was 1974 and it had seen better days. However, the condition was good enough for me to familiarise myself with the geography if nothing else.

One of the books contained the speeches of a previous president. Hardly riveting stuff apart from appreciating the art of bullshit. He'd screwed the country out of millions and yet to read his words you'd have thought he taught Nelson Mandela everything he knew.

Another was about the fauna and flora of the delta region of the country written in quaint nineteen thirties colloquial French. I guessed the author was an expat colonial who saw himself as a Jacques Cousteau.

The third book held my interest for quite a while. Again written in the 1930s it was a travel guide to the colony as it was. A chapter caught my eye, on the prisons of the country. Four major ones were mentioned in different provinces, each having the capacity for about five hundred prisoners. The Central Prison of Kanina looked to be about a mile from the church. Mention was also made of many small town jails under the auspices of the Gendarme.

With little else to do and as the rain had stopped I decided to walk up to the prison. I didn't expect to learn much but it filled time before dinner if nothing else. Back on the main road I walked in the opposite direction to the port so it gave me an opportunity to see more of the town. As I walked away from the centre the buildings quickly fell into disrepair with squalor and poverty appearing in abundance.

I remembered Henri's words from last night, 'The UN has made the city centre look pretty but the people are still starving, corruption is out of control and the place is totally fucked.'

I soon felt very threatened with street beggars shouting at me and children demanding money. So different to how I felt in the market that morning, less than a mile away. Within minutes I had about twenty people surrounding me, jostling for position and I felt genuinely threatened. They were shouting and screaming at each other, fully expecting me to become a major benefactor to them all. I kept my hands in my pockets, not wanting to lose my watch or my money. It was all too much to handle so I pushed my way through quite forcibly and hailed a passing cab. He screeched to a halt scattering the people around me. I climbed in and we drove off at break neck speed.

'What are you doing walking around there man?' he asked, 'Are you a suicide merchant?'

'I've just arrived in the city and was having a look round.'

'Man, you don't walk around this place unless you have a death wish.'

He'd continued to drive out of town and I noticed a big building on the left with a high wall surrounding it.

'What's that?' I asked.

'Man, that is the prison, and you don't wanna go there either. Five thousand people are locked up and it is horrible. They are starving, they have diseases, it is inhuman what goes on in there.'

'That's a lot of people for a small country' I said, 'What have they done?'

'Most of them are Muslim and have done nothing, apart from not liking the politics of this place.'

'Is it mixed?' I asked trying to sound like a naive tourist.

'No, it is just men, the women's prison is just as bad.'

'And where's that?'

'About twenty miles out of town and if you wanna go I'm not taking you.'

'No no, just take me back to The Christian Missionary Society, I've had enough of sightseeing for one day.'

As he pulled up outside the church he turned and said, 'You go careful man, this is a dangerous place. Five dollars US please.'

For once I didn't argue and gave him a ten dollar bill. 'Keep the change' I said, 'And thanks for your help.'

He grinned, 'Here's my card man, any time you wanna taxi you phone me. My name is Sarab.'

We shook hands.

'Salaam.'

He was obviously a Muslim and I filed that bit of information, not knowing whether it would be of use or otherwise. Climbing out of the car I was just relieved to be away from the filth of the city. I rang the bell and Yvette opened the door.

'You're looking happier than earlier Monsieur.'

'Yes' I said I'm fine, 'I think it must have been something to do with the long journey.'

She smiled, 'Dinner is at eight'.

'Thanks,' I replied and climbed the stairs to my room. With a couple of hours to kill, I went online. Surprisingly the signal was strong, much better than on the boat in Amsterdam. Idly I typed into Google 'Prisons in Zambola'. Seconds later I was reading a UN report written ten years previously.

'Amazing' I thought, 'Why the hell hadn't The Organisation found this.'

The report was 22 pages long and went into a fair amount of detail. I started to note down the salient points:-

1. *Prisons can be under the authority of*
   - i. *Courts and Tribunals*
   - ii. *Police*
   - iii. *Army*
   - iv. *All prisons are overcrowded, with up to six people in a   cell designed for one.*

2. *Prisoners in the Court jails are predominately criminals.*

3. Prisoners in the Police and Army jails are predominately political.

4. There are 12 declared prisons and three suspected political prisons not declared. Six of the declared prisons are old and decaying, having been built in colonial times. The others are camps hastily thrown together using predominately containers as cell blocks. There are also an unknown number of army jails not considered in this report.

5. Out of a population of approximately 5 million, there are 54,000 criminal and 142,000 political prisoners, 3.8% of the population, as compared with 0.72% in the USA. Muslims account for over 40% of the prison population but only 15% of the country's population.

6. Nine of the prisons are for males and three for females.

7. Most prisons are single sex, but that is not always the case.

8. The inmates are kept in inhumane, cruel and degrading conditions.

9. On the prison diet, prisoners are confronted by acute malnutrition, due, principally, to the lack of basic food.

10. Many detainees, appear skeletal and are suffering from tuberculosis and dysentery with Cholera regularly raising its ugly head.

11. The medical dispensaries rarely have pharmaceutical products at their disposal.

12. Cases of death through illness, starvation and disease are daily occurrences.

13. *Some cells are equipped with beds and mattresses,
    however due to overpopulation most prisoners sleep on
    the ground.*

14. *Water is available in sanitation blocs but is often
    stagnant.*

15. *Showers and toilets are dilapidated and badly
    maintained.*

16. *The overpopulated cells, are neither aerated nor lit, and
    emit a sickening smell of urine and stagnant water.*

17. *Inmates are kept in overwhelming heat, and are subject
    to mosquito bites, lice, and ticks.*

18. *Electric lighting is spasmodic.*

19. *Hard labour, chores, physical punishment and other
    physical tortures are regular practice.*

20. *Iron bars, batons, thin cords, metal chains, cattle prods,
    mechanical clips and other slicing and cutting
    instruments are used as objects of torture.*

21. *Political prisoners are prohibited from any kind of visit,
    even those of close family members, lawyers, doctors
    etc.*

22. *Criminals are allowed visitors every Sunday between
    12midday and 3 pm. Visitors are allowed to bring food
    but have to bribe guards to take food to the inmates.*

The report went on to list known prisons including the male
prison in Kanina and the female one in Nabila, several miles
south of the capital. It named several hundred people believed to
be incarcerated but whose whereabouts were unknown.

I felt quite depressed, with the number of prisons scattered
across the country trying to find Caterina would be like looking

for a needle in a haystack. Also only known prisons were mentioned in any detail and the report was years old with much of the information no doubt way out of date.

However it did confirm conditions were intolerable and I doubted things had changed. If I couldn't find Caterina quickly there was little chance of her being alive. *Where the hell do I start?* I thought.

I forwarded the report to Mark and asked if he could get his boffin's to try and glean more information. With the resources The Organisation had at their disposal I hoped they could find something. However, I wasn't going to hold my breath.

Just before eight I went down for dinner and Father Steve stood waiting for me in the dining room.

'Would you care for some wine?' he asked filling a glass from a decanter.

'Thank you.'

Handing it to me he filled another.

'Good health' he said draining half the contents. 'Have you had a good day?'

I told him about my conversation with Fei Yen and my trip through the town.

'Go careful young man, otherwise you may disappear as well.'

While eating I told him about the UN report. He was genuinely interested and asked many questions.

'I don't think things have changed much,' he said after a while. The political prisoners will be of a different persuasion but I reckon the numbers will be about the same. The politics change but the culture doesn't.'

'Which means Caterina is going through hell.'

'If she's in a government prison.'

'What do you mean?' I asked.

'Well it could be the Chinese have got her holed up somewhere.'

'Yeah,' I said feeling somewhat deflated not honestly knowing which way to turn.

'Young Man,' said Father Steve, 'I think you have to face facts, the chances of finding your friend are slim, she may well be dead already. Judging by how you were when I came to your room earlier I think you need to slow down a little. I don't know what you've been through and it's none of my business but you have to give yourself a chance.'

'You're right' I said, 'I think I'll turn in, early start tomorrow. Thanks for dinner and listening to me'

'That's what clergy do in the Catholic Church,' he said grinning. 'The bus to the school will be here at about 6.15, there'll be some breakfast laid out before then.'

'Good night,' I said. Closing the door, I noticed him pouring another glass of wine. 'Poor old soul', I thought, 'he must spend so much time on his own contemplating the world. Is he really helping anyone or is it all a delusion?' I was too tired to think about it and went straight to bed.

Chapter 8

The following morning I woke at 5.30 feeling remarkably fresh. I showered, dressed and headed down to the dining room. Father Steve sat eating a croissant and he beckoned me to join him.

'So how do you feel about today?' he asked.

'Good,' I responded, 'It'll be nice to see the kids and a bit more of the country.'

'I'll introduce you to the school at Assembly and then you can take a couple of classes. You'll find them a bit more responsive than in the West, they are programmed by their parents to learn and get out of the poverty trap.'

'Is there any language you want me to focus on?'

'It has to be Chinese sadly, if that's okay with you?'

'Fine.'

'Let's go, we can talk more on the bus.'

Dawn had just broken as we stepped outside and I immediately felt the warmth of the sun. An old yellow bus pulled up outside half filled with children of all ages, immaculately dressed in yellow shirts, with brown shorts for the boys and skirts for the girls. They were laughing and shouting but as we climbed on board the noise level subsided and in unison they said, 'Bonjour Papa Steve.'

He smiled, 'Bonjour mes enfants, sa va?'

As one they replied, 'Sa va bien merci.'

We sat at the front as the bus started to move. With Father Steve on board the children were somewhat quieter; they obviously had enormous respect for him.

Within minutes we were back in the world of the shanty towns Children were picked up at various stops, and as each one got on they greeted Father Steve.

'Tell me about the school.' I felt a bit guilty as I hadn't asked before. However I wasn't here to teach, that was very much a side issue as far as I was concerned.

'It's actually two schools,' came the reply, 'Junior and Senior, both have about 500 pupils They come to us aged six, most cannot read but learn quickly. We take children of all abilities and are popular because parents don't have to pay.' He laughed. 'However, it is a strict regime. If they don't work they are asked to leave, That might sound tough but these kids are the ones who may eventually help this God forsaken land. In reality, we only lose about five percent due to laziness. Parents push them hard, We teach up to their ability level and build on strengths. If someone shows ability with their hands we focus on carpentry, metal work etc. If someone shows ability with their head we focus on the world of academia, and that's where you'll be focused. We don't stream as such in that academics are not singled out as being the elite. In a country like this you are more likely to survive with carpentry skills rather than media studies. The junior school takes the kids to eleven and the senior school to sixteen. There are heads for each school who teach as well and there is a fair amount of cross fertilization with regard to staff. So one lesson you may be teaching six year olds and the next kids ten years older. They have classes from 7.30 to 3.30 so it's a long day by Western standards. Class sizes can be a problem. In an ideal world you want no more than twenty, we have forty plus. It's reality and we have to live with it.

'How involved are you with the school?'

'I'm here three days a week teaching Religious Knowledge. I don't just tutor in Christianity, I look at the complete spectrum, I can't then be accused of favouritism by the authorities.'

'What about the Church?' I asked, 'What support do you get there?'

'Good question' came the response as Father Steve guffawed. 'I'm supposed to have an assistant priest but the last one disappeared back to France eighteen months ago. I do have a fair amount of lay support which helps, be it in terms of the choir, cleaning, flower arranging etc. Between the church and the school I have a pretty full week.'

We arrived at the school to see a dozen or so single story buildings surrounding a larger central structure. Everything looked to be in pristine condition with manicured lawns and paths.

'Each block has two classrooms' said Father Steve, 'The hall in the middle is used for breakfast, assembly, overspill classes, lunch and sports. Students come out from Europe and the States on a regular basis to help maintain the place. They pay for the privilege which keeps the cost base down. We also have an educational garden where we grow our own crops, cabbages, carrots, tomatoes, eggplants, maize, fennel, potatoes, beans, maize etc. The kids get quite a buzz eating the food they grow for lunch. It's probably the most useful educational exercise we carry out, teaching them to be self sufficient.'

The bus drew to a halt and the children sat without moving. Father Steve stood and I followed, the kids then rose.

'You have them well trained,' I said.

'Discipline is paramount in this society, correction, in any society'.

We walked across the campus and into one of the smaller huts.

'This is the staff room and headmaster's offices. We currently have twenty five teachers including the heads and me.'

The staff room was packed and I recognised a few faces from the church service. People shook me by the hand and introduced

67

themselves along with their subjects. Every discipline seemed to be catered for, from physics to farming.

'Good morning,' said one in English as we shook hands, 'I am Patrice Umgali, head of languages, I gather we are going to be working together.' He was a tall thin man in his late thirties, obviously educated with an air of quiet authority.

'Looking forward to it, Father Steve says you want me to focus on Chinese.'

'That would be wonderful, but if you could take some English classes as well I would be very grateful.

'No problem,' I said smiling.

Father Steve came over, 'It's time for assembly, we do seniors Monday, Wednesday and Friday, juniors Tuesday, Thursday and Saturday. The seniors don't come to school on Saturday in order that they can work.'

I fell into line with the teachers as we made our way across to the central assembly hall. The noise level was deafening but immediately fell to a virtual silence. Children stood in rows with a central walkway and we made our way as a procession onto the stage.

Father Steve stood at the centre of the stage with a lectern in front of him. The teachers spread out behind him.

'Let us pray' he said and everybody bowed their heads.

We sang a hymn accompanied by an old lady sitting to one side of the room playing an out of tune upright piano. Father Steve introduced me to the assembly and I got a round of applause. Sports results were read out together with notices on various activity groups and following another prayer the kids shuffled out of the back of the hall.

Patrice came over, 'Follow me and I will take you to your first lesson.'

Having not prepared anything I went into a mild panic. I then thought of a favourite expression, 'In the land of the blind the one-eyed man is King.'

'Your first class will be year eleven, that is our most senior students. They are hard working and most want to go to university. Sadly due to the cost only two or three will do so. However they are all good kids.'

I smiled and started putting a few thoughts together as to how I was going to approach the lesson. We walked up to one of the huts, and into the classroom. Again the kids went quiet.

'Bonjour' said Patrice, 'You've already met Monsieur Simpson. This morning he is going to teach you the rudiments of Mandarin Chinese. Enjoy the lesson.'

Turning to me he said, 'I will come back and show you to your next class.' I was left with about forty beaming faces.

'Zǎo ān' I said, 'Which is Chinese for?'

The kids looked at me not quite knowing what to say.

'It's Chinese for Good Morning.'

'Now all together - Zǎo ān.'

Everybody joined in and so the lesson went on for the next 40 minutes. The kids were incredibly responsive and as the bell went I said, 'Now you all speak Chinese, not a lot but if you see a Chinese person you can at least say hello in their own language. Well done.'

They all seemed delighted as Patrice beckoned me from the door.

'Are you ready for another class or do you need a break?'

'No let's go for it,' I said. 'How many lessons in a day?'

'We have nine, but not on your first day I think.'

I ended up taking seven covering all age bands. At 3.30 Father Steve appeared, 'How are you feeling?'

'If I'm honest, knackered!'

'Welcome to teaching in Africa.' He bellowed followed by a mighty laugh.

We caught the bus back to the Mission chatting about the school and the day's events.

'They are so keen to learn' I said, 'It must be a joy to watch those kids develop.'

Yvette had tea and cakes waiting for us and I asked Father Steve where I could meet Fei Yen the following day.

'Try the Hotel Justice, they do traditional afternoon tea and often have a pianist playing. It's quite acceptable.'

'Thanks,' I said, 'I think I'll go down to La Maison tonight if that's OK, try and meet a few more people.'

'That makes sense, see you at breakfast.'

I went up to my room and checked the 'O' phone for messages. Mark had replied, 'No more info on jails, will pursue.'

If there was anything, I knew he'd find it, if nothing else I had confidence in the man.

I phoned Fei Yen and told her about the Hotel Justice. She seemed genuinely pleased that I had contacted her and we agreed to meet at 5.30 the following afternoon. I then lay on my bed trying to find a way forward with regard to finding Caterina. I was frustrated as hell because I couldn't begin to see a starting point.

I remembered the words of a wise man I had worked with previously in The Organisation. 'Slowly slowly.' The trouble was I knew that if I took too long I'd be too late for Caterina.

I counted out fifty dollars and left the rest of my money in the room. I assumed I could trust people in the Catholic Church if not outside in the big bad world. I started to walk up to 'La Maison' when I heard a screech of brakes and a taxi pulled up beside me. Sarab opened his window.

'Man, I told you not to walk these streets, now get in.'

'I'm only going round the corner.'

'I don't care, any fare is a good fare and I haven't had one today. I was hoping to see you, now where are you going?'

La Maison, it's really not necessary' I said.

'Two dollars US because I like you and I can see I'm going to have to be your guardian angel.'

For two dollars I couldn't be bothered to argue so I opened the back door and climbed in. I decided to pump him a little for information.

'So you've not been to the prison today?' I said as if making a joke.

'No man, I wanna keep away from that place, too many of my friends are in there and they have done nothing, apart from being Muslim.'

Trying to sound as casual as possible I said 'Is that where they put bad westerners as well?'

'Yeah man so that the embassy staff can go see them. That's about the only good thing about the place, it's a good fare.'

'Better if you take them to the women's prison?'

'That would be nice but I only ever took one person. To see a German woman who had been caught smuggling diamonds out of the country.'

'What happened to her?'

'No idea man, why you ask.'

'No reason,' and with that we drew up outside the restaurant.

'Give me five dollars and I'll wait for you.'

'I don't know how long I'll be.'

'No problem, there won't be any other business tonight.'

I gave him the money and as I knocked on the restaurant door I turned.

'How do I know you'll still be here?'

'Trust me' he said laughing.

Climbing the stairs of 'La Maison' I wondered whether I'd ever see him again. However I wasn't too bothered as I'd learnt something very important, Caterina could well be in the women's prison twenty miles away. It was a start at least.

I was welcomed by Henri like a long lost brother.

'Tom, it is so good to see you again, a beer for my friend,' he said turning to the barman.

'So what have you been up to since we last met?'

I told him about my trip to the prison.

'Oh be careful my friend, this is a dangerous city, the prisons house mainly good people who don't agree with the authorities. All the bad guys walk the streets.'

The barman handed me a beer while Henri spoke.

'Salute mon ami.'

I then mentioned my taxi driver chum. 'Whether he'll still be waiting for me I've no idea,' I said laughing.

'He will be, you'll be seen as a long term customer and he'll look after you. Keep him onside, people like that are useful.'

'Sounds good, he was telling me about a German woman who was locked up for smuggling diamonds.'

Henri's eyes closed for a second as if he was in pain and he shook his head sadly, 'She is a friend of mine, Tanja Westermann. All her papers were in order, but she didn't bribe the right people. She's now two years into a five year sentence.'

I felt saddened for the man. 'How's she doing?'

'Not well, I go to see her once a month. I take food which she rarely sees, cigarettes to bribe the guards and medicines when required. I doubt she'll survive another three years. If I'm honest Tom, she's the only reason I stay in this God forsaken hole.'

'Is there no way you can get her out?'

'Oh I've tried, believe me, I've tried. We're caught in the middle of a political quagmire and nobody is prepared to make the decision to release her. I've talked to the German embassy time and time again. I've even had a meeting with Michelle Kasenga our glorious leader. I showed him all the evidence I have, proving beyond doubt Tanja's innocence. He promised to look into it. That was six months ago.'

'Is there no way you can bribe people at the prison to get her out?.' Although I was sorry to hear Tanja's story I was also thrilled. This information could be invaluable with regard to Caterina.

'The prison officers are terrified of making mistakes. If she were to escape they would soon become inmates. The regime is intolerable.'

'Where is the prison?'

'La Croix? It's about thirty kilometres from here and set up like a concentration camp. Barbed wire fences, turrets with guards, containers for accommodation, sanitation at the most degrading level, you don't want to know.'

'I am so sorry, there's no way you could smuggle her out?'

I would if I could believe me, but I'd need a small army. It's just not possible.'

'Are there any other westerners with her?'

'Not that I'm aware of, why do you ask?' he was suddenly on his guard.'

'No reason, I'm just trying to visualise what the poor girl is going through.'

'We've been together for nine years,' I could see the tears in Henri's eyes, 'She's my soul mate, friend, lover and there is nothing I can do to help her. I'm sorry I shouldn't be talking like this.'

I desperately wanted to tell him about Caterina, but I knew this wasn't the time. I had to establish first that she was in the same prison. It seemed likely but I couldn't just act on a hunch. I needed hard evidence and then I could provide the small army Henri needed.

That night he introduced me to a couple of journalists, one French and one Belgium. They were on the lookout for stories and had little interest in me. Conversation was polite but laboured.

I left at about ten and Sarab was outside.

'I told you I'd be waiting,' he said as I climbed into the taxi.

'Thanks Sarab, you're a good man.'

'I am your guardian angel.'

Chapter 9

I got back to the mission and emailed Mark.

"I'd be grateful if you could find out as much as possible about La Croix women's prison. It's about thirty kilometres south of Kanina and I believe this could be where Caterina is being held. I can confirm a German woman Tanja Westermann is imprisoned there. It may be worth checking her out."

His response was immediate, "I'll have something for you by tomorrow morning."

I slept, deeply and woke with a start as the alarm went off on my 'O' phone.

There was an email waiting for me from Mark:-

> "La Croix prison is home to about 1500 women. Conditions are appalling and the UN is trying to send in monitors. Their request has so far been declined. The camp is approximately three miles from the village of Tsheka with dense forest surrounding it. Access is by one road in poor condition. The camp was originally set up by the French during colonial days for political protesters. There are seventy five containers which are used as sleeping quarters. Approximately twenty women sleep in each container on mattresses with little if any bedding. No electricity is available in the containers. There is one sanitation block where prisoners shower weekly, if there is water. There are approximately fifty guards on duty at any one time. Most are armed and ruthless. Beatings, torture and rape are common place.
>
> The German embassy is well informed with regard to Tanja Westermann and has made regular visits. They are aware that her health is deteriorating.

Despite protests for her release all requests have been ignored.

> *We are working behind the scenes to try and confirm Caterina's whereabouts. Keep up the pressure at your end. Once we have confirmation as to where she is we will send in the necessary resource to release her."*

School was very similar to the previous day. I took eight classes, six Chinese and two English. The staff were kind and welcoming and the head of senior school insisted I joined him for lunch. We sat at a long table with kids of about sixteen and ate ugale, a kind of porridge. It wasn't exactly appetising but the warmth and camaraderie of teachers and children made me feel very comfortable. I began to think that if I found Caterina maybe I could help these kids on a longer term basis. That would be for the future, for now I had to have total focus on the job in hand, finding Caterina.

I got back to the mission at about quarter past four and Sarab was parked outside.

'Give me ten minutes,' I said, 'And you can take me to Hotel Justice.' I was determined to arrive on time, knowing how important punctuality was to Chinese people.

'No problem boss.'

Having washed and changed Sarab drove me towards the docks. A mile down river we pulled into the grounds of what once upon a time must have been a most elegant hotel. Now it was in desperate need of a face lift. We swept up to the main entrance where a doorman opened the car door and stood to attention as I climbed out.

'Welcome to Hotel Justice Monsieur' he said in perfect French with just a hint of an African intonation.

Walking into the hotel it was as if a full party was in swing. Ladies of all ages were dressed in what looked like their Sunday best, sitting at tables of two, three and four people. One large rectangular table seating about twenty people stood in the middle of the room where a large black elderly lady was in full flow as if lecturing the others. A pianist accompanied two singers performing Lakmé's Duo des Fleurs, the quality was quite remarkable considering we were in the middle of Africa.

'Can I help you sir?' I was asked as I stood taking in the scene.

'I'm waiting for someone, could I have a table for two please?'

I was ushered towards a table and passing the big lady heard her pontificating about 'filthy Muslims', totally unconcerned about who heard her. The table was set with a linen table cloth, napkins, silver cutlery, and bone china crockery. I felt as if I'd walked into another age. As I sat Fei Yen appeared at the door. I stood and beckoned her over. She smiled and walked towards me. We shook hands and I nodded my head as is the custom in China.

'This feels like an English tea party' I said in Mandarin as we sat down, 'So how its been transported to a former French colony is beyond me.'

'It looks very pleasant' replied Fei Yen coolly.

The waiter came across and asked in French, 'Would you care for afternoon tea sir?'

Fei Yen looked at me blankly, she obviously didn't speak French. I translated, 'What is it? she said.

'What's on the menu?' I asked in French.

'Tea, sandwiches and cakes sir,' came the response.

Again I translated, 'This sounds interesting, I would like to try.'

'For two please,' the waiter scribbled our order on a pad, smiled and walked away.

'Do you ever eat western food?' I asked.

'No never, this is the first time.'

'I feel honoured,' I said and smiled.

I really wanted to say, *'What's happened to Caterina'* but I knew I had to be a little more subtle.

'So what are you doing in Africa?' I asked.

'I'm working in computer development at The National Mining Company,'

'Sounds interesting,' my heart started beating fast, knowing Caterina had been based there.

Are there many in your department?' I was trying to sound interested without being obvious.

'About twenty five.'

'Are they all Chinese or do you employ locals?'

She burst out laughing, 'No no, the locals couldn't help us, although we do have some Americans.'

'I think I'd prefer locals,' I joked trying to bring her out of herself.

The food arrived and we spend the next few minutes selecting sandwiches and cakes.

While the waitress poured tea I said to her, 'You're busy today.'

'We are honoured to have Madame Kasenga with us. She is the mother of our illustrious president.'

'I take it she is the lady in full flow sitting on the big table?'

The waitress scowled, 'Our leader is a good man and the saviour of our country.' With that she put the teapot down heavily and stormed off. I translated for Fei Yen.

She looked at me in a none committal way and grimaced as she tasted the tea.

'I'm sorry,' I said, 'the tea here is more for European tastes than Chinese.

'That's fine, it is interesting to try. You do not like the people of Zambola?' She asked.

'I haven't been here long enough to form an opinion. The children and staff at the school seem very friendly and hard working.'

'What about Americans?'

'They're OK, a bit loud and a little inward looking. How do you find them?

'I do not understand them, they are not very friendly towards us and keep themselves at a distance. I only ever spoke to one girl socially, and she was originally from South America.'

'Oh,' I said, trying to play the inscrutable card with my heart pounding. *At last I was onto something.*

'Perhaps she could join us next time we meet?'

'No that will not be possible.'

'Oh what a shame, where is she now?'

'Why do you ask' she snapped and suddenly looked uncomfortable.

My heart was beating ten to the dozen. *Don't push it too hard* I thought.

'I'm sorry, It's just interesting to hear about the people you work with.' *One final try* I thought. 'Has she gone back to America?'

'I do not know,' the response was final. I decided not to take the line of questioning further so I changed the subject.

'What do you do socially while in Africa?'

'We have Chinese cinema and satellite TV.'

This gave me a good opportunity to lighten up a little. We went on to discuss Chinese film stars and music. I was able to tell her about my visit to Shanghai the year before and she became quite animated as this was close to her home city.

'What do you think of Zambola' I asked.

'I do not like it, the people are lazy and the government is corrupt.'

I looked across at the president's Mother who was stuffing what looked like a large slice of French custard tart into her mouth.

'I was told about someone who was locked in a prison for five years because she didn't bribe the right people.'

'Exactly and this is why I do not like the country.'

While being polite and sociable I kept thinking, *how can I glean more information about Caterina?*

'I hope your American friend didn't end up in prison here, it sounds ghastly.'

'I do not know, now I must go.'

I'd pushed things too far and started to back track. 'I'm sorry if I offended you, It's just that I find everything about this country fascinating. I've enjoyed talking in Chinese, thank you so much, I don't often get the opportunity. Perhaps we can do it again sometime.'

'Perhaps, I will phone you, good bye.' With that she stood, shook hands very formally and left the restaurant.

I had the feeling she knew more than what she told me. *Bugger,* I thought as I paid the bill.

Chapter 10

For the rest of the week I got into the routine of teaching during the day and then eating at La Maison. I found the school to be quite an enjoyable experience but the evenings were tedious. Sitting with sad old expats getting pissed and reminiscing about the good old days bored the hell out of me. I was learning nothing new and I worried that time was slipping away. I spent Saturday morning teaching at the junior school and Jacques invited me to his farm that afternoon.

Sarab had all but become my personal chauffeur so he drove me out there. After about half an hour he pointed to an unmade road, 'That's La Croix, the women's prison.'

I feigned disinterest but my heart was pounding. I couldn't see anything apart from the track surrounded by forest.

Jacques entertained me superbly well. We dined as if in a Michelin restaurant with cordon bleu cooking and fine French wines. He introduced me to his three wives and a dozen or so mixed race sons and daughters.

'These are the people who will save our country' he said proudly. 'They are educated and understand the culture of both the white and the black man. Maybe he was right, all I knew was that he lived his life his way and he seemed quite content.

I asked about Tanja Westermann.

He sat silently for a second and then said, 'A fine woman and a good friend. If I could do anything to get her out I would. Henri is my best buddy and it breaks my heart because I know on the back of this he's drinking himself to death. It's a toss up as to which one dies first. She doesn't deserve a prison sentence and truth be told, it's nothing to do with her, it's political, a warning to the white man. They want us out.

After a couple of large brandies I got up to leave.

'Englishman, I don't know what you're doing here but watch yourself. They don't like outside interference and they're ruthless. Look at Tanja, it makes me sick.'

We said our good byes and Sarab took me home. He was happy having been given a good meal by a couple of the sons. I knew I was the worse for wear and as I staggered up the steps to the mission Father Steve opened the door.

'You better sober up quickly, I've got something to tell you.' I followed him into his library and he poured me a cup of strong black coffee. As I took a sip he said,

'You are aware that I am unable to break the seal of the confessional?'

I nodded, I knew that whatever was said in the confession box stayed in the confession box.

He went on, 'According to Roman Catholic canon law, "The sacramental seal is inviolable; therefore it is absolutely forbidden for a confessor to betray in any way a penitent in words or in any manner and for any reason.' He paused for a couple of seconds. 'However, a priest may ask the penitent for a release from the sacramental seal to discuss the confession with the person himself or others.' He paused, 'I have that release.'

'How?' I asked.

'He wants absolution.' He's a simple man and it wasn't hard to convince him to help himself.

'Go on.'

'Your friend is in La Croix. She's in a bad way having been beaten and raped. I'm sorry.'

'Who is this man?'

'I'm not prepared to say anymore, you have the information you need.'

'And you're going to give absolution?' I asked incredulously.

'Which would you prefer that I maintain absolute secrecy?'

He was right, even though it sickened me. He hadn't broken the rules of the church and he was giving Caterina a chance.

'Sometimes' he said, 'We have to take a pragmatic approach, that way people live who may otherwise die.'

'And those who commit the crimes walk away free.'

'Life's a long song, trust me, they usually get their cum uppence.'

I nodded, 'Thank you' was all I could say. He bid me good night and left the room.

My mind went into overdrive. I poured more coffee and a tumbler of water. I had to sober up quickly. Caterina was in La Croix. Somebody had confessed to something which confirmed where she was. I ran upstairs and grabbed my 'O' phone.

Mark answered immediately, 'I'm pissed and I don't apologise because I've found her, she's in La Croix women's jail. Don't ask me how I found out, just believe me.'

'Superb work Jonathan, I'll rally the troops, get some shut eye, something tells me you're going to need it.'

I slept but was woken at four thirty by the 'O' phone ringing. It was Mark.

'We're going to fly in a platoon low so they won't be detected and get her out. But we need to land somewhere quietly, any ideas?'

My head was throbbing and I felt like shit.

'There are two expats I've met, well one is third generation African. I told him about Jacques, Henri and Tanja Westermann. 'If I could convince Henri that we can get Tanja out at the same time as Caterina they may well be helpful. They know the geography of the place.'

'Sounds as good an option as there is. Let me check them out.'

I gave him all the information I had on the three. Admittedly it was pretty scant but Mark said he would be back to me within a couple of hours. I drank some more water, swallowed a couple of ibuprofen tablets and dozed off. There was little I could do at that time of the day with a raging hangover.

Zan was making love to me, then she was Caroline and then Caterina. All three were laughing as I woke in a cold sweat. Dawn was breaking but my head was throbbing. I phoned Mark and again he picked up immediately.

'Anything?' I asked.

'Not really, neither of them appear to have many physical assets, apart from the farm in Jacques case. La Maison is rented and looking at the bank accounts it scrapes by as a business.'

Even though I knew precisely how The Organisation was able to hack into bank accounts I still marvelled at the approach.

He went on, 'They haven't made the papers, the French Embassy know them both but have no real information on either. Quite frankly in a country like Zambola we're not going to find much more. The German embassy has confirmed Tanja is being used as a political pawn but there's little they can do. She seems straight enough.'

'I'll go and see Henri at eight o'clock, hopefully he'll be up by then.'

'There is a risk, you may find they don't want to play and report you to the authorities.'

'I doubt it, everything fits together, we're the only hope Henri has to save Tanja.'

'Watch yourself.'

I showered and dressed quickly. Father Steve was in the hall as I descended the stairs.

'You look as rough as old boots' he said grinning. 'There's fresh coffee and croissants. I have early morning Mass, if you'll excuse me.'

'Thanks again,' I said as he turned waving his hand in acknowledgement.

I walked up the road, people were making their way to the church. One of the teachers came across to me.

'Are you going to Mass?' she asked.

'Later' I replied I have to see someone now.

'The kids love you at the school, I hope you can stay forever!'

I smiled and felt as guilty as hell knowing that I may not even return. Knocking at the door of 'La Maison' I felt a little pissed off as there was no reply. I was about to leave when the hatch opened.

'I need to see Henri, it's important.'

The hatch closed and I stood for a couple of minutes watching the market in full swing.

Eventually the door opened and an old woman beckoned me in. I guessed she was the cleaner. As I walked through the bar Henri appeared wearing a dressing gown and looking somewhat dishevelled.

'What the hell do you want at this time of day?'

'Sit down and listen,' I said quite forcibly.

'Coffee?' he enquired.

I nodded and he ordered the cleaner to make a pot.

''I'm trusting you,' I said, 'As I think we can help each other.'

'Go on' replied Henri raising an eyebrow.

'I work for an agency connected to the UN. I've been sent here to find one of our people who has gone missing. I have it on good authority that she's in La Croix.'

'How have you established that?'

'Don't ask but take it as read.'

'We will be sending in a team to get her out, if you help we'll get Tanja out as well.'

Henri looked at me, I could see tears welling up in his eyes,' My God this is incredible,' he immediately pulled himself together, 'Yes, yes, yes of course, what do you want me to do?'

'I need to land a plane somewhere which isn't going to alert anyone, preferably close to La Croix. Do you know of anywhere?'

He sighed, 'There's an old French airbase about fifteen kilometres east of Jacques farm. It was used by the FAZ, the government air force until all the planes were destroyed in the last uprising. There has been talk of re-establishing it but nothing has happened. The base is in ruins and I've no idea whether the runway is still serviceable.'

'Can we go and take a look?'

'Sure give, me ten minutes to change.'

I sat drinking my coffee formulating a plan.

Whatever happened I didn't want to implicate Father Steve and the mission. I wasn't being altruistic just sensible. The Christian Missionary Society had been more than helpful, without them we wouldn't be in this position. If their movement was compromised in Zambola they would never help us again.

I realised that I would have to stay for a period of time to ensure there was no connection between Caterina's release and my disappearance. I wasn't unhappy as I enjoyed teaching at the school and knew I'd be doing something useful. *Who knows?* I thought, *I may stay here for the duration.*

My mobile rang. 'Mark,' I said.

'We've found an old French airbase about twenty miles from Kanina.'

'I'm ahead of you,' I said grinning, 'I'm on my way to check it out.'

'Henri playing the game?'

'Yep, I'll phone later.'

I cut the call as Henri shuffled into the bar fully dressed. 'Let's go,' he said.

We went down the back stairs into a courtyard where a tired looking Land Rover stood.

'Nearly forty years old but still going strong,' laughed Henri. He suddenly looked serious.

'I don't know how to thank you.'

'We haven't got her out yet,' I replied, 'And if we do, you may well have to stay here for a while. I can't have local people compromising the operation.'

'If I know she's escaped and alive I'll do anything. I've waited so long, I can wait a bit longer. Jump in.'

We drove out of Kanina heading towards Jacques's farm. A plan began to formulate in my mind as we bounced along.

'Tell me about the Muslims,' I said.

'The government is terrified of them. They're persecuted for no reason and Kasenga is paranoid they'll take over the country. Not a bad thing from my perspective, they couldn't be worse than this lot.'

'How many are there?'

'Difficult to say, government figures suggest five percent of the population, Comizan say fifteen.

'Comizan?'

'La Communauté Islamique en République Démocratique du Zambola.

I'd say they were probably about right but with ethnic cleaning it could be lower.'

'And is Comizan powerful?'

'Should be more powerful than it is, but there's too much infighting between the Sunni's, the Shiites and the Ahmadi. It was set up to bring all Muslims sects together, help the people with their problems and provide a communication point with the authorities. Sadly the government has accused them of being a terrorist force and arrested many of the people associated with it. Why do you ask?'

'I'm not sure yet, but they seem to be a group of downtrodden souls who could possibly help us.'

'How?'

'No idea, I'm thinking out loud that's all.'

'I know the Imam of Kanina vaguely.'

'I'll come back to you on that one. 'Why's he not been arrested?'

'Not sure, political dynamite to imprison a religious leader may be? Mind you give it time.'

We pulled off the main road and went along a track which to a large extent had been taken back by the forest. After a hundred yards of weaving between potholes weeds and branches we arrived at wire mesh gates, one of which hung off a post and had a tree growing through it, the other lay on the ground covered in undergrowth. It had been trampled down a long tine ago.

We drove slowly around potholes and a couple of craters with Henri looking closely at the ground.

'I don't want to wreck my tyres on that barbed wire,' he said pointing at the undergrowth.

The aerodrome stood in ruins, everything had been destroyed long ago. Henri pointed out where the infrastructure had once been. The control tower was now a heap of rubble, the remains of the main terminal had been totally destroyed, wreckage and debris was scattered for hundreds of yards. There was an eerie silence where no life appeared to exist.

Henri drove around and eventually we came to the runway. At least what was left of it. Craters, potholes and cracks ran the length of what had once been the lifeline of the country.

'This is a microcosm of what has happened to my country.' Henri said sadly. 'It sums up everything that is wrong. Here we had a perfectly good and operational airport, totally destroyed by the ridiculous political factions. And what have they achieved for the ordinary Zambolan? Absolutely fuck all, in fact the place has regressed a hundred years.'

'I need to make a call' I said hitting the satellite app on my 'O' phone.

Almost immediately I was put through to Mark's answerphone. Again I marvelled at the technology. Here I was in the middle of the African jungle making a phone call.

'Mark the airport is totally destroyed, there's no way a plane could land, we'll have to think of something else. Also, can you check out Comizan, La Communauté Islamique en République Démocratique du Zambola. It's a Muslim political group. They're downtrodden and abused. Do we have any contacts, could they be of use? Speak later.'

I killed the call and surveyed the derelict vista, it was quite depressing. 'Let's get out of here' I said.

'Maybe Jacques could help us' said Henri who'd suddenly become my right hand man, 'there's nobody I could trust more.'

'Let's go see him,' I said.

Twenty minutes later we arrived at the farm. Jacques stood with his head under the bonnet of a vintage Citroen truck. One of his sons was standing next to him. Turning round he grinned.

'Fancy a drop more brandy?'

'No, I think I had enough last night.'

'We need to talk,' said Henri.

Jacques looked at him quizzically and handing a spanner to his son said 'Let's go inside.'

We sat in the living room as Henri outlined the day's events. Jacques said nothing, he just listened. As Henri spoke I received a text.

Jacques looked up quite surprised, 'Satellite phone,' I said.

The text said, 'We'll use helicopters, just sorting refuelling points. Will the airbase be suitable for night landing? Imran will be contacting you re Comizan.'

I smiled, that could only mean one person. Imran had been on my initial training course with The Organisation. We called him our Middle East expert. He'd worked with the likes of Hezbollah, the Israel defence force, the National Liberation Army in Libya and the Syrian rebel forces. His experience was all a bit north of Zambola but obviously he had contacts within the Muslim world.

I told Jacques and Henri about the helicopters.

'They can land here' said Jacques.

'No' I replied, you'll be immediately implicated, there's enough land around the airbase. It'll be much safer.

Jacques nodded, 'You'll need landing lights, I can organise that. Let me know how many helicopters are coming in.'

'I don't want you getting into trouble' I said. 'People talk.'

'Only my sons and I will be involved, don't worry. Besides I'm fed up looking at this ugly git every time I go into town, I'll be glad to get rid of him.'

We all laughed and shook hands. Henri and I headed back to town. On the way my phone rang.

'Imran, how are you,' I said. I liked the man, he was a serious character but extremely able. We hadn't been that close but always got on well enough. The sadness was eight people had attended our initial training course, two were now dead and a third missing.

'I'm good,' he said, 'And glad you're back with us.' His Middle Eastern intonation was always pleasant on the ear and I felt somewhat reassured he was now part of the operation.

'So tell me about Comizan,' I said.

'Not a lot to tell at the moment. I'm just ringing to touch base. I'll be spending the rest of the day talking to people to see what I can come up with and I'll be in touch as soon as possible.'

'Good man,' I replied, 'Speak soon.' I killed the call and relayed the details to Henri.

'This is all moving so fast' he said, 'When do you think the action will start?'

'Given that they have to plan the mission, resource it, bring the team into Africa, I'd have thought Friday, maybe Saturday.'

'Incredible,' he said smiling, suddenly looking ten years younger.

Chapter 11

Henri dropped me off close to the Church. The morning service had obviously just finished as people were streaming down the road. I saw Fei Yen and went up to her.

'Hello,' I said remembering just in time to speak in Mandarin, 'I was hoping you'd be here' She looked genuinely pleased to see me.

'I thought you weren't at the service.'

I ducked that one, 'Shall we go for a walk?'

'That would be nice'

We started strolling towards the docks.

'You must speak English' I said trying to steer the conversation around to Caterina.

'Why do you ask?'

'Well you said you had an American friend and I don't know many Americans who speak Mandarin Chinese, or any other language for that matter.'

'Yes I speak a little' she said laughing in heavily accented English, 'But not well, your Chinese is much better.'

'I am happy to speak Chinese' I said.

We walked passed the market stalls and created a fair amount of interest amongst locals. They'd probably never seen a Chinese girl with a white man. Chatting about nothing in particular Fei Yen seemed more relaxed than the last time we met. I stopped at one stall and bought two fruit drinks, they were squeezed in front of us from fresh papaya and oranges. She smiled and seemed to appreciate the gesture.

'I must apologise for being rude when we last met' she said having taken a sip.

'I wasn't aware you were rude.'

'We were talking about the American girl and I found it difficult.'

I tried to be non committal but my heart skipped a beat.

'I did not mean to be rude but she did something very bad.'

I stayed silent, hoping she would say more.

'I thought she was my friend but she was an enemy of The People's Republic of China.'

Fei Yen looked angry but at the same time upset. I tried to be as nonchalant as possible in the hope she'd say more.

'Goodness me, what did she do?'

'She tried to steal state secrets.'

'What in Africa?' I replied showing my genuine surprise.

She remained silent for a few seconds before she spoke again, 'I have said too much, I am sorry.'

'Don't worry,' I held my hands up. *One last try* I thought.

'So has she gone back to America?'

'I do not know,' the response was terse and followed by silence, it was time to back off again.

'I'm sorry if you have been hurt or feel betrayed' I said and tried to lighten the atmosphere by making a joke, 'Americans, who'd trust them eh?'

'I thought English and Americans were all the same, but you are different.'

I turned and looked at her, she wasn't the most attractive girl in the world, but there was something that appealed. I took her hands and she blushed.

'May I buy you lunch?' I asked. Apart from anything else I felt bloody hungry.

'No' she replied pulling away from me, 'I must go.'

'Why Fei Yen, I'd like to get to know you.'

'No, it's not possible.' She turned and hailed a passing cab which screeched to a halt in front of us.

'Can I see you again?' I asked, 'Please?'

'I do not know' she said climbing into the car.

'Not all Westerners are like Americans you know.'

'I know, perhaps I will phone you.'

'I hope so' I said grabbing her hand again through the open window as the cab started to move off.

She pulled away and smiled sadly. I walked back to the Church feeling perplexed. I knew I didn't want a relationship with the girl but something about her disturbed me. Was it because she was Chinese like Zan? Was it because she was the only girl I'd really met since coming to Zambola. Was there an attraction? Was it purely lust? I didn't really have an answer, but I felt as guilty as hell for using her to gain information. I felt very confused. But then, I wasn't hurting anyone, and she had helped me fill in the pieces with regard to Caterina.

Truth be told, it was the guilt trip I was still on for Zan. My guilt for her having died and me having lived. *Was it always going to be like this whenever I met a girl* I wondered? I began to hate myself and The Organisation for putting me in this position.

Yvette opened the door at The Missionary Society.

'Would you like some lunch Monsieur?' she asked.

'I would thank you.'

'Go and sit in the dining room I will bring some soup, cheese and bread.'

While waiting I phoned Mark and told him about the conversation I'd had with Fei Yen.

'What the hell did Caterina find I wonder? asked Mark.

'Long shot,' I said, 'Can you see if she downloaded anything onto her 'O' phone?'

'We've done all that, if there'd been anything the boffins would have found it.'

94

As he spoke I could see Imran was trying to get through. I told Mark I'd touch base later.

Imran came straight to the point.

'I'm coming over with a colleague. He's a senior member of The Muslim Brotherhood and has worked with me several times, We're going to set up a meeting with the Imam of Kanina and a few of his Comizan cohorts. For information the Muslims in Zambola are on the verge of revolt. Arms have been smuggled in over the last couple of years and they are now all but in a position to help overthrow the government. They're working with a political faction called Parti Chrétien Républicain or PCR. So we have Christians and Muslims working together to oust the current regime. They're not exactly friends but fate makes strange bedfellows. To be fair both factions want a peaceful and honest government to run the country so the alliance may just work. Between them they have enough manpower to give Kasenga's army a run for their money. It won't be easy and will probably be extremely bloody. However they need to release many of their people currently locked up in Zambolan prisons to provide manpower. Once they're out the overthrow should take place quickly. Now this will happen with or without our involvement. So we can't be accused of manipulating the overthrow of a nation state. The PCR have been pushing for months but Comizan have been slowing the process down to ensure they have enough weapons in place. With our help we can get them operational within a week.

'Why the hell didn't we know about this before?' I asked feeling a little pissed off that I'd come over to Zambola knowing only half the story.

'To be fair,' responded Imran, 'Zambola has never really been on the Organisation's radar. It's too small, our brief was to find out what the Chinese are up to in Africa. Local politics are very much a side issue.'

I put my personal feeling to one side and tried to think through any floors in Imran's plan. 'The central prison is in the middle of Kanina,' I said, 'How do you propose to take that?'

'There'll be a mass demonstration organized during which the prison will be attacked. Trained snipers will be put into position to take out government forces if they start firing. It won't be pretty but it will be effective. As the prisoners are released they'll be placed into military units to fight with us. With a belly full of food those not already on our side will soon come over. The hope is Kasenga's men will defect on mass, although that is far from a given.'

'Why should they?'

'Poor conditions, and they haven't been paid for months.'

'This all sounds very good, are we still sending in a force?'

'Oh yes, The Organisation will be taking out the women's prison, that way Caterina has more than a fighting chance of survival. Make no mistake there are going to be a lot of casualties in this little fracas. By putting in pros we can minimize losses in this one area. Hopefully by having trained personnel on board together with the right equipment casualties will be kept to a minimum. That's why I need to link up with the Imam to ensure we're all working together and not falling across each other.'

'What can I do?' I asked feeling a little redundant.

'We're flying into Kinshasa tomorrow, from there we'll travel by helicopter to the base you saw earlier. Otherwise it's an overnight in Kinshasa and we haven't got time to waste. Arrange pick up to take us into Kanina. We aim to arrive at 2am local time. I'll tell you where to drop us in town. That's all I need presently. We'll keep in touch by 'O' phone and no more. We need to keep contagion to a minimum, if we're caught nobody can track us back to you. If I could arrange a pick up excluding you I would but we need to get in quickly and with minimal local knowledge.'

'No probs, I'll be there, but I didn't realise helicopters had that sort of range.

'They haven't, we're currently arranging refuelling stops. Tomorrow will be a test run for the main force which arrives on Saturday.' My phone cut out, the battery had died.

'Shit,' I thought. I ran upstairs and plugged it in to charge.

There was no need to phone back, we'd said all that was needed. As usual, The Organisation's attention to detail was exemplary. Laying on my bed I tried to find any flaws in what had been planned. I couldn't so I dozed for a couple of hours and woke feeling tired. The stress of the last few days was taking it out on me. I walked up to La Maison, Henry was out.

'Bierre?' said the barman.

'Non, café s'il vous plait' I needed to keep my wits about me. I sat half reading the local newspaper for about twenty minutes at which point Henri and Jacques came in. I looked at them and gestured to the back door, in other words, *we need to talk.*

'Mon ami Anglais' Henri said grinning from ear to ear, 'I am so glad you are here, come and see the book I have found in the market, I think it is just what you are looking for, an introduction to Niger Congo languages. It is very old but like me still useful.' He laughed at his own joke and ushered me into his private quarters.

'I'd actually quite like that book', I said.

He smiled again, 'How can I help you?'

I outlined Imran's plan. Henri pursed his lips while Jacques sat down looking pensive.

'Wow' said Henri, 'this is incredible. I had no idea, in the past when we have had revolutions the whole country knows about it before it happened.'

'Will it work?' I asked.

'I am no military expert, but what I have learned over the years is that the incumbent army becomes lazy and disenchanted. Your men will be lean and hungry but untrained. It could well be messy. But if it gives Tanja a chance I'm with you.

'You'll need transport to the airport,' said Jacques. 'What I suggest is that my son uses his passion wagon as we call it. He'll take his supposed girlfriend with you in the back. If he's stopped by the police they'll think he's joy riding and going for a bit of nooky. A bribe will keep them quiet.'

'And the girl, will she be reliable?' I asked.

'No problem.' grinned Jacques, she's my daughter.

'I can't let you do that' piped up Henri. This is my problem, I'll take Tom.'

'No,' said Jacques quite forcibly. You'll have no excuse for cruising the streets in the middle of the night, a young couple is perfect cover. It'll be water tight, trust me.'

'But...'

'No buts, this is how it's going to be.

Henri nodded in a resigned manner, we both knew Jacques's plan was as robust as we could make it.

'You eat with us tonight?' asked Henri.

'No thanks', I replied, 'I have a few things I need to sort out.' Truth be told, I felt knackered having been on the piss the night before, with little sleep and quite a jam-packed day. I decided on an early night realising that the following week was going to be full on.

By the time I left La Maison darkness had fallen. For the first time that week Sarab was nowhere to be seen. I wasn't particularly bothered and started strolling back to the Church. As I rounded the corner from the main road I heard a voice in the darkness speak in French.

'Give me your money and there'll be no problem.'

I spun round and saw three people in silhouette. I wasn't about to play the hero so I took the money I had in my pocket and held it out.

'Fifty US dollars, that's all I've got.'

'Don't fuck with us white man, we want proper money.'

'I work at the Christian Missionary, we don't have a lot of money.'

'Search him.'

With that heavy hands grabbed me and started ripping at my clothes. *Discretion is the better part of valour*, I thought as they threw me to the ground, cut open my shirt, pulled off my shoes and slashed at my trousers with what was obviously a sharp knife.

They pulled away and one of them snarled, 'You must have money, where is it?' with that he kicked me in the groin, just missing my vital parts.

I got up onto my knees and said 'Guy's I haven't got anymore money.' With that I felt a blow to the side of my head and everything went black. The next thing I remember was opening my eyes and feeling the sensation of movement. I was lying in the back of a car and heard a voice.

'I am so sorry Sahib but I was waiting for you at the church, I didn't know you'd gone out.'

It was Sarab talking at me.

'Where are we going?' I asked feeling punch drunk and dizzy.

'You're alive, praise be to Allah. I'm taking you to the hospital.'

'How did you find me?'

'I had my window open and heard the commotion at the top of the street, I drove up to see what was going on and in the headlights the three men ran. I found you lying on the road and put you in the car.'

'I'm glad you were there.' I croaked coming round a little, 'But I've got no money to pay you for the ride.'

'Do not worry, another time. These people who attacked you, do not hate them. They have nothing, no work and no hope. This country is finished, the politicians take everything and we have nothing. It cannot continue.'

I began to feel nauseous as the cab came to a halt. Sarab climbed out.

'Stay here Sahib, I will get help.' As he spoke I threw up, *that'll cost me another twenty bucks* I thought.

After what seemed like only a few seconds the back door opened and heavy hands dragged me onto a stretcher. I felt myself being wheeled up a ramp and then the smell of hospital disinfectant hit me. A male nurse wearing a white tunic and dark trousers started asking questions. Name, address, where I worked etc. He seemed more intent on finding out whether I had medical insurance than anything else.

'I will have to ring The Missionary Society to confirm who you are,' he said, 'Do you have their number?'

I looked at him, 'I've just been robbed of all my possessions and no, I don't know the number, can't you find it?' I was getting a bit pissed off and just wanted to see a doctor.

'Leave it with me,' he said.

I lay there for ten minutes or so thinking about not very much. My head was splitting and I could feel my body stiffening. I'd suffered a real pummelling but thanks to Sarab I reckoned I'd be okay. The door opened and he came rushing in.

'Sahib I got the number for the Mission and Father Steve wants to talk to you.'

He handed me a mobile, I put it to my ear, my arm hurt like hell.

100

'Tom are you alright?'

'I've been better, but I think it's just a few cuts and bruises.'

'This is terrible I'll be right over.'

'Father Steve there's no need, I'm in safe hands.'

'There's every need I have to sign for you otherwise you'll only get emergency treatment. Tell your taxi friend to come and get me.'

'Thank you, I appreciate your help, could I ask you to bring my mobile, you'll find it charging in my room.'

'Hello I am Doctor Nkodia,' I heard from behind me, 'You teach my son at the Mission school, he tells me you are a good man. I am so sorry this has happened to you in my country.'

For the next few minutes he prodded and poked. 'You'll need stitches in your arm, apart from that a bit of mild concussion and a few bruises. I'd like to keep you in overnight just to make sure you're okay but I should be able to release you in the morning.'

He shook me by the hand and wandered off. The nurse reappeared, stripped off what was left of my clothes, cleaned me up and then helped me into a hospital robe.

'I'm now going to stitch your arm' he said, 'with a little local anaesthetic this shouldn't hurt at all.'

I hadn't really been aware of the problem but when I looked I could see a deep cut where the knife must have slashed me.

'These guys don't mess about do they?' I said.

'You cannot blame them,' came the response. 'Sadly the government keep all the money so people starve. There is no real investment in the country, anyone who complains is locked up, it is terrible. We were better off as a French colony. At least we had laws which people respected.'

I didn't really expect this tirade but the man's comments on top of what Sarab said intrigued me. I was building a real picture of hate for the governing classes.

'Is there any hope?' I asked.

'The PCR is our only hope. Who knows, maybe one day we'll have a government that want to help all people, not steal, murder and destroy anything that is decent.'

'How can they take power?' I asked.

'Revolution, it is the only way.'

'Is that likely?'

'Soon my friend, soon.'

I thought about what my Muslim taxi driver Sarab had said together with the nurse's comments. Muslims and Christians working together to make a better society. Perhaps by getting involved The Organisation was actually helping to make a difference. Maybe Caterina's disappearance would actually assist this country to move forward.

The nurse wheeled me into a private room. As with the rest of the hospital it was very well appointed and not what I expected in the middle of Africa. Money talks I thought as Father Steve and Sarab came rushing in.

'Okay' said Father Steve, 'I've brought clothes, shoes and the modern appendage you call a mobile. Cell phone in my language.'

'You should come to my lessons at school' I quipped, 'I'll teach you to speak the Queens English.'

We talked for a few minutes at which point the doctor reappeared.

'Gentlemen could I ask you to leave please, my patient needs a good night's rest and hopefully tomorrow he will be fit enough to leave.'

Father Steve shook me by the hand, I grimaced as the pain from the cut kicked in.

'I will be hear for you tomorrow Sahib,' said Sarab and with that the two of them left.

The nurse reappeared and gave me some pills, 'For the pain and to help you sleep,' he said.

'Is there really going to be a revolution?' I asked.

'Oh yes, we have had enough. Too many good people are in prison and too many bad people are running the country. How many millions have been siphoned abroad? With that money we could be a rich country.'

I decided at that point, no matter what, I would use The Organisation to get that money transferred back from France, Switzerland and wherever else Kasanga and his cohorts had hidden it. I realised that for once I really could make a difference.

The pills kicked in and I slept.

Chapter 12

The following morning I woke at about 7.30 as a pretty nurse wheeled in a trolley on top of which stood a coffee pot and a large jug of orange juice.

'Bonjour Monsieur Simpson', she said, 'Would you like some breakfast?'

I blinked a couple of times and realised I was as parched as hell.

'Orange juice would be wonderful' I croaked. She poured a glass and handed it to me. My right arm had really stiffened up overnight and felt sore. I took it with my left hand and drank.

'Thank you, I said, 'May I have some more?'

She poured another glass, 'Croissant and cheese?' she asked. I nodded and she rolled a hospital table up the bed and put the food on a plate before handing it to me.

'When will the doctor be here?' I wanted to be out of this place as soon as possible. My head still throbbed and my body ached but I had too much going on to worry about such irrelevancies.

'In about half an hour.' She had a delightful smile which lit up the room.

'How long have you been a nurse?' I asked.

I am not a nurse, I am an orderly, but I have been here for three years. I have to work to look after my children.'

'How many have you got?'

'Three, two boys twelve and ten and a little girl aged four.'

'What does your man do?'

'Sadly he died, that's why I work here.'

'I'm so sorry, what happened?'

'He was a doctor who disagreed with the government. They put him in jail and he died. I'm a qualified surveyor but because of my husband's politics I cannot get a job. If I apply for one the powers that be have a conversation and I get a rejection. The only reason I am here is that friends of my husband quietly employ me. That's how things are in this country.'

'I hope it changes soon.'

'I think it will'.

'What do you mean?'

'I don't know' she replied guardedly.

'Henri and Jacques may not know about the coming revolution.' I thought, *'But the local populace do.'*

She left the room so I rang Mark and brought him up to speed.

'One thing' I said Kasanga has siphoned millions, probably hundred of millions out of this country. We need to ensure a stable government is put in place and the money invested back into the economy. We've got the power and resource to do it.'

'We'll need the political influence as well, easier said than done.'

'That's surely what we are about.'

'Maybe, but one step at a time, a change of government doesn't often lead to a change in culture. Invariably the replacements are as bad as the previous incumbents. Enough of that, how are you feeling? If you're not fit I'll find another way to get Imran in.'

'I'll be fine, the doctor is going to release me after a final check in about twenty minutes.'

'Keep me in touch, I don't need heroes, we've lost too many recently.'

'Tell me about it.' I thought.

'I'll phone when I've seen the Doctor.'

I lay on the bed, my head was beginning to clear, apart from a few bruises and a bit of discomfort in my arm I felt good enough. Doctor Nkodia arrived.

'You work long hours,' I joked.

'I have to, sadly a doctors pay in this country doesn't cover the bills.' He gave me the once over. 'You'll live, I'll release you once the nurse has changed your dressing but take it easy for a few days.'

'That'll happen,' I nodded and smiled.

He left the room and a couple of minutes later the nurse I'd seen previously came to change my bandage. He handed me a couple of packets of pills.

'Antibiotics and painkillers,' he said,' Take them until you run out and we'll see you this time next week to check your arm. Don't let the bandage get wet and don't do anything strenuous.'

The fact that I was in the middle of helping to promote a revolution made me smile.

'Thanks for your help' I said.

'Do you want a hand dressing?'

'I should be OK.'

I phoned Sarab and asked him to pick me up in fifteen minutes. Trying to shower while keeping my arm out of the water jets proved challenging. As did doing up my trousers and even putting socks on. Finally ready I collected my possessions left the room and signed out at reception. Sarab was waiting and greeted me like a long lost friend.

'How are you Sahib?' he said with a look of genuine concern on his face.

'I'm okay thanks, can you run me to the mission and then up to the school?' He nodded while opening the door.

'I am so sorry this has happened,' he said as we set off.

'What's going to happen to this country Sarab?' I asked, trying to establish what else the common man knew.

'I tell you because you are my friend. There will be revolution. The Muslims and Christians will fight together to get rid of these monsters. Many will die, but we will be free.'

'When will this happen?'

'Soon, I do not know.'

'Do you know people in prison?'

Sarab stayed silent for a few moments, 'My brother, and he is a good man, he has done nothing.'

'I am so sorry,' it was all I could say. We arrived at the Mission and as I knocked on the door Yvette opened it.

'Monsieur I am so relieved to see you. How are you feeling?'

'I'm a bit sore Yvette but okay. I have a few things to do and then I will go to the school.'

'Shouldn't you rest? Father Steve said I should look after you.'

'I'll be fine, a cup of coffee would be appreciated though.'

She smiled, I'd really won this lady over, 'I will bring it to you.'

I went up to my room and phoned Mark. He got down to business straight away.

'Imran is on his way, I can get him in tomorrow without a problem if you're not up for it.'

'I'll be fine.' I was already a bit pissed off that I was only picking Imran up and not working with him directly, Mark knew me too well to argue.

I phoned Henri, he was appalled when I told him what had happened but confirmed I'd be picked up outside The Mission by Jacques's son at midnight. A wise man would have rested, but I was too pumped up for that and decided I'd be better focusing on the school. At least that would give me something to think about.

As I got back into the taxi I handed Sarab a hundred US dollar bill.

'Thanks for looking after me' I said.

'No no this is too much.'

'Just take it.'

'You are a true friend' he said stuffing the note into his top pocket.

I arrived at the school just before the mid morning break and went straight to the staff room. As the teachers filed in they all hugged me and shook my hand, horrified at what had happened. Father Steve beckoned and we went into a private office.

'Isn't it a little soon to be back?'

'What am I going to do instead? Sit in the Mission feeling sorry for myself?'

'There's no point in arguing is there?'

'I have to ask you something Father Steve, You mentioned about the possibility of an uprising. I've talked to quite a few people who seem to agree with you. Would a PCR and Comizan alliance make for stable government?'

'Well well, for someone who's only been here five minutes you are remarkably well informed.'

He thought for a second. 'In theory it could work as long as the moderates are in control. Put it another way they couldn't be any worse than the current regime, but many innocent people will die in an uprising and that I have difficulty with.'

'Many innocent people are currently dying in prison.'

'Indeed, and that is the conundrum.'

I spent the rest of the day teaching. Staff and pupils were so kind towards me, appalled at what had happened. They asked me to forgive their countrymen who had committed this crime. I kept being told it wasn't their fault but the fault of the system. It was obvious these people needed a government free from corruption to stand any chance at all. I had serious doubts that much would change post revolution. It was as frustrating as hell but obvious the status quo couldn't survive.

By the time I got back to The Mission I felt shattered. I went to bed and set my alarm for 11.30. Although it was only early evening I slept. The alarm woke me with a jolt. My head ached and my arm felt sore. I took more pills than I should have to kill the pain, dressed as quickly as the restrictions of my arm allowed and headed downstairs.

I hoped like hell nobody would be around as I quietly opened the front door. A Nissan van was parked outside and a gorgeous girl in her late teens climbed out. She could have been Caterina's younger sister with Latino looks and long dark hair.

'Hi Tom' she said smiling while shaking hands, I'm Marianne and this is my brother Gilles.' I peered inside and a very handsome young man waved in acknowledgement from the driver's seat. Marianne slid open the side door and pointed at three mattresses.

'If we are stopped,' she said, 'these have been hollowed out underneath so you and your friends can hide while we do the talking.'

'Thank you.' I replied.

'No no, thank you, I gather you're helping our friends Henri and Tanja. Jump in before anybody sees us. It won't be very comfortable I'm afraid.'

The side door closed behind me and Gilles set off immediately. Within minutes we were out of the town travelling at a good speed towards the derelict airport. Conversation was kept to a minimum, I think we all felt anxious and the nervous tension could be cut with a knife.

There was little traffic apart from the odd truck and within forty minutes we turned off the main road and onto the overgrown airport track. Marianne jumped out of the van and walked ahead checking for barbed wire and debris. Twice she steered us away from possible dangers. Eventually we crawled past the gate, Gilles pulled up cutting the engine and lights. We sat in darkness, it was just before one o'clock and the silence was deafening. No animals could be heard, nothing, just an ominous calm.

'It's so quiet' I whispered.

'I know' replied Gilles at the same level.

'Why are we whispering?' asked Marianne.

We all giggled like school children. Sitting in silence the tension was too much. I decided to lighten things up a little.

'So did you two go to the Mission School?' I asked.

They both nodded, 'And I then studied agronomy at the AgroParisTech.' said Gilles. I knew it to be one of the 'Grandes Ecoles' where the directors of French industry are moulded.

'And what about you Marianne?

'I'm off to study law at the Sorbonne later this year.'

'Good girl,' I said, 'Paris is a fantastic city.'

'It certainly is,' replied Gilles.

'Do you miss it?' I asked.

'Of course, but we have much work to do here and with the right government we can make it happen.'

We chatted quietly for nearly an hour when the mood was broken as my 'O' phone vibrated. In the silence of the night it sounded like an alarm clock going off, startling the three of us.

'Hi,' I said, conversation in a situation like this was always kept to a minimum. It had been instilled during training. Although confident our lines were secure, there was no point in taking risks.

'Five minutes' came the response and the line went dead.

'How will they know where to land?' asked Marianne.

'They'll know' I replied.

Moments later the sound of the helicopter broke the silence. Landing lights came on and the Super Puma hovered about half a mile from us.

'Go' I shouted. Gilles started the engine switched on the headlights and drove as fast as the undergrowth would allow.

'Steady,' I said, 'We want this little baby to stay in one piece.' As we approached the helicopter touched down and two people could be seen climbing out. They dipped their heads and started running towards us. As soon as they were clear of the blades the aircraft was airborne again.

'Sweet' said Gilles.

I fumbled for the side door. My arm frustrated me but eventually it slid open. The two men clambered in and we were off before I'd shut it again. Marianne again got out and walked in front of the van checking the track leading to the main road. A minute later we were heading towards the city.

'Hi Imran' I said switching to English as I shook him by the hand, 'Great to see you again.'

'Tom, can I introduce you to Imam Ahmad al-Maturidi.'

'Asalaamu alaikum' I said 'Good to meet you.'

'Alaikum asalaamu' came the response, I am pleased to be here.' The accent suggested the man had been educated in England.

'Do we have an address?' asked Gilles also in English. *A bit if one-upmanship* I thought and smiled in the darkness.

'On Rue de la Vielle Mosque.' replied Imran, 'there is a restaurant called Aladdin. If it is quiet drop us on the next block.'

'That's a tough area,' replied Gilles, 'Will you be okay?'

'We will be tonight' replied Imran.

As we approached town a blue flashing light could be seen behind us.

'Beneath the mattresses you three, now,' suddenly Gilles was in total control. We ducked under the mattresses and the cold hard floor jarred against my recent cuts and bruises. I felt the van slow down and heard the indicator as we pulled in. Seconds later a strong beam penetrated through the back window. Footsteps could be heard moving along the side of the van.

Gilles opened his window. 'Bonne Soirée Monsieur' he said sounding very cool and calm,

'Bonne Soirée,' came the curt response. 'What are you doing out at this time of night?'

'Well my girlfriend and I, we've just been cruising.'

'And what have you got in the back of the van?' I could see the torch light shining through the mattress.

'Just a place to relax, you know?' Gilles laughed. *He's a bloody good actor* I thought.

'And who is this?'

'She's my girlfriend man.'

'She looks like a prostitute to me.'

'Hey no man,' replied Gilles with a hurt tone, 'She's a good girl, goes to church every Sunday.'

By now it was getting hot under the mattress and my heart was beating ten to the dozen. I felt almost surprised the police couldn't hear it.

'And what would her Mother say if she knew she was out with you at 3am?'

'I'm not going to tell her man, you know?'

After a moment's silence the policemen said, 'She looks about fourteen so I could charge you with having sex with a minor.'

'No man, we got our papers here, we are legit, just been having a good time together you know?'

Again there was silence. 'Well you went through a red light, that's a spot fine of five hundred francs.'

'Oh come on man no, we just had a nice night.'

I wanted to scream *Pay the bastard and let's get the fuck out of here.*

'Five hundred francs or a night in the cells, which would you prefer?'

'Merde' came the response as I heard a rustling of paper.

'Have a good night and watch the traffic lights in future.'

I didn't dare move. Silence prevailed 'Stay where you are' said Gilles quietly as he started the engine. We moved off slowly and I could feel sweat pouring off my face.

'OK you can come out but don't sit up, they may well follow us for a while.'

I shuffled out bumping into the Imam. I noticed he too was covered in sweat.

'Are you alright?' I asked.

''I have been in much worse positions,' he replied.

After a couple of minutes Gilles spoke, 'They've gone, you can sit up.

'Did you get a receipt?' I asked.

'Yeah right.'

After turning down a couple of streets the van came to a halt.

'Gentlemen. Welcome to Rue de la Vielle Mosque.'

Imran and the Imam climbed out of the van quickly. Again we drove off before I had time to slide the door closed. I turned and watched them walk down the street towards the restaurant.

Putting my arms around both Marianne and Gilles and grimacing with pain I said, 'Thanks Guys, you were bloody marvellous.'

'All part of the service.'

Within a couple of minutes we were back at the church. As the van came to a halt I dived out, ran up the steps and into the Mission. Before I had opened the front door the van had moved away. We'd delivered part one of the plan. I text Mark to update

113

him and went straight to bed. The thought of getting up in a couple of hours didn't inspire me, I felt knackered, but I had to keep up the pretence of everything being normal for as long as possible.

Chapter 13

The alarm went off at 5.30 and I lay in a comatose state for a couple of seconds. I knew if I stayed there I'd be back to sleep in no time. My head throbbed and my arm was sore. I hoisted myself out of bed and immediately felt dizzy. Logic said I should climb back into the pit, after the beating I had the perfect excuse. However I was determined to put on a good show so I dragged myself to the bathroom, swallowed a few pills and showered.

It didn't really help much and after dressing I staggered downstairs. Father Steve sat eating breakfast.

'If you want some advice,' he said, 'Go back to bed.'

'Do I look that good?' I croaked.

'No and that's the problem.'

I helped myself to a cup of coffee, I couldn't face food.

'I'll be fine,' I said, 'Early morning have never agreed with me.'

'Especially after late nights and beatings,' He didn't miss much.

We sat quietly on the school bus and the kids seemed to know that I wasn't in a fit state to be hassled. If I'm honest I drifted through the day, six lessons, but I let the kids do most of the work. We did revision classes so I didn't have to think too much.

I actually fell asleep on the bus back to the Mission and on arrival went straight to bed. I slept through the night and the following morning woke feeling a bit muzzy headed with my arm hurting like hell. Again I took more pain killers than I should have, showered and struggled downstairs. I knew I was far from one hundred per cent and again couldn't face the thought of dried up croissants.

'Would Monsieur prefer an omelette? asked Yvette.

'I'll be OK and we haven't really got time.'

'Make the man some eggs' said Father Steve taking control, 'the bus can wait for once.' He paused, 'I'm not at the school today so enjoy your breakfast and I'll see you as and when.' With that he left the room and within a couple of minutes a steaming omelette appeared which must have been made out of at least half a dozen eggs. I tucked in and realised that I was actually damned hungry.

Mark and Imran had left messages to phone and without Father Steve on the bus I was able to speak to them. '

I rang Imran first. 'How are you feeling? he asked.

'I'm fine, on the school bus at the moment.'

'OK, difficult for you to talk but I can. Let me update you. As I said, a mass demonstration has been organised for late Saturday in Kanina during which the prison will be attacked by rebel forces at 0200. The other three major prisons across the country will be hit simultaneously. Trained snipers that we're providing will take out the prison guards in Kanina along with any military that appear. As the prisoners are released they'll be placed into military units to fight alongside the rebels. Trucks have been sourced to bring troops and weapons into the city and the other complexes from holding areas.

'Where are they?' I asked trying to give nothing away to the kids on the bus.

'They're out of town, that's all you need to know. During the prisoner release the Comizan and PCR forces intend to secure the army base where much of the fighting is anticipated to take place. The released prisoners will be split into units to march on government buildings and the national TV station. A separate task force will take control of the Kanina Power Plant which produces most of the electricity for the city, the reservoir and sewerage plants. The Imam of Kanina is to be appointed interim President with the head of the PCR, Renee Ndebele his Prime Minister. Their aim is to secure the country with as little bloodshed as possible and to keep casualties to a minimum. It's hoped that government forces will stand down peacefully with many of them coming across to join the rebel army.'

'What's the weather forecast?'

'Dry and cloudy, we couldn't have asked for more.'

'What about Caterina?'

'Mark will give you details.'

'I'll phone you back when I can talk,' immediately I phoned Mark.'

'The Organisation are going to take control of liberating LaCroix.' he said, 'That way we are more likely to find Caterina alive. Four platoons are to be flown into the airbase using Chinook and Sikorsky helicopters. That's around one hundred and twenty men along with weaponry. Six container trucks are currently being driven overland from Kinshasa to the airbase to provide transportation to the prison. Without being able to land planes it's the only way we can provide transport.'

'What about landing nearer the site?' I asked looking around to ensure no one was listening.

'With half a dozen helicopters coming in the element of surprise would be compromised. This way we can transport the troops to within a mile of the camp and nobody will be any the wiser.' I could tell I wasn't at my best, I'd used the same argument the day before with Jacques.

'What happens if the trucks are caught?'

'They are just normal supply trucks delivering into Kanina. Supplies will be offloaded leaving the trucks empty for our use.

They even have a contract to take stuff back to Kinshasa. Whether that happens is another story. The important thing is all the paperwork will be legit.'

'Where do I fit in?'

'You arrive at the airport at midnight and ensure it's quiet. Confirm all is okay with the lead truck and they should join you by 00.45. ETA for the helicopters is 01.00. Our people will unload and be in the trucks by 01.15, twenty minutes to the prison and in position by 01.50. The fireworks will start at 02.00.'

'We need to clear the gates at the airport to ensure clean access.'

'I'll leave that to you. Details are on the 'O' platform under Operation Caterina.'

'I'll look at it today and get back to you.'

There were loose ends which I realised could be thrashed out during the week. For example, I needed transport to the airport, we had to clear the access, what happens if the helicopters are discovered while we're chasing across the countryside, how the hell was I going to find Caterina with bullets flying around, what were we going to do with 4000 women after they were released?

We arrived at the school and I breathed a sigh of relief. By focusing on teaching I knew that when I came back to think about this I would find solutions.

It was as if I'd never taken the beating. I felt alive and rejuvenated. The adrenalin had kicked in and I was raring to go.

The omelette had obviously done a good job!

There are some days when you know you're on top form and this was one of them. I'd done no planning for the lessons but I could tell the kids were really motivated by my performance. I was energised and vibrant. My enthusiasm cascaded to all those around me. As Patrice Umgali the head of languages said, 'Man

I don't know what they gave you in that hospital, but I want some.'

We high fived each other and burst into fits of laughter. On the way back to the Mission I even organised a sing song on the bus. I got a round going with each year group singing a verse of Frère Jacques. As I stepped off I got a round of applause.

'Well I've never seen that before' said Father Steve as he walked out of the church.

'They're lovely kids,' I said, 'I can't tell you how much I enjoy teaching them.'

'I hope you can stay a while,' said Father Steve.

I went up to my room and on impulse phoned Fei Yen.

She was very curt as she answered.

'I was wondering if we could meet for tea tomorrow?' I asked.

'No that will not be possible.'

'Oh, what about Thursday?'

'No I'm sorry.'

'Have I offended you?'

'There was a long silence, I was about to blurt out something when she spoke,' I'm going home tomorrow.'

'That's very sudden.'

'This country is no good, Chinese are leaving, goodbye.' With that she hung up. I tried phoning back but the call went straight to answerphone.

I phoned Mark, 'I think the Chinese know something's going on.' I related the conversation I'd just had. Mark stayed silent.

'Can someone talk to the American contractor?' I asked.

'I'll get back to you.' The line went dead.

My mind started to race, if the Chinese do know how will they react? It appeared they were pulling the civilians out of the fray, but, if they decided to back the government forces this threw in another dimension and could mean a total massacre of the Christian and Muslim militia.

I dozed off and woke to the phone ringing. It had gone dark and I realized I'd been asleep for over two hours.

'Our summation is,' said Mark, 'that the Chinese are going to sit it out and then deal with the winning party. We don't believe they are lovers of Kasenga but they don't want to be seen as taking part in what could be a very bloody civil war. The thought is that if they are seen to be openly supporting the present government even if they were to remain in power there could be a global backlash. In their normal pragmatic manner, we believe they are thinking this country is small fry and not worth the condemnation of the world. Especially as they'll probably be able to do a deal with whoever comes to power. It is critical therefore that our part in these hostilities remains covert. Imran knows that if anything goes wrong at his end he's on his own. Operation Caterina as we're calling it is totally independent of anything else. The troops will be seen as mercenaries, they'll carry no regalia and the arms used will be untraceable.'

I shook my head feeling a little groggy.

'Now if I know you' continued Mark, 'You're probably pissed that you're not centre stage this week. Truth be told, Jonathan you've done a damn good job but now it's time to come home.'

'No chance,' I said suddenly wide awake, 'I need to ensure there is access to the airport and I've come this far to find Caterina so I'm not walking out on her now.'

There was a moment's silence.

'I thought that would be your reaction and I'm not going to stop you, but go carefully this week, just teaching and listening. No more, no contact with Imran, there's no need, and you make sure Jacques and Henri keep it buttoned too.'

He was right of course and as long as I was staying until the fireworks on Saturday I felt pretty relaxed. Beyond that I wasn't sure. In the few days I'd been in the country I'd grown to like the people and felt I could be a lot more use here than in the world of espionage.

We agreed to talk daily and as I hung up I thought about going to La Maison. If I'm honest, I didn't feel that good, my arm was throbbing and I felt a little muzzy headed. I went downstairs and Father Steve was sitting in his office. He beckoned to me.

After the usual pleasantries he looked me in the eye. ''I bent the rules to help you, now it's payback time and I don't want detail. One question, should I close the school at any point this week?'

His eyes bored into me and I felt a little lost as to what to say.

He tapped his fingers waiting for my response.'

'I'll be in school all week including Saturday' I said with a slight emphasis on Saturday.

'So it's Saturday night' he replied his eyes penetrating deep. I looked back saying nothing but decided to open up a little.

'Obviously the grapevine is talking, that is not going to help.'

'Trust me, my sources will not compromise the situation.' After a second he said, 'Are you eating out tonight?'

I shook my head.

'Good, I could do with some company, let's open a bottle of wine, 'Yvette,' he boomed. She appeared seconds later.

'Un bouteille de vin rouge, s'il vous plait et deux verres.'

'And will Tom be staying for dinner.'

'Oui merci' I responded.

'You've got a friend there' chortled Father Steve. 'She's never called one of our interns by their Christian name before!'

I could feel myself going red as the Yvette reappeared with the bottle and two glasses. 'Your complexion is the same colour as the wine,' boomed Father Steve as he guffawed. Yvette looked on with a faint smile not having a clue as to what Father Steve was saying.

We ate together making polite conversation but saying nothing about what was on both of our minds. The following day I played the dutiful teacher and if I'm honest took a lot of satisfaction out of what I was doing. That night I decided to go to La Maison as I knew I had to draw Henri and Jacques into our plans. Sareb was waiting as I opened the front door. He seemed somewhat pensive.

'Are you alright?' I asked.

'Oh yes, but there are things happening that I cannot tell you, I am sorry.'

I didn't push him, that could come later I thought. When and if I need his help.

Henri stood talking to Jacques at the bar. As I walked in he handed me a beer and motioned for us to go to his private quarters.

'Just the one beer for me' I said, 'we have important things to discuss and I need all my wits around me. Truth be told, I was saying *You need to have your wits around you* and at that point I wasn't too bothered about whether I upset them or otherwise.

I went through Mark's plan. I knew I was taking a risk as I didn't really know either of them. However so far they had come through and I needed their support. 'Two things you can help me with' I said, 'One, we need to ensure the access road to the airport is cleared in order that the trucks can get in and out without any major calamities. We don't need tyres being ripped apart on barbed wire. And two I'll need a lift to the airport on Saturday night. I could use Sarab and I do actually trust him.'

Jacques shook his head and butted in, 'Come up to the house on Saturday morning and we can then get you across to the airport later on. If there's going to be trouble in town the odds are the authorities will know something's afoot and crack down on movements early on.'

He paused thinking things through. 'I would suggest we clear the access road after dusk on Saturday night, that way we shouldn't be discovered. If we attempted anything before somebody may just stumble on it and the game's over. I'll go out later, see what needs to be done and what equipment we'll need. My boys can do the donkey work.

'I can help clear the access road.'

Jacques nodded.

'I want to be involved' piped up Henri, 'I have to be there for Tanja.'

'I don't have a problem' I said. We agreed to meet again on Thursday for an update and as I got up to leave Henri gave me a bear hug.

'How can I ever thank you?' he asked as his eyes filled up.

'We're both here to help someone we love,' I replied, 'Lets hope we're successful.'

Wednesday and Thursday dragged by and I could feel the stress levels mounting. I wasn't directly involved which was particularly frustrating and all I could do was listen to Mark who kept me updated.

'Do you want me to map the airport' I asked desperately trying to find something to do.

'No need, we've had a couple of Predator drones flying across all day building a complete picture of the area, the airport, the roads and the prison camp. We probably know more about the region than anyone. Just ensure the access road is clear.'

'Can you email me pictures of the prison camp, I'll talk to Henri to see if he knows the whereabouts of Tanja within the complex.'

'Good thought, I'll send it straight away.

'What about medics for Caterina and Tanja?'

'They'll be part of the task force.'

I was floundering while trying to get more involved. 'The supply trucks' I said, 'Jacques said there may well be a crack down on movements in and out of town early on that day if the authorities suspect anything.'

'See if you can find an out of town place where they can park up safely, and keep thinking. Any holes you see I want to know about. This operation has been put together at speed which means there will be things we've missed. Keep thinking, it's one of your strengths.'

Back at La Maison that night Jacques spoke.

'I was up at the airport today looking at access. I was also able to test a plan I've been formulating. I hid one of my sons in the bushes a kilometre up the road from the airport and another a kilometre the other way. They had walkie talkies and kept us in touch with any traffic coming up and down. I concealed my truck in the undergrowth and having been given notice by my lads that traffic was coming hid as well. The good news is we can clear the road without any great problem. All we need is to remove the gates, the barbed wire that's buried in weeds and there's a few potholes to sort out. Nothing that an hour of hard labour won't sort out on Saturday night. The road will be quiet at that time of night so we should be able to get on with the job without too many disturbances.'

'It'll be dark,' I said stating the obvious.

'A couple of spots and helmets with torches will sort that. The access road will be cleared and by the time we've finished nobody will be any the wiser. Once cleared long grass will be used to cover the road so without looking too closely the world will be none the wiser.'

Jacques looked very pleased with himself as I thanked him.

I then asked about parking the trucks.

Henri piped up, happy to get involved. 'There's a lorry park on the road out of the city towards the airport. It'll be perfect cover, the majority of drivers sleep in their wagons and it's become quite a meeting place. Lorries come and go at all times of the day and night. There's a food market and a couple of bars together with toilets and showers. They're crude but functional. Prostitutes do a roaring trade.'

'Henri' I said, 'I've been emailed some aerial shots of the prison camp, you've been there and know the layout. I need to print them off somewhere and go through them with you.'

'Sure, I have an old pc, it's slow but works. Come into my office.'

We went through to a small room which looked surprisingly orderly. An old pc monitor stood on a desk. Henri sat down and switched it on. Jacques and I stood behind him.

'It'll take a couple of minutes for the valves to warm up,' he joked.

I pulled out my 'O' phone and rather than having a trace I emailed the photograph to a gmail address.

Henri vacated his seat, I hit the google icon, went into gmail and punched in the email address and password. I'd set it up in Tom's name for this sort of situation, it was part of out training. As with so many things we'd been taught, simple but effective.

There were four aerial photographs. The camp perimeter could clearly be seen together with about forty odd oblong blocks in neat rows of eight.

'These are the prison huts.' said Henri pointing at the screen as I hit the print button. 'This is the road in and what they call the reception area.'

From the shot it looked like a smaller oblong block.

'You can see the turrets around the perimeter.'

There were twelve of them.

'These buildings at the front of the camp and to the right and left of the road are the guards quarters and administration offices. As you can see, apart from the road in, the prison is surrounded by forest. There is no way in or out apart from the road.'

'What's that building?' I asked curious about a block slightly distanced from the admin building but outside the prison perimeter.

'I'm not sure.'

I zoomed in, I could see fuel tanks adjacent to it.

'That must be the power plant' Jacques exclaimed.

'Yes you're right.'

'Okay so where is Tanja kept?'

'I'm not totally certain,' said Henri, 'I think it's one of these two. He pointed at a couple of blocks which were to the right and left of what appeared to be a central walkway behind the reception area.

'I'm sure she once said she was in the first block two down. She may have been moved however.'

'That'll do,' I said, 'invaluable information. Give me a minute please, I need to make a call.'

The two obligingly left the office, I phoned Mark and gave him the low down on the prison camp.

'I'm having a brainstorming meeting tonight in Geneva,' said Mark, 'With fifteen of our top operatives. We'll be going through the operation in minute detail to ensure no stone is left unturned. Keep asking yourself and me questions, we need to ensure we've covered everything.'

I found Henri and Jacques drinking coffee.

'Guy's' I said,' if there's anything you think we may have missed, no matter how small you must let me know. The devil is always in the detail and one slight mistake can and does cost lives.' I thought back to my previous operation, people had been killed because we didn't ensure we weren't being followed. We'd become a bit too clever for our own good. I was determined that would never happen again.

'Let's have a little wine,' said Henri smiling, 'to lubricate the brain. It may help us think of something.'

With that one of the waiters appeared from nowhere with three glasses and started to open a bottle. The label read 'Chateau Petrus'. I was far from a wine expert but I knew this stuff cost more than five hundred quid a bottle.

'I don't think I'm qualified to drink this' I said.

'My little English friend, with what you are doing I can't think of a more qualified person.' Henri picked up a glass and held it out, 'Here's to Tanja and Caterina.'

We all drank, it was the best wine I had ever tasted.

Chapter 14

On Friday before leaving for school I had a long and detailed conversation with Mark. We went though every facet of the next couple of days and questioned each other until we were as certain as we could be that nothing had been missed. Mark's biggest concern was getting the trucks across Zambola and into position. He fully expected to lose at least one but knew he still had enough capacity to carry the troops. It had been agreed at the meeting in Geneva the night before that the trucks should come in separately over the next twenty four hours rather than as a convoy to reduce any suspicions that may arise.

Imran was having separate briefings with Mark, there was no need to include me, I was better focusing on my own operation. With Imran's experience and the backup in Switzerland I felt comfortable knowing that I was working true professionals and little would be missed. I just hoped the coup would be reasonably peaceful and that the government troops capitulate quickly.

Mark gave me two contacts. Firstly the leader of the military operation, a Swiss given the name Nico Wegmann and secondly the lead driver of the convoy, a Zambian, Boniface Nondo. I knew both names were aliases, 'to avoid contagion' as we always said. In other words, if any one member was caught he or she could give nothing away.

I put my heart and soul into the school day in the hope that if I turned my mind away from the operation when I came back to it I could see any flaws. As had become my habit I had lunch with Patrice Umgali the Head of Languages. We'd taken to speak in English as he wanted to practice. Apart from a thick French African accent he spoke the language well.

'What are you doing this weekend?' I asked politely.

'Not too much' he replied airily, 'What about you?'

'I'm going to see my friend Jacques at his farm tomorrow, so no doubt I'll have a raging hangover come Mass on Sunday morning.'

Patrice looked at me pensively, 'My friend I like you and I want you to be safe. If I can advise, stay at your friend's farm on Sunday.'

'Why?' I asked playing the daft laddie, intrigued as to how he was going to answer.

'Things are going to happen that I do not want you to be involved in. Serious things, which will help this country. Keep away from the city, please. I want you back here on Monday. Now no more questions, I have said too much.'

With that he stood up and walked out of the room. I went and gave my final three lessons of the day, impressed at how far most of the students had come in just a few days.

That night I spoke to both Nico Wegmann and Boniface Nondo. I've always tried to see the best in people but I found Nico a strange man. He spoke German with a Swiss intonation and did his utmost to get me off the line as quickly as possible. His only concern was the clearance of the access road to the airport. There was no humour and he made his disdain clear for using unauthorized personnel. The conversation was cut very short when he said, 'I will see you at 01.00 on Sunday morning. Ensure the access road is clear and the trucks are in place.'

'What about lighting for the landing areas?' I asked.

'That will not be necessary, the helicopters have there own landing lights and we have detailed information regarding the airport. We know where we are to land. When we land ensure the trucks come to us immediately.'

129

Boniface was a totally different person. He was information overload giving details of all the trucks, the drivers, their phone numbers. what they were carrying and estimated time of arrival for each vehicle. 'They should all be at the truck park by 10am tomorrow' he bellowed. 'Anyone who fails will have me to answer to. Tomorrow night I will be the lead driver. We won't be in convoy but two minutes apart. It's less obvious that way. I'll phone you as I get close to the airport.'

'Text me with the order you are coming in,' I explained about the lookout system Jacques had devised. 'I can talk to each driver as they approach the airport and tell them if it's clear to pull in. If there is traffic they'll have to drive on, turn around and try again.'

I decided he must have been a sergeant major in the Zambian Army in a previous life. The British had taught them well and their influence had obviously been felt across Zambian military life. He agreed to contact me as each truck arrived.

Father Steve was out that night so I dined alone which suited as it gave me the chance to gather my thoughts. I'd come a long way in recent weeks, both personally and in finding Caterina's whereabouts. I'd found a future and decided that once everything had died down I would return to Zambola. I knew I could make a difference here and really wanted to help these people. I said a silent prayer that there wouldn't be too many casualties and went to bed. I was teaching the juniors the following morning, kids who were so eager to learn. I hoped I could get back to them quickly.

My phone rang at 4am. For once I wasn't dreaming about Zan, maybe I was in too deeper sleep, maybe I was beginning to move on.

'We've got a problem,' it was Mark.

'An opportunity as Frank used to say.' Frank being my boss who'd sadly been blown away during my last operation.

'Imran's sources have discovered the Chinese are backing Kasenga's government.'

'How?' I asked.

'With arms and ammunition, they're being transported to the main army base in Kanina as we speak.'

I went cold. It had all been too easy, something had to go wrong.

'Any chance of air cover?' I asked.

'No, too far from any military airbases and NATO aren't going to be drawn into anything like this.'

'Can't Imran do anything?'

'He hasn't got the man power or equipment needed.'

'What about sending in a smart bomb? We could deploy it from the airport and blow the army base sky high.'

'Good thought but we won't be able to get the gear in place for tonight.'

I was getting frustrated, all I could hear was negativity. It was then as if a light bulb turned on in my brain.

'Listen Mark, they won't be expecting retaliation; I doubt they'll even suspect the opposition forces are aware of the situation. Can you get a couple of thermobaric bombs brought in? We can load them into the trucks that are being driven across, drive the trucks to the army base in Kanina and blow the place.'

I could almost hear Mark gasp at the audacity of the plan.

'What are you suggesting, we drive straight into the base with suicide bombers?' I detected a hint of sarcasm.

'I'd have thought we could use mobile launchers from the back of the trucks' I said evenly.

Mark went silent for a couple of seconds 'I'm playing devils advocate because there maybe something in what you are saying. What happens if the trucks are stopped driving into the city?'

'We'll have a couple of guys on board who are well armed. The other thing is, morale in the government forces is rock bottom. They're underfed and haven't been paid since God knows when, those who survive won't be in a hurry to fight when that lot goes off.'

'Hang on' said Mark, 'We need the trucks for Operation Caterina, I can't put that in jeopardy, my honest thought is that we let the country sort itself out.'

'It'll be a bloody massacre,' I said almost shouting, 'We can't Mark, it's obscene.'

'In this case, the needs of the few outweigh those of the many.'

'Woe, I'll hire a couple of trucks locally, there must be a way.'

'We haven't got time Jonathan, you're going to have to let it go.'

'Give me a couple of hours Mark.'

'I don't think so Jonathan, this time I'm going to have to overrule you.'

'I'll get two trucks to the truck park. You provide the drivers.'

'I'm not going to be able to get people in until tonight Jonathan, it's a non starter.'

'It can't be' I said desperately trying to find a solution.

Another thought came to mind, 'Our drivers will be in place by 10am this morning. Towards dusk they can drive two trucks up to the airport, we conceal them and take the drivers back to the park to pick up the other trucks. It's simple.'

I heard Mark breath in, 'You've got two hours.' The line went dead.

I sat on my bed and rubbed my eyes, where the hell was I going to find two trucks?

I went through my contacts in Zambola. Father Steve, the school staff, the hospital staff, Henri, Jacques, Sarab.

Henri and Jacques were the obvious ones but I didn't want to implicate them more than I had already. I needed a cover story.

On impulse I picked up my phone and dialled. 'Sareb, I need to ask you a question and I need an honest answer, I will pay you well for the information.'

'How can I help you Sahib?'

'Will there be fighting tonight?'

'I cannot answer that Sahib.'

'Sareb, you have to help me, I may need to get children out of town quickly to save them from what could be a bloody civil war, I don't want them caught up in the middle of this, I need two container wagons to transport them without raising any alarms. I can find drivers. Should the trucks be damaged the Mission will pay for repairs or replacements. You have my word. All I ask is that the trucks be left in the truck park.'

'It will cost money.'

'Lives are worth more than money.'

'I'll phone you back.'

'I need an answer within thirty minutes.'

'I will try Sahib, I will try, I promise.'

I showered and dressed. Downstairs, croissants and coffee were laid out. There was no sign of Father Steve. My phone rang.

'Sareb?'

'My cousin will do as you say, but he wants two thousand US dollars.'

'He is a thief and not a good Muslim but he will get his money, thank you Sareb. Pick me up at the school at 12 noon, you can then take me to the Truck Park where we will do the deal with your cousin. He will show me the trucks and give me

133

the keys. Tell him if it all goes to plan he will get a one thousand dollar bonus and so will you.'

I rang Mark and gave him the news. He was silent for a long time. 'I'm not happy Jonathan, but I'll go with this because I trust you, good luck.'

'Thanks, you'll need to transfer four thousand dollars to the Western Union office in Kanina.'

'Will do, I'll text the tracking number to you.'

I punched Boniface's number into my phone. He was full of the joys of spring.

'I'll be in place by 8am Tom, then I can get some shut eye.'

'Maybe not,' I outlined my plan.

'Oh this sounds fun man,' said Boniface chortling.

'So at dusk two of your drivers will take the new trucks up to the airport, I'll ensure transport back so you can bring the rest of the trucks in. I'll be at the Truck Park at about 12.30 and text you on arrival. I doubt there'll be too many other white men around so I should be reasonably easy to spot. If not text me with an obvious place to meet, for example the bar. I'll go for a wee, you can follow me and I'll hand over the keys. I don't want you and I to be seen together, if you see what I mean.'

'No probs man.'

Yvette appeared, 'the bus is waiting for you Tom.'

I acknowledged her, killed the call and went to catch it. The young kids were noisy and excited, Saturday had a completely different atmosphere to the rest of the week without the presence of the seniors.

As we wound our way around the slums of Kanina I wondered what the city would look like the following morning and where I would be. I wasn't sure whether I'd be flying out with Caterina or staying. I was playing that one by ear. If she was sick I would go with her, if not I'd stay. Sadly I felt I would be on the flight out.

I went through the revised plans and felt comfortable. My cover story to Sareb was reasonably watertight.

I did three lessons that morning and put the kids through their paces. I was delighted with their progress and felt as if I was really achieving something. I had seven and eight year olds who were so keen to learn. I knew I'd found myself and my way forward. I also knew I had more than a little task to carry out before I could really settle into this country.

At 12 noon Sareb was waiting.

'Thanks for your help' I said.

'It is I who should be thanking you for saving our children.'

I felt a slight pang of guilt for having lied, but then thought, actually that's precisely what I am doing, by destroying the army barracks I will save many lives.

Twenty minutes later we pulled up outside the Western Union office. There were three people inside and the first was taking an eternity as his money hadn't arrived from France. He kept arguing with the cashier who was powerless to do anything. Eventually the man in front of me shouted in a local language. It was pretty obvious what he was saying by the timbre of his voice and the first guy swept out of the office in high dudgeon. Eventually my turn came.

'Bonjour' I said to the teller, 'My name is Thomas Simpson I am here to collect four thousand US dollars. The tracking no is CX45463BW2Y.'

I handed over my passport and within seconds the money in crisp twenty dollar notes was handed to me. I marvelled at the efficiency of the operation.

'Merci Mademoiselle.'

'Have a nice day,' she said in English with a big smile.

Back at the car I sent a text to Boniface, '*Be with you in 5 mins*'

The response was immediate, 'I'll watch you into the park. Once you have the keys make your way to the Ntemba Bar. I'll see you for a wee!

I smiled, simple but effective. Within minutes Sareb turned into the truck park. Dozens of vehicles were parked, container wagons, low loaders, removal trucks and vans of all shapes and sizes. Men stood in groups chatting and we drove past the Ntemba Bar. It was little more than a shack made of corrugated iron and through the door I could see little, just people moving in and out, smoking and drinking from beer bottles.

We parked at the far end and Sareb greeted a small skinny man in his mid thirties dressed in a khaki jubba and charcoal trousers. 'Salaam Haaziq,' he said as they shook hands while putting their other hand on their hearts.

'Haaziq, this is my friend Tom Simpson.'

'As-salaamu alaykum.' I said being slightly more formal than Sareb and again shaking hands. The greeting was returned with a smile. The man had mean eyes and I immediately didn't like him.

'You have the money?' he asked with an evil smile.

I nodded, 'You have the trucks?'

He held out two sets of keys.

'Show me,' I said.

We walked across to a couple of Renault container wagons. He unlocked one and climbed in. I got in the other side.

Surprisingly it was in reasonable condition. He started the engine and looked at me.

'Is it fuelled' I asked.

'They both are' came the response along with a smarmy smile.

'Let's have a look at the other one.'

We went through the same process. As I climbed out I said, 'I trust you because I trust Sareb. You are of the same blood, I hope you have the same level of honour.'

'He is fine,' said Sareb.

I pulled out the cash and handed it to Haaziq. He in turn gave me the keys.

'I need them back here at 5pm tomorrow' he said.

'It shall be so, As-salaamu alaykum.'

'As-salaamu alaykum,' he responded and we shook hands. He turned and disappeared behind a couple of wagons. *Probably the easiest couple of grand he'll ever earn,* I thought.

'Are you sure he's okay?' I asked Sareb.

'On my Mother's grave.'

'I need a piss' I said, 'take me up to that bar.'

Sareb dropped me outside and I walked in. It was dark and full of smoke. Forty or fifty men sat at tables drinking, playing cards and dominoes. A couple of women in their early twenties sat at the bar, their intentions pretty obvious. I idly wondered how much they charged. Being the only white I created a bit of a stir. People glared as I walked through to the toilet. A dirty green sign pointed the way.

I went in and the stench hit me, there were two urinals, both were taken. Eventually one guy left and I took his place. As the other one moved away I heard, 'Give me your money or you're a dead man.' He was standing behind me and for a split second I pondered what to do. My training kicked in and wheeling around, I kneed him in the balls while punching him hard on the chin. As he collapsed into a cubicle the door opened again.

'What's going on man?' I recognised the voice, it was Boniface. I put a finger to my mouth as if to say 'be quiet'.

'That shit tried to jump me.' I said. 'He obviously thought a white man can't fight. Somehow I don't think he'll be producing bastards for a while.'

With that I winked at Boniface, handed him the keys and walked out. My arm was till sore from the beating but I thanked God quietly that I had made a reasonable recovery. *Good enough to sort that yob,* I mused.

Sareb was waiting for me, 'Take me to The Mission.'

I let myself in, ran up to my room and deposited the remainder of the money in my wash bag. Yvette looked at me as I ran back down the stairs.

'See you later,' I said as I headed out of the door and into the taxi. 'Jacques's farm please Sareb.'

Chapter 15

Jacques and Henri sat on the veranda and stood in unison as we drove up.

'Assuming your cousin doesn't let me down I'll give you the rest of the money tomorrow.' I said to Sarab as I climbed out of the car.

'How can he let you down Sahib? You have the trucks.'

'As long as they're not stolen or a pile of shit.'

'Don't worry, they will be fine. Look after the children, please.'

We shook hands, he reversed and drove off. I told Jacques and Henri about the turn of events.

'I need another driver' I said, 'My colleague Boniface is to organise two guys to take the trucks up to the airport after it goes dark. We need to conceal the trucks and take them back into town so they can bring two more trucks to the airport. A couple of extra drivers will be flown in with the rest of the troops.'

We went through the detail for that night with a fine tooth comb. Jacques had planned to bring his seven sons and two daughters to clear the road. Gilles was to drive an ancient digger come bulldozer to drag the remnants of barbed wire away. Another son, Andre would be in charge of a truck carrying sand to clear any potholes. The rest of the boys were going to lay the sand and smooth out a temporary road surface. The two girls would be lookout sentries at each end of the road with Jacques controlling operations.

'Now with the change of plan,' said Jacques thinking on his feet. 'Giles and Marianne can take your boys back into town in the passion wagon. If stopped the boys can duck under the mattresses as before. I'll handle the digger and Henri you can be lookout.'

'Happy to be doing something' said Henri.

'Great job Jacques, I can't thank you enough.'

'Neither can I,' piped up Henri again in tears.

'Let's have some lunch,' Henri wanted to change the subject quickly to save his friend any embarrassment. He stood and strolled into the dining room where a buffet had been set. More like a gourmet meal truth be told, plates of French saucisson, salami, chicken, cold roast pork, salads, cheeses and French bread.

'Just a snack then,' I quipped.

'It's going to be a long night' replied Jacques seriously, 'I haven't provided wine, I think we'll need all our wits around us. Hopefully we can celebrate tomorrow, with something more than wine. Eat and enjoy.'

We ate and made small talk. Mark rang and rattled off details in brisk military style about the plan to blow the base.

'Imran has found a vantage point for us to blow the army base. The city is in a slight basin and we can access a position that looks down on the location. The good thing is that it's a country track so it's unlikely there'll be anyone around. I've managed to get hold of two lightweight multiple launchers which will be brought in tonight. These will fire three Starstreak High Velocity Missiles automatically from the containers before reloading. Each container will house three men, one to fire the launcher and two as backup armed with sub machine guns. Six missiles should blow the place, we will have twelve. Once the deed is done the trucks will disappear. If they are compromised Imran is providing two eight seater vehicles again, as backup.

Now, I want you to forget about that side of things, Imran has control. Your job is and always has been to get Caterina out.'

That afternoon we had time to kill. I'd been hard at it one way and another for quite a few days. I felt knackered.

'Jacques, would you mind if I lay down somewhere for a couple of hours. I think a bit of shut eye would do me the world of good.'

'Your right, I'm going to do the same, as I said, I think it's going to be a long night. I'll show you to a room.'

I set my alarm for five and lay on the bed. Within minutes I was fast asleep. I didn't dream, I was too tired for that.

When the alarm went off I woke immediately. I don't know if adrenalin had kicked in or if it was just sleep reviving me, but I felt alive and all set for whatever the nights activities brought. There was a basin in the room, I washed my face and combed my hair. My arm had enough movement, I was ready for action.

I walked onto the terrace, the digger and sand truck were parked in the yard together with the passion wagon and an old Renault mini bus. As predicted it was cloudy but dry. The humidity was still high but more than bearable.

'We'll be leaving in about forty five minutes.' Jacques said handing me a cup of coffee. 'I just hope to God we can get those girls out safely.'

I nodded and drank, there was little more to say. As dusk fell we all assembled by the trucks. Jaques handed out builders helmets with torches attached.

'Good luck everyone,' I said 'And thank you for your support.'

'Thank you' they all said almost in unison.

Andre climbed into the sand truck, Giles and Marianne into the passion wagon and Jacques onto the digger. I clambered into the mini bus along with Henri and the rest of the team. I formally introduced myself to those I didn't know. Jacques's second son Charles was driving, his daughter Odette sat next to him in the front.

Jacques set off first, his cover story was that he was lending another farmer the digger to help knock down an old farm building. Why was he travelling at night? Because he'd been using the digger during daylight hours. A friend had been organised to provide the alibi if necessary. Andre was using the same cover, sand was needed for the new building. In the minibus we were heading for a night on the town. We'd even booked a table at a restaurant. We tried to cover every eventuality. Giles and Marianne were using the same cover as before, a night of passion.

As we set off I had a real feeling of anxiety. Had we covered every eventuality? What could we have missed?

Henri read my thoughts, 'Young man, I am sure you have done everything possible to ensure this operation is successful. Whatever happens, thank you for trying.'

He shook my hand as we trundled towards the airbase. The road was quiet. I imagined this was partly due to it being Saturday and much of the commercial traffic having a day off. Secondly word would have got around that there was going to be trouble tonight.

Even though the road was quiet we didn't want to be seen driving in convoy so after a few minutes we overtook Jacques in the digger but kept at about forty five miles per hour. We didn't want to alert anyone. The four parties stayed in touch using walkie talkies, not everyone had the luxury of a satellite phone. Boniface rang to say he and one of his drivers would bring the two trucks up to the airport.

'You've not delegated that responsibility then' I quipped.

'And miss out on the fun? No chance.'

By now it was dark, after twenty five minutes Charles pulled in. As Odette clambered down I whispered, 'Bon Chance' I watched her disappear into the undergrowth by the side of the road. The first lookout was in place and could never be seen. *Simple but foolproof,* I thought and hoped.

We drove past the entrance to the airport. In the dark it could hardly be seen and about a half a mile down the road Charles pulled in again.

I shook Henri again by the hand as he climbed out. The second lookout was now in place. Charles swung around and headed back to the deserted airport. As we approached he spoke on his walkie talkie.

'All Clear?'

'Non,' crackled the response from Odette, 'Truck coming your way.' Charles kept driving until it past him. He swung around again and asked the same question as we approached the airport.

'Oui bien.' Odette's voice crackled through the ether, 'Oui bien' said Henri.

We turned into the road leading up to the airport. Everyone got out to walk ahead of the minibus to ensure the tyres weren't ripped apart by barbed wire or damaged by potholes. I could see the importance of clearing the road, we needed quick access in and out for the heavy trucks.

Once the bus was beyond the link road Charles parked half in the undergrowth. As we started to clear the area lights flooded onto the scene. My heart started to race until I realised it was Andre followed by Giles in the passion wagon. We helped them through the undergrowth and they parked next to the minibus.

We immediately started to clear the road and as we were working Charles spoke in a clear voice without shouting.

'Father has just past Odette.'

Thirty seconds later he turned into the slip road, headlights blaring. Charles pointed at the undergrowth and ushered us all back. Jacques brought down the bulldozer blade and began driving slowly forward. We heard a ping as the buried barbed wire snapped. That's why we'd been ushered back, the whiplash could have done severe damage. Within thirty seconds Jaques was up to the broken gate. Charles raised his hand and pointed towards the airport. That was our signal to hide, there was obviously a vehicle coming. Jacques immediately drove forward killing the lights and his engine. We stepped back into the bushes and by the time the vehicle drove past he would have suspected nothing.

`All clear?' asked Charles.

'Oui' said Henri, 'Oui' said Odette.

Jacques fired up his engine again and began clearing the slip road from the other end. The broken gate was pushed to the side in one easy move. *The joy of technology* I thought. Five times we had to hide because of traffic. It slowed us down but that was not an issue, we had plenty of time. Eventually Jacques drove up and down the slip road three times to ensure he was happy with his work.

We then set about clearing the snapped and broken barbed wire, ensuring it was rolled and left at the side. Andre ran from person to person using metal cutters where the wire was trapped or stuck. After twenty minutes or so Jacques pronounced himself satisfied so he moved the digger away and Andre reversed his truck up the road towards the main gate. He then lifted the tailgate and started to drop sand as he moved forward. Half way up the road he revved the engine lowered the tailgate and moved forward quickly while killing the lights. Again we melted into the forest.

This time two vehicles came past before we were able to continue. We then filled the potholes with sand and spread it as evenly as we could over the road. Jacques again drove the digger up and down several times until he declared himself satisfied with the surface. We all then went to collect long grass and leaves from the bushes and spread them across the road.

This was incredibly time consuming, hard work and not really necessary but Jacques was determined to ensure that to the casual eye nothing had been altered. I admired his professionalism and eventually the job was finished.

We were admiring our handiwork when my mobile rang.

'Boniface' I said.

'We're about two kilometres from you is everything in order?'

'Yes, keep this line open, as you approach the entrance road I'll tell you whether there is any other traffic around. If there is drive on for a kilometre and turn round. I don't want you being seen turning in here.'

'Understood.'

After about thirty seconds Odette spoke over the walkie talkie.

'Two trucks approaching.'

'Ask Henri if it's clear his end.' He heard me.

'No problems here.'

'Boniface drive straight in, you are clear.' I ran to the entrance and saw the trucks coming. I beckoned them in, they drove over the virgin road and Andre pointed them in the direction of the other vehicles. They parked alongside, Boniface and his colleague jumped out and following a brief handshake I introduced them to Giles and the passion wagon. Nobody was there for niceties and the two men climbed straight into the back, Giles and Marianne got into the front and they headed back to town.

The team replaced the leaves and long grass that had been disturbed on the new road, it was eight thirty. We had several hours to kill before the helicopters arrived.

Torches were switched off and we sat in the dark. There was no point in taking any chances, Jacques poured coffee for everyone from a couple of flasks. He'd taken command and was

145

revelling in the situation. I had no problem, his knowledge of road building was far superior to mine. I was happy to delegate, I knew I was in safe hands.

After a few minutes Odette and Henri appeared. There was no point in having lookouts for the next couple of hours. We chatted idly about what the future held for Zambola and if the alliance of Muslims and Christians could work. In the meantime I phoned Mark and updated him. He sounded quite relaxed. He'd touched base with Nico Wegmann and the platoon was on its way. No real problems had been encountered.

Time dragged interminably. I discussed the possibility of sending some of Jacques's kids home. He shook his head. By now we were well accustomed to sitting in the dark and I could see the group of people sitting and lying around me.

'No' said Jacques, 'let's stay put, we might be needed. Having come this far I don't want to wreck the operation for no good reason.'

He was right, I was just concerned for the safety of his family. He had thrown everything into this. If anything happened I could never forgive myself.

At half past eleven Boniface phoned. 'Clockwork man. The kids dropped us off at the Truck Park and we're on our way back, each truck two minutes apart. The roads are quiet, everybody is tucked up at home I think, keeping well away from the city. See you in about thirty minutes.'

Henri and Odette headed back to their lookout posts.

So far so good I thought.

Conversation had become forced and we sat in silence apart from the odd comment. The tension was becoming too much to bear and a couple of times I got up and walked around just to break the monotony. Eventually the phone rang again, 'Yet again I'm two kilometres away.'

'Stay on the line' I said trying to sound as cool as possible.

146

Jacques spoke to Odette and Henri.

'Trucks on their way.'

'Ready' crackled Odette, 'Ready,' said Henri.

'Truck approaching' said Odette.

'Clear this end.'

'In you come I said to Boniface.'

I killed the call and rang the second truck. We went through the same procedure. Again, there was no traffic to worry about. Only one truck encountered traffic and had to carry on down the road. He turned round and came in last. The six trucks parked up next to the rest of the vehicles. If anyone came in now we'd be caught red handed. It was impossible to provide cover for eight container wagons. The walkie talkie crackled into life, 'Hi it's Giles, we're just approaching.'

'All clear' said Odette, 'All clear' repeated Henri.

We were becoming a well oiled machine. I looked at my watch, it was 12.15, well on schedule. Jacques and his boys were checking the newly built road and camouflaging it again with leaves and grass. Now all we could do was wait for the platoon. We had delivered it was up to them from here on in.

I text the information to Mark and Nico. 'All eight trucks in place, we are ready.'

Nico responded immediately, 'We're on schedule for 1am.'

At twelve thirty Odette and Henri headed back to their lookout posts. Come five to one the rest of us were sitting apprehensively. Hardly a word had been said for half an hour. All that could be heard were strange African birds making sounds I didn't recognise. It was still humid and I felt hot and sweaty. Gilles handed me a bottle of water.

'How are you feeling,' he asked in English much to my surprise.

'I'm fine, just a little anxious. I'll be glad when we get this show on the road.'

147

As I spoke I heard a low drone in the sky. 'They're here.'

The sound grew louder until it blotted out everything else. Suddenly light cascaded from the sky as the helicopters switched on their landing lights. We could see as clearly as if it was lunchtime. They started to land about half a mile from where we stood, the drivers jumped into the trucks. The vehicles started their engines and moved slowly towards the aircraft. The fear of a pothole or two was ever present and they weren't about to drive into one and wreck the operation.

Within minutes there was a sea of activity. Soldiers poured out of the helicopters carrying guns and all sorts of paraphernalia. The trucks were directed to park in a row and equipment was unloaded and brought across to them. These guys knew exactly what they were doing. I could see one in conversation with Boniface. I went across to see what was happening.

I recognised the voice, it was Nico. I introduced myself, he nodded and carried on talking.

'The lorries for town are leaving first. They should be loaded within the next five minutes,' he said pointing at the two trucks standing closest to us. They were two of the vehicles that had been transported across. I felt relieved as I didn't want Sarab's trucks being used for blowing up the army base. If they were seen it could have created all sorts of complications after the event.

I saw the missile launchers being loaded and put into place.

Within minutes the troops climbed into the back and one in the front with the driver. I radioed Odette and Henri.

'All clear,' they both responded, the trucks moved off.

'What an operation,' I marvelled to no one in particular.

'These are the best soldiers you can get' said Boniface stony-faced, still standing at my side. *My crew aren't bad either* I thought.

Less than ten minutes later with the troops and equipment loaded onto the trucks we were ready to roll. I'd been directed to the first truck and the feeling of standing on a London tube in the dark came to mind. I was surrounded by a sea of bodies. All silent, all still, the calm before the storm I thought.

'All clear?' I spoke in the walkie talkie.

'No' replied Odette.

'Hang on' I shouted.

My nerves were jangling, I could hear the crackling of the walkie talkie and eventually Odette's voice came through the ether.

'Clear,' she said.

'Clear' said Henri.

The engine started and we began to move forward.

'This is where I'm uncomfortable' whispered Nico. 'We have one access road and are cover could quickly be blown. We will stop two hundred meters from the prison camp on the main road. With luck at this time of night we won't be noticed.'

'How can you not notice a bloody big truck?' I asked.

'That is the point, why should anyone think this is anything but a bloody big truck that's pulled off the road? Once we have disembarked the truck will move away turning round a mile up the road. Each truck will carry out the same exercise. The drivers will continue up and down the road until we have control of the camp. At which point they will pull up at the entrance ready to transport us back.'

We stood in silence as the truck trundled along, I'd estimated a journey time of about thirty minutes. Standing in darkness I could feel sweat dripping down my back, the smell of human bodies was more than perceptible in the heat and humidity. I went into something like a trance like state and started thinking about how far we'd come in recent weeks. From being a lost soul living on a Dutch barge I'd been on quite a journey. I'd

149

found Caterina, whether she was still alive I had no idea. I hoped and prayed that within the next few minutes I'd find her, safe and well. I was jolted out of my thoughts as I felt the truck slow down.

'You stick with me' whispered Nico, 'If I lose you don't play the hero, make your way back to the road and wait for transport, that's an order.'

I nodded, there was no need to argue.

The truck came to a standstill and I heard the word 'Go' in a low clear rasp.

We poured off immediately and started jogging up the road. Within seconds the truck was on its way and overtook us. Headlights could be seen ahead of us. I was grabbed and forced into the undergrowth. The training was immaculate, the vehicle drove past suspecting nothing.

We turned off the road and started pacing up the track towards the prison, hardly a sound could be heard. These guys were fitter than me and by now I felt breathless. The camp was clearly visible, bathed in a sea of electric spotlights. The main barracks and administration block stood in front of us, to the right and left. I knew the power plant was across to the right as well. As we stood I became aware of other troops joining us as the trucks dropped them off. Some of them began moving forward. We stood still.

'Three guys will be positioned near each of the twelve turrets ready to take the guards out.' whispered Nico,' Immediately after the main barracks and administration block will be blown. Any survivors will be casualties of war. We haven't got time to take prisoners.

We stood quietly for several minutes. I was aware of Nico looking at his watch.

He started a countdown.

'Five, four, three, two. one.'

Chapter 16

I heard the crack of rifles and a second later it was as if Armageddon had begun. The buildings exploded in front of me and to the right, the sound was deafening, the heat frightening and the screams terrifying. Men could be seen running out, some on fire and as they came into view they fell in a sea of bullets. It was mass carnage but I felt no sorrow. These degenerates had incarcerated and killed too many innocent people and were getting their just deserts.

The action didn't take long, within a few minutes only the fires burned and there was an eerie silence.

'We're moving in' said Nico in a calm detached manner. 'Lets see if your friend is where we think she is. Watch out for snipers.'

About thirty troops ran forward with Nico and I shielded in the middle. The main entrance had been blown along with the rest of the carnage and troops were already clearing a path. We ran through aware of women screaming in the huts that stood before us.

Henri thought Tanja was in the first block, two down either to the right or the left. Troops swarmed into both buildings, Nico held me back.

'Here' I heard and we ran to the building on the left. The stench hit me first, human excrement and foul smelling sweat made me want to vomit but adrenalin had kicked in and I fought off the sensation. Strong torches lit a scene straight out of Auschwitz or Dante's Inferno.

Dozens of women lay huddled together on the floor, some were ill, very ill, several appeared lifeless, many had sunken eyes and just stared, unable to comprehend what was happening. All were so thin and dirty, suffering from extreme malnutrition.

'Over here,' I heard the same voice as before. I made my way through the sea of women towards the back of the hut.

Apart from the fact that she was white I didn't recognize her. She lay with her eyes closed, sunken cheeks and a very pale complexion. She was in rags lying on a filthy piece of cloth not moving. Her hair had been cropped short and she was so thin. I thought back to the Latin beauty, she was little more than a shell of her former self. For a moment I felt lost. I'd found her but I felt sick. I knelt down and put my hand on her brow. There was no movement and she was running a temperature, I didn't have to be a doctor to realise she was damned ill.

'Caterina' I said, 'I've found you.' There was no response and I didn't feel any elation, she was too sick for that.

Another white woman lay next to her, eyes half open just staring at me.

'You must be Tanja,' I said in German. We're here to get you and Caterina out,' She put her hand out to me but the effort made her slump back.

By now several paramedics and a doctor had arrived. The two women were put on stretchers and taken out of the hell hole where a couple of small vans were waiting.

I followed, 'You in the front' said the doctor. I climbed in by which time he was examining Caterina. As we started to move off I could see him working feverishly connecting drips, putting a thermometer in her ear and taking a blood sample.

'How is she?' I asked.

'Alive, just. Too early to say anymore. Just thank the Lord that ebola hasn't hit this God forsaken place. All we've got to worry about now is malaria, tetanus, TB and God knows what else. If she's been raped which is more than likely syphilis, gonorrhea and HIV. I'm doing some rapid diagnostic testing so I'll know more in about twenty minutes. She's got a temperature of 41 degrees centigrade, my best guess is that we're dealing with malaria at least but maybe a hell of a lot more.'

We sped back to the airbase. Outriders flanked us on powerful motorbikes. They were armed and ready for all eventualities. The Organisation had found Caterina and they weren't going to lose her at this stage.

The van was warm and I suddenly felt tired. I'd been on the go for a long time not forgetting a little spell in hospital. It was if my body was saying, '*You've done your job, now it's payback time.*' I dozed off and was woken by the driver shaking me.

'Come on we're getting on the Chinook.'

Caterina was already being unloaded along with Tanja from the other van. Henri and Jacques were walking alongside Tanja as she was taken towards the helicopter. Henri was holding her hand as our eyes met. He ran over and gave me a bear hug. I could hardly breathe.

'I can never begin to thank you, my dear dear friend.'

I struggled out of his grasp and we shook hands.

'Come on Jonathan, we've got to go.'

I looked around, troops were swarming onto the Chinook. I patted Henri on the shoulder waved to Jacques and ran up to the helicopter. Inside it reminded me of the prison camp with dozens of troops crammed in, sitting on their equipment cases. They were incredibly orderly, knowing exactly the procedure to board the machine ready for a quick take off. I was ushered towards the back where behind a makeshift curtain lay Caterina and Tanja. I was amazed as I looked at the equipment surrounding them. It was like a mini critical care ward with electronic monitors, drips, suction pumps and a myriad of other equipment I didn't begin to recognize.

153

'Star Wars has nothing on this' I said to no one in particular. Caterina was being connected to all sorts of tubes, wires and cables at incredible speed. Three people were working with her, the doctor who'd accompanied us from the prison camp, a pretty looking nurse and a young man. The doctor was splitting his time between the two patients with two more paramedics working on Tanja. They were leaving nothing to chance.

'Malaria has been confirmed' the doctor said glancing at me, 'I've given her artemisinin-based combination therapies or ACTs as there known as well as clinically assisted nutrition, hydration, saline etc. We'll do all we can. If you have a God, pray. She's not good, and you don't look great either, get some sleep.'

'Tanja?' I asked. 'Similar but more resilient, been out here for a long time. She'll pull through.'

I looked at the two of them, there was little I could do apart from get out of the way. I ducked behind the curtain and a couple of the troops looked up making space for me on the floor.

'Good job guys' I said.

'Lets hope they pull through,' replied one of the men in a southern American drawl.

He handed me a beer. It was cold and tasted good.

'I wouldn't have thought you guys would be allowed to drink on duty,' I quipped smiling.

'The jobs done', was the simple response.

I finished the beer and closed my eyes. It was warm in the helicopter and although I was sitting on the floor I slept, waking a couple of hours later feeling stiff and dying for a wee.

Standing I hobbled through the curtain trying to shake off the stiffness. A sense of serenity stared back at me. Two of the nurses were sitting with Caterina and Tanja. They lay peacefully with oxygen masks covering their mouths and wired up to the machines bleeping and flashing. The male nurse was feeding information into an iPad.

'How are they?' I asked.

'Considering what they've been through, remarkable,' said the pretty nurse with a soft French accent. 'They are both stable. Hopefully the drugs are starting to take effect. All we can do now is wait.'

'When will we know?'

'The next few hours are make or break. We may have to give Caterina a blood transfusion, it's difficult to say at this stage. If they are still with us tonight hopefully they'll be okay.'

'I need the loo,' I said sheepishly.'

'I can offer you a bottle but we'll be landing within half an hour.'

'I'll wait' I said grinning.

I went and sat down. By now I was wide awake and sat thinking about the last few weeks. I knew I'd done a good job and to be fair to The Organisation they'd pulled out all the stops to get one of their own back. The cost of the operation defied comprehension. *Having said that* I thought, *these people would already be employed so the budget wouldn't be much bigger than a training exercise.* Crikey I thought, I'm beginning to think like an accountant!

I could feel the Chinook dropping and within a matter of minutes we hit the ground. The girls were stretchered off first and I followed.

'Good luck,' said one of the men I'd been speaking to.

'Thanks Guys,' I shouted above the noise of the engines, 'You've all been bloody marvellous. They cheered as one. I clambered out into a tropical rain storm and immediately relieved myself getting soaked in the process. This was no time for politeness. The girls were being carried over to a small jet. I assumed it to be an air ambulance. I followed seeing little apart

155

from the fact we were in what looked like a clearing with a runway and a small control tower. Some sort of army base I assumed. I didn't even know which country we were in.

I ran up the steps of the plane and inside it was kitted out like a proper hospital. A row of half a dozen seats stretched out across the front of the plane behind which Tanja and Caterina were being transferred from the stretchers onto beds. The doctor who'd accompanied us was talking to two men, he called me across.

'You're in good hands now. I'll be taking my leave off you, good luck.'

'Where are we going?' I asked feeling particularly stupid and somewhat out of touch.

'Geneva' he responded smiling, 'Let me introduce you to Doctors Breuer and Baumann.' We shook hands. Both men had that pleasant benign look of medical practitioners well in control of their surroundings. I pitched them to be in their mid thirties, fit and healthy, they obviously looked after themselves.

I thanked the doctor as he disappeared out of the door. Immediately it was shut and I was asked by what I presumed to be an air steward to sit down and put on a seat belt. Within seconds we were taxiing and moments later airborne. The girls were again connected to all sorts of sophisticated machinery and I began to feel surplus to requirements. The steward handed me a cup of coffee and a copy of The International New York Times. I idly surveyed the headlines and felt little enthusiasm for reading any further.

'Jonathan?' I looked up to see Dr Breuer smiling at me.

'Caterina's temperature has fallen slightly. It's a good sign but she's not out of the woods yet. She's semi conscious.'

'Can I talk to her?'

'Just for a few minutes, I don't want to tire her.

I walked to the back of the plane. Her eyes were closed and her skin had a yellow hue, she looked terrible.

'Caterina,' I said, 'You took a bit of finding.'

Her eyes half opened, 'Jonathan,' she whispered, 'You got me out?'

'As the songs says, with a little help from my friends.'

She tried to smile but struggled and her eyes closed again. I held her hand and she squeezed it tight. I was surprised at her strength.

Her eyes opened again, this time much wider. 'You must check my email account,' she said weakly but clear and precise. '*rodriguezluciana889@gmail.com*, please, it's important. Password, *Jonathan01*. Despite the state she was in, she looked embarrassed.

'Sorry,' with that she slumped back her eyes closed.

'Let her rest' said Doctor Breuer.

I sat for a second trying to remember the email account. *rodriguezluciana889@gmail.com*. Whatever it was it had to be important.

'Do you have internet access on board?' I asked the doctor.

He nodded. I took out my 'O' Phone made the connection and went into Gmail. Accessing the account I found the usual amount of junk awaiting deletion. On a hunch I skipped through and went back to the day Caterina disappeared. I found an email she'd sent to herself which had an attachment but no title. My pulse began to race, *was this why she'd been kidnapped? What the hell was in the attachment?*

Sod was up to his usual tricks, the attachment hung and I couldn't open it.

'Are there normally problems with emails up here?' I asked the steward.

'Yes sir we drop the connection every so often. It should be backup again in a couple of minutes.'

157

I sat tapping the phone in frustration. Eventually the attachment opened. I couldn't believe what I was reading. *How the hell did she get hold of this?* I wondered.

It was an email written in Chinese. I read it with incredulity and disbelief:-

Top Secret

Distribution to African and Middle East Regional Party Secretaries only

The Chinese African Union

You are aware of the investment we have put into African countries over recent years helping them to build their economies. This has been part of a long term plan to gain control of resources across Africa and The Middle East and keep them out of Western hands. Many of the smaller countries in Central Africa are now totally dependent on Chinese investment and this together with The 'Arab Spring' project to destabilise Northern Africa has been particularly successful in giving us the opportunity to take control of Central and Northern Africa. Our 'Islamic State' unit has thrown the West into disarray and severely weakened any opposition to our presence and planning.

The peacekeeping Chinese military presence gives us the opportunity to create puppet states which will be used as a springboard to destabilize economies that don't wish to work with The Chinese African Union. This will give us the opportunity to bring in resource which will move into the Northern African countries and then the Middle East.

The aim of the exercise is to give us control over oil supplies and ensure we do not become reliant on Western governments.

While they may be unhappy with our approach given that Europe is reliant on Middle Eastern oil they will have to learn to work with us. The Americans will create but they do not have the military capability to take on China with its enlarged presence across the world. The Russians will be given loan enhancements and territory guarantees to ensure a non aggressive stance.

Your immediate cooperation is paramount and attached to this email are plans for your region. Please implement these plans with immediate effect to ensure the success of The Chinese African Union.

Your Central Committee Party General Secretary will be contacting you to discuss the contents of this email within the next twenty four hours. Please have questions ready for him.

General Gao Xiang

I read through the attachment. It started with the withdrawal of civilians from Zambola. Fei Yan flashed through my mind. Another innocent pawn I thought. The report went talked about arming the government to overthrow the proposed revolutionaries. One sentence sickened me. *'The internal fighting will weaken local militia on both sides reducing casualties of Chinese military as they take control.'*

So the Chinese had helped set up the Zambolan revolution, probably working with both sides. This I surmised was what had probably happened in Tunisia, Libya, Egypt and Syria. Brilliant but simple. Arrange for the countries to implode and then walk in.

After a safe period the Chinese were to use troops they'd trained to take control of Zambola. Similar instructions would have been sent to Regional Party Secretaries across Africa and the Middle East.

I began to feel physically ill. I was reading a report suggesting global domination by the Chinese. Did they really believe the West would just lie down? I shuddered, maybe the West wouldn't have any choice. What could they do without oil? Effectively I had control of world events in my hand. Me, just an ordinary bloke from a provincial town in England. *No pressure then!* I smiled grimly.

There was only one thing I could do at this stage. I translated the email as quickly as I could and forwarded it onto Mark.

'I find this incredulous,' I wrote, 'It's all a bit above and beyond me and bloody terrifying. Your thoughts would be appreciated.'

I went back to Caterina, Tanja lay awake. She had more colour and looked alert.

'How are you?' I asked in German.

'I'm okay, thanks to you I think.'

'Not forgetting Henri and Jacques, they were instrumental in this exercise.'

She smiled, 'My dear Henri, how is he?'

'He's was fine as we left Zambola, I hope he remains that way.'

'I must get back to him as soon as possible.'

'Give yourself a few days to recover.'

'Jonathan' I heard. Turning I saw Caterina awake, still not looking good but at least she looked more alert.

'You got me out?'

'We've had this conversation.' I said sitting down and holding her hand.

She looked a little confused, 'Did I tell you about the Gmail account?'

'You did, how did you get it?'

160

'Such a stupid story. I was working on a computer programme in the general office with a Chinese girl I'd befriended.'

'Fei Yen' I said

'You know her?'

'That's another story, let's hear yours first.'

The assistant to the local Party Secretary came in and started shouting at me in Chinese. I don't speak the language so Fei Yen translated. Apparently the laptop of the local Party Secretary had frozen, a regular occurrence because the equipment they use is old and cheap. However he had an important email to read. I asked why none of the Chinese technicians could look at it which was the norm in these situations. He screamed at me that I was not to question the Party Secretary. Realising there could be something in this I followed him to his boss's office. A Buddah like figure sat behind the desk and glared at me.

'You fix this?' He barked in pigeon English.

'I should think so' I said picking up the machine.

'What you doing?' He screamed.

'I need to take it back to my workstation to have a look at it. All my equipment is there.'

He scowled and said, 'My assistant will go with you.'

The assistant followed and I set to work. The problem soon became apparent. So much porn had been downloaded the laptop was full of every kind of virus you could think of.

'No wonder he didn't want his own people to look at it' I said.

Caterina nodded and continued,' To get rid of the viruses I started by deleting the porn. After about an hour the machine was working well enough so I had a look at the email traffic. Given that everything was in Chinese it didn't mean a lot but there was one that had come in earlier that morning with an important sign next to it. By now the assistant had become bored and was paying no attention to what I was doing. I copied the contents of the 'C' drive onto a portable hard drive and then to the company system for future reference. I then thought if this email is so important it's worth taking a copy as backup.

So I copied it onto a memory stick, then onto my laptop and emailed it back to myself.'

'Clever old you,' I said holding her hand.

'Was the email anything important?' she asked innocently.

'Only something that may avert World War Three, and I'm not joking.'

She looked at me with horror in her eyes.

'Why were you arrested?'

She laughed, a little of the old Caterina was coming back, she was gaining strength.

'They knew nothing of what I'd done, I handed the machine back to the assistant fully operational. When the Party Secretary realized his beloved porn had disappeared he ran into my office screaming, "You have stolen state secrets, you are an enemy of The People's Republic of China". With that two guards appeared, I was handcuffed and locked in a room. Several hours later the door opened and two local militia men dragged me to a van and I was taken to La Croix. No trial nothing. The only saving grace was that I met Tanja, without her I would have died.'

She reached out and took Tanja's hand. At that point my phone rang, It was Mark.

'Excuse me' I said walking back to my seat at the front of the plane.

'My God' was all he said.

'Where now?' I asked.

'Before I start a war how confident are we this is genuine?'

I told him Caterina's story. 'If I was a betting man,' I said, 'I'd put my shirt on this, it's genuine alright.'

'Not the answer I was hoping for, but I believe you're right. You'll be in Geneva in about six hours. I'm going to set up a conference and I want you here. Needless to say Jonathan you have done an outstanding job.'

'I get the feeling it's not over yet.'

'Get some shut eye, you're going to need it.'

Caterina had drifted off again so I left her to it. The steward handed me a plate of lamb stew and rice together with a large glass of red wine. The food wasn't very appealing but I ate. I then slept in the chair waking a couple of hours later, still feeling tired. Caterina and Tanja were both asleep so I left them to it. The doctor's were reasonably confident that they were recovering. If I'd have had a God at that point I'd have said thank you. Instead I just asked the steward for a glass of water. Wine would have been more agreeable but I wanted to keep my wits about me for whatever lay ahead.

To kill time I started making phone calls. Firstly I rang Father Steve but couldn't get through. Obviously the lines were down in Zambola. This was confirmed when I tried to get hold of both Henri and Sareb. I then phoned Caroline and gave her edited highlights as to what had happened. I couldn't tell her about the Chinese plans, she was just relieved to hear that Caterina was out. I pondered over Caroline for a few minutes. I liked the girl but knew that nothing could come of our relationship. I just hoped we could remain friends after our one night stand.

Chapter 17

Mark rang to confirm that I'd be picked up from the private terminal at Geneva Airport and that a conference had been planned for eight o'clock the following morning. People were flying in from all over the world to attend. He wanted a pre meet meeting with me on arrival. It was going to be a long night, I tried to sleep again. After half an hour I was still wide awake so drank coffee. I felt fidgety and hyped up. I had no idea where this was going or what part I would play. All I knew was that I wouldn't be seeing my beloved school in Zambola for quite a while.

I chatted to the steward about nothing in particular. Caterina and Tanja continued to sleep. The doctors advised me to leave them that way. Eventually I was asked to fasten my seat belt, we were coming into land.

The joy of flying in a private jet is that you don't have the usual ridiculous landing procedures. Within minutes of touching down we'd taxied up to the terminal and were off the plane. Caterina was half awake as I went to say goodbye. She put her arms around me and we kissed. For a sick lady she was very passionate.

Holding me she said, 'How can I ever thank you?'

'I can think of ways.' I said smiling ruefully.

'I look forward to them,' her warmth had returned, hesitating she went on, 'Jonathan, I know you lost Zan, and that you loved her dearly, but I'm here for you. You've saved my life twice now and there must be a reason for that. I'm a fatalist,' she hesitated, 'I care for you deeply Jonathan, and thank you.'

I held her and it felt good. Had I not cared I think I would have been shocked by what she had said. Instead I just felt happy, a sensation I hadn't felt since Zan's death.

'Look after yourself,' I said squeezing her hand, 'I'll see you soon I promise.'

I climbed down the steps from the plane feeling a spring in my step. Yes the world was on the verge of war but maybe I could help stop it, and with a girl like Caterina by my side, life could be a hell of a lot worse!

The cold hit me immediately, Geneva was a far cry from the humidity of Africa. As I approached the terminal a familiar face smiled at me.

'Heinrich,' I said giving him a bear hug. He was the driver, come odd job man, come steward working for The Organisation in Geneva. A man who'd had an interesting military career I'd been told which I hadn't yet bottomed out. All I knew was that he was totally trustworthy. 'God it's good to see you, how are you?'

'I am well Jonathan and you?'

'Better for seeing you.'

'Your passport' he said quietly handing me an envelope. It'll make life easier going through immigration.'

'I was hoping you'd sort something out,' I said laughing, 'I had to leave in somewhat of a hurry.'

Opening the envelope I realised I'd use this one before, in Paris after my last exploit with The Organisation. It was in the name of Andrew Harrison. What's in a name? I thought.

I was whisked through passport control with the immigration officer showing no interest whatsoever. Heinrich directed me out of the building to a small car park where his beloved BMW 5 series stood.

'Is this old wreck still going?' I laughed.

'This car will still be operational long after you and I have left this world.' We were both laughing as we got in. Heinrich started the engine and we drove off.

'Do you know what's been happening in Zambola?' I asked.

'Mark updated me this morning but I am sure he can tell you more. The government has been overthrown and the Christian Muslim Alliance has formed a government with the Imam as temporary president. The army barracks were blown as planned and after that many of the government troops capitulated to the other side. There was little resistance. A curfew is currently in place which the authorities hope to lift in a few days time. Swiss banks are being very helpful in returning funds to the government which had been taken by their predecessors.'

'What about the prisoners?'

'I'm sorry I imagine Mark has that level of detail.'

I sat in silence for a few minutes and decided to try and phone Father Steve again. This time I got through and after three rings I heard Yvette's voice.

'Bonjour Yvette,' I said 'Tom Simpson ici, I'm just ringing to make sure you and Father Steve are okay.'

'Ah Tom, we were so worried about you, we are fine I'll get Father Steve.'

'Tom,' hearing the big American's voice made me smile. 'How are you fella?'

'I'm good, I got Caterina out, she's not well but hopefully will pull through. I'm afraid I had to leave in rather a hurry but hopefully I'll be back in a few weeks. How is everything?'

'Well we have a new government and the town is quiet. People have been instructed to go about their normal business tomorrow but we're keeping the school closed until Wednesday at least. The power and phones have been back on for a few hours so life could be worse. For a revolution its been remarkably civilised. There was some rampaging through the streets last night as the prisoners were released but most fell into line with the troops supplied by the Alliance. Already that's what we're calling it. Casualties were light thank God, mainly Kasenga's men.'

'What's happened to Kasenga and his Mother?'

'No idea and as a Christian I should be concerned but they've created too much pain in this country and maybe, just maybe now we have a chance.'

'One thing, could you get hold of Sarab the taxi driver and give him two thousand US dollars from me. You'll find the money in my washbag.'

'That's a lot of money.'

'He's earned it Father Steve, trust me.'

'You're a good man Tom, I'll make a Catholic out of you yet.'

'Look after my stuff Father, hope to see you in a few weeks.'

'God bless you Tom, you look after yourself.'

I hit the redial button and this time got straight through to Henri. The new authorities had done a wonderful job putting the infrastructure back together.

'Henri, its Tom, just to say that Tanja is improving, as is my friend Caterina so things are very much on the up.'

'Oh mon ami what can I say? I have been crying with happiness ever since I saw you last. Where are you?'

'Geneva, and Tanja is in the best possible hands. If she's well enough tomorrow I'll get her to phone you.'

'That would be wonderful my friend, I can't begin to thank you.'

'How are things in the town?'

'Remarkably quiet, there are a few troops on the roads, people have accepted the new government and hopefully life will return to normal quickly. The new president has just appeared on television to say that emergency funds are being released quickly to get the infrastructure up and running, he wants all banks, shops and markets to open tomorrow morning as normal. Early signs are good but I'm not naive enough to think that everything is going to be wonderful from now on. I believe we have a long way to go.'

'Are you going to stay?'

'The first and only thing as far as I am concerned is Tanja. We'll make that decision together.'

'Good luck' I said, 'hopefully see you in a few weeks.'

I killed the call and turned to Heinrich, 'Sorry that was rude, do you speak French?'

'Yes but not well. Your friends are alright?'

'Everybody seems fine,' I said while thinking, *apart from the fucking Chinese wanting to take over the world.*

Less than half an hour later we drove up a gravel path to a large mansion The Organisation used as one of its bases. I knew the smaller house to the right currently covered in darkness was also part of the operation. Truth be told, I knew little more than that. The Organisation was a need to know operation and I knew little about its size and scope. However I did know that it had major influence across the world and that the man I called Mark was a key player.

As we drove up the door to the house opened and Mark came out. Shaking me by the hand he spoke.

'Jonathan, it's so good to see you, what an operation, well done my friend. Finding Caterina and getting her out was fantastic in itself. Then, your idea to blow the army based saved thousands of innocent lives and you've also discovered exactly what the Chinese have been planning. Come on in and have a drink, you deserve to celebrate.'

'I thought we were having a pre meet meet.'

'We can do that at the same time. Two whiskeys please Heinrich.'

168

Mark ushered me through to the drawing room, beautifully furnished with expensive antiques and tasteful murals. I felt a pang of sadness thinking about the last time I had been here. I was with Zan, we'd just lost several of our friends and colleagues in a bloody massacre. It was as if Mark was reading my thoughts and immediately he started talking. He basically repeated what Heinrich had told me.

'How's Imran?' I asked.

He's fine, working with the Imam on the fiscal arrangements. Again, I took your advice and the banks have agreed to release Kasenga's money. We however are controlling it and will be putting our own people into Zambola to ensure it is used wisely.'

'I'd like to apply for that job' I said.

'If it's a way of keeping you in The Organisation I think I could arrange that.'

Heinrich arrived with the drinks, 'To the Organisation' toasted Mark.

I raised my glass, everything was falling into place too simply and too quickly. I felt it couldn't last.

'So who's coming to the meeting tomorrow?' I asked.

'There'll be about a dozen of us, pretty big hitters but don't feel intimidated I beg of you. Firstly the President of the United Nations Security Council, The Secretary General of Nato, The Secretary of State for Defence in the UK together with the head of MI6, US Secretary of Defence, the Assistant Director of the CIA, the French Chief of Defence, the German Defence Minister, the Japanese Defence Minister and I'm still waiting on confirmation from a couple of others.'

'Wow,' was all I could say as I took another sip of whisky.

'In theory nobody will know they are here. In practice of course one leak to Facebook and the press will have a field day.'

169

'What's the aim of the meeting?'

'To establish an understanding and a way forward. The great thing is these people don't want detail. That's for us to work out. We give them an overview of our plan. Needless to say nothing is written down and no party would suggest the meeting ever took place. That gives us the freedom we need to operate. As long as we're successful there will never be a problem. If we get it wrong that will be the end of The Organisation.

Mark sat quietly for a second and then eyeballed me. 'What do you make of it all?'.

'My concern if I'm honest is the credibility of that email. Let's be honest it went to a pretty low level Party Secretary. And to release such information in that format staggers me.'

Mark nodded, 'Yup you're so right, but then Imran confirmed the Party Secretary in question doesn't just control Zambola, he also covers about half of the countries in Central Africa. He's a bigger fish than we thought. The Imam has been talking to his sources and apparently our man has flown to the Congo and is basing himself there for the time being. With regard to the format, secure emails are as good a form of communication as any other. It's obvious why he wanted Caterina to look at his laptop, he assumed she was just some computer whizz from the US who couldn't read Chinese. Much better that than letting one of his own technicians see what was going on. He obviously never suspected Caterina to be anything other than a computer technician. His mistake was letting his perversion get in the way. How the hell the Chinese didn't put a block on porn sites is beyond me. Maybe they did, and he found a way around it. But you're right, getting such information from only one source is worrying. Ideally we like to triangulate as you know and confirm information from three different areas. That way we are watertight, at the moment we could be leaving ourselves wide open. But this is too bigger situation to ignore or wait. That's why we've got the big boys joining us tomorrow.'

What's your plan?' I asked.

'I was hoping you'd have one' Mark was grinning which was most unusual. He was normally very seriously minded.

We looked at each other for a few seconds in silence. 'Should we get as many of our own people together as possible and brainstorm.' I said, 'hopefully something will come out of it.'

'Funny you should say that.'

'Go on'.

'The meeting starts in fifty minutes. I'd like you to attend. There'll be fifteen of us. Some of the best operatives from around Europe. I didn't have time to pull resource from elsewhere.

'And here you are filling me up with whisky.'

'One won't do any harm. Heinrich will take you to your room. There you'll find some food and a change of clothes. I suggest you shower, it may be a long night.'

Chapter 18

'When you're ready Jonathan.'

I turned to see Heinrich waiting for me. I left half the whisky, knowing that I needed my wits around me. In the bedroom there was a plate of sandwiches, some quiche and a small bowl of chips. Clothes hung on a couple of hangers. I didn't have to look at them, I knew they'd be designer gear and a perfect fit. Having not changed for a couple of days I was glad to strip off and shower. Following a shave and a couple of sandwiches I felt good enough. I was actually quite excited about what was to come and couldn't wait to get involved. I ran down the stairs nearly colliding with Heinrich. We both burst out laughing, there was a feeling a déjà vu about all of this.

'Are we in the meeting room?' I asked.

Heinrich nodded. it only seemed like five minutes since I was there before. The pain of losing Zan swept over me again. I shook myself and made my way to the room.

It was full of people who turned and looked at me as I walked in. Suddenly I felt depressed, this was the same room I'd been in less than a year before doing a similar exercise but with my beloved Zan. I even recognised a couple of the faces. Mark was standing at the far end and when he saw me he tapped on a table.

'Ladies and Gentlemen may I introduce you to Jonathan, the man responsible for finding one of our own and bringing this vital piece of information to our attention.' Everyone started applauding much to my embarrassment.

Mark went on.' I'm not going to do introductions it will take too long and there is no need. Suffice to say you're all operatives with The Organisation and you are here to try and formulate a plan that we can present to the big hitters tomorrow morning. As usual in these circumstances I want every stupid idea that comes to mind to be put on the table. One stupid or funny idea may just spark something from someone else. You've all seen the brief, apart from Jonathan but he knows it because he wrote most of it. So let's start the ball rolling. We're looking for ways to stop the Chinese from taking control of Africa and the Middle East. Who's going first?

There was silence for a few seconds until I heard.

'We drop our troops into Africa?'

'That's no good,' came a response, 'How can we muster an army big enough to take control of Africa, it's impossible.'

Mark stepped in, 'I want ideas at this stage no matter how outlandish. We can discuss the merits once we have them up on the wall,'

He wrote on a flip chart *'Drop troops into Africa'*.

'Create a buffer zone along the Suez Canal.'

Again Mark wrote on the flip chart.

'Nuke Beijing.'

A few people tittered, Mark just wrote.

'Threaten them at the UN with serious economic sanctions.'

'Cut all credit lines to Chinese companies.'

'Impound all Chinese assets in the West.'

'Send a delegation of world leaders to Beijing.'

'Send a fleet of warships out to the Pacific.'

'Tell all the countries threatened what is going to happen and provide them with weapons so they can defend themselves.'

I rather liked that idea but realised the cost and logistical implications would be dire. Still better that than Chinese domination.

'Put all Chinese living in the West into prison camps.'

'Start a cull of Chinese in the West.'

173

'Poison water supplies to city's across China.'

'Create a virus to kill them off.'

We were beginning to slip into the realms of fantasy, still this is what Mark wanted. The brainstorming went on for nearly an hour with nothing definitive coming out of it. Mark clipped each page of writing onto the wall so that we could survey our work.

Coffee and sandwiches were laid out so we didn't break. People helped themselves while we carried on talking and throwing out ideas. I began to feel tired and frazzled.

I kept looking at one line, *'Nuke Beijing'* There was something in this, not actually killing millions of people but.... I knew there was the kernel of a plan but I couldn't quite see it.

'You look deep in thought Jonathan,' said Mark, 'What is it?'

I said what I was thinking,

A couple tittered, *moron*s I thought.

Someone said *'Bomb a smaller city'* and then it clicked.

'That's it, I said, that's what we do.'

'Are we really going to suggest to the UN tomorrow that we're going to nuke a small city in China? Come on Jonathan.' Mark sounded exasperated.

'No listen,' I was trying to formulate a plan but it was hazy in my mind. 'What we need to do is scare them off with a series of explosions.'

Then I had it, total clarity, and it frightened me.

'We front China at the UN, tell them we know what they're doing. Explain unless they pull back there will be severe consequences and then leave it. We then monitor troop and arms movements closely. That gives us time because, and this is the clever bit, we plant small nuclear devices in far reached places across China well away from populated areas.

If they ignore us and I'm assuming they will we begin to set them off, one by one with each one closer to a major conurbation. There will come a point when they will be forced into submission.'

'They could retaliate,' someone said.

'That's why we need to put the bombs in place first, we're talking hours between detonations, they wouldn't have time to retaliate.

'They could send missiles across to the western seaboard of the US or Australia.'

Explain if they do that both Beijing and Shanghai will be blown immediately while at the same time exploding another bomb in an outlying region to show we mean business. They wouldn't dare send missiles, it would be tantamount to suicide.'

'Jonathan there may be something in this,' said Mark, 'but we haven't got the manpower to go scurrying around China planting bombs.'

'Surely the US and Europe could provide men and equipment?'

'Yes they could but getting troops in and out as well as bombs and equipment would be a logistical nightmare. It couldn't happen without us being caught. Don't forget China is a very closed society, and the territory is huge.'

I put my head in my hands trying to think. If it was simply a matter of logistics there had to be a way.

It was then I had a eureka moment. I stood up in excitement.

'My enemy's enemy.' I shouted as my chair fell back and crashed to the floor.

Everyone looked at me as if I'd lost it.

'My enemy's enemy is my friend, it's thought to be an old Arabic saying.'

'I know the expression' replied Mark derisively, 'And I know the concept has been used throughout history, the second World War being a prime example when the British and Americans fought with the Russians against Nazi Germany.'

'And that's precisely what's happening in Zambola with the Muslims and the Christians working together to overthrow the Kasenga regime'

'Go on' said Mark humouring me. The others just looked confused and embarrassed. I'm sure some thought I'd cracked.

'Who in China is going to be anti the current regime and their plan for world domination?' I asked looking at no one in particular.

'Businessmen,' said one, an Asian looking chap with a Nordic accent.

'Human rights activists,' shouted another.

'Journalists and ethnic minorities.'

'The Triads' bellowed an attractive blond woman in her thirties sounding German.

'Exactly,' I said clicking my fingers and pointing at her.

'The Triads, do they want their markets destroyed? Do they like the present government? Do they want to lose billions? No, so we work with them. They'll have the infrastructure to import equipment quietly and distribute it around the country. They're enormous and they'll have the capability to act quickly.'

'Do we know anybody associated with the Triads.' an Englishman called Ben asked, I'd worked with him briefly the year before.

'No' said Mark, 'And I very much doubt the people we're seeing tomorrow would sanction us to work with the Triads.'

'Two things' I responded, I was on a roll and wasn't going to give way. 'Firstly we give them concepts tomorrow, not details, secondly we do have a contact.' I felt sick as I said it.

'Go on,' replied Mark gaining interest.

I looked at him, the rest of the room faded into a blur. I felt sick with what I was about to say. However I knew it was the only way forward.

'Maybe now is the time I go and pay my respects to Zan's family. It's pretty obvious that her connection to The Triads was through them.'

Mark looked at me and half nodded, I could almost hear the cogs turning in his brain.

'We have a plan,' he said quietly. The room burst into applause again. I sat back and wanted to burst into tears.

Chapter 19

'There's one thing still worrying me,' said Mark after everyone had quietened down. 'We only have one email confirming all this. I really need to triangulate, that is confirmation from at least three sources. Otherwise we could end up with egg on our faces. We believe the information to be genuine. In theory it could be a spoof but that's most unlikely. It is a logical conclusion given the Chinese approach to Africa in recent years. However, the evidence is all circumstantial and I'll have to state this at the meeting tomorrow. For two reasons, firstly I'm covering our backs and secondly it's too important to suggest otherwise. The meeting has to decide whether we take a calculated risk. However I would be happier if we could find a way to get confirmation.'

I looked at Mark, 'Shit I've been stupid.'

'Why' he said.

'Caterina told me that when she was looking at the Party Secretary's computer she copied the contents onto the Joteque system for future reference. There may well be something more. We need to access that info.'

'Who are Joteque?' someone asked.

'The company Caterina was working for in Zambola. They're based in California'.

'I'll get onto them now' said Mark.

'While you're doing that I can go to the hospital. If Caterina is conscious she can tell me where the file is stored.'

'In the meantime the rest of you continue brainstorming and see if you can find something, anything.'

Mark picked up his mobile phone, 'Heinrich I need you to take Jonathan to the Générale-Beaulieu Clinic straight away.'

Looking at me he said, 'You really need sleep.'

'I'll power nap in the car.'

'Phone when you've spoken to Caterina. In the meantime we'll start looking for the file from this end. Probably be quicker if Caterina can help. I'll organise resource to disseminate the info and start putting the presentation together for tomorrow morning.

Heinrich appeared.

'Off you go and thanks.'

'Good luck,' I heard as I left the room.

I felt absolutely knackered and even the cold air didn't help as we left the house.

'Heinrich, while you drive I have to sleep.' I climbed into the back of the car and lay down. 'Wake me when we arrive.' I slept, a deep sleep. I didn't dream but woke to Heinrich shaking me.

'Hello,' I shouted totally confused.

'Have some water Jonathan.' Heinrich handed me a litre bottle. I swallowed a few mouthfuls poured some over my head and rubbed it in. Still feeling groggy I climbed out of the car and followed Heinrich up a path to the hospital.

I wasn't really paying much attention but in the dark I could see a four storey faceless seventies building in front of me. At eleven o'clock at night the reception area was empty but a young nurse appeared.

'You are here to see Caterina?' she spoke in almost perfect English. I nodded.

'Follow me please.'

'I'll wait in the car.' said Heinrich.

'How is she?' I asked as we walked along a corridor.

'She is doing well, her temperature has come down and she is conscious. Hopefully with time she will make a full recovery.'

The nurse opened a door into a room where Caterina lay in bed. Nothing much had changed from the flight, she was still surrounded by a sea of monitors, an oxygen tube was hooked round her ears winding into her nostrils and a couple of intravenous drips pumped fluids into her. As we walked in her eyes opened and she smiled.

'I didn't expect to see you tonight Jonathan, how lovely.'

I felt a pang of guilt and turning to the nurse I said, 'Could you leave us please?' She scowled, 'Five minutes, Caterina is still very weak.'

I sat down and held her hand, she looked far from well. 'It's not exactly social my darling,' I said in Spanish as the nurse closed the door. 'Things are hotting up but I don't want to trouble you with detail. I'll fill you in when you're strong enough. However, we need to know where you stored the Party Secretary's file. You said it was on the Joteque system. The information could be crucial to stopping World War Three, I jest not.'

'And I thought you'd come to make love to me.' Caterina joked squeezing my hand.

'Nothing would give me greater pleasure' I said, only I wasn't joking.

She looked serious for a second, 'In the company 'C' drive you'll find my private file. I was known as Camila Sanchez. Password - *jonathan111*. The file is named *Background Africa*.

'Thank you, I must tell Mark.' Picking up my phone I relayed the information.

'I'll get the boffins on it straight away,' he said.

'How many speak Chinese?' I asked.

'I've no idea. I'll see what resource I can get hold of quickly. You'll be a useful pair of hands, can you come straight back?'

'Will do.'

'I've got my marching orders,' I said turning to Caterina.

'I understand, don't forget I still work for The Organisation.'

'I know, and you've done a truly miraculous job.'

I kissed her on the mouth, even though she was far from well she responded and I could feel the excitement rising.

'Hopefully see you tomorrow.' I said pulling away.

I headed back to the car where Heinrich was waiting.

'It's going to be a long night.'

'Try and get some sleep on the way back.'

I was too wound up to sleep and sat looking out of the window, vaguely aware of the late night Geneva traffic.

Arriving back at the mansion Mark was sitting at his desk.

'We've got the file, I've got the CIA, GCHQ and The Public Security Intelligence Agency in Japan working on it. They're our best bet.'

'I'll have a look as well,' I said.

'I think you should sleep, you look shattered Jonathan.'

'Thanks I replied,' I can sleep tomorrow. Give me a laptop and I'll see what I can find.'

'You'll find one next door, The file is on the 'O' drive under "Correspondence Caterina". I'll organise coffee and sandwiches.'

I was getting a bit fed up with sandwiches but felt now wasn't the right time to start complaining.

'Did the guys come up with anything?'

'No, we went round and round in circles and gave up half an hour ago. They're reconvening at seven to have another go. Sleep may just help.'

I went and sat down next door and stared at the screen. I was bushed and could hardly think straight. Heinrich appeared with a tray.

'Don't you ever sleep?' I asked.

181

'It varies,' came the response,' Sometimes it is like this, then I may go for weeks doing nine till five.'

I started rifling through the files. After a few minutes it became obvious this was far more than a one man job. I could see why Mark had brought in several agencies to work on it. Ferreting around for an hour or so I found nothing of significance. Mark came through the door.

'The Japs have found something,' he said, 'Go into Documents/Correspondence/Meeting/ Politburo/November.'

I opened the file and there were the minutes of a meeting held the previous year. Copies had been sent to members of the Politburo Standing Committee including the **General Secretary of the Communist Party**, the **Vice Premier of the Peoples Republic of China**, the Chairman of the Central Military Commission, the Head of the Central Politics and Law Commission, Chief of the General Office of the Communist Party, Regional Party Secretaries and various ambassadors from around the world. I translated for Mark as quickly as possible cutting the irrelevancies and the massive amount of Chinese sycophancy. Eventually I found the confirmation we needed and paraphrased for Marks benefit.

'It talks about Chinese investment in African countries and the long term plan to gain control of resources across Africa and The Middle East. The reason being to keep them out of the hands of capitalist states. It talks about the dependency of African Chinese investment, the 'Arab Spring' and 'Islamic State' projects to destabilise Northern Africa. The aim is to give China control over oil supplies and ensure they do not become reliant on Western governments. They believe the Americans will create but they do not have enough military capability to take on China with its enlarged presence across the world. Future projects will also ensure America becomes a puppet state. The Russians to be paid off with loan enhancements and territory guarantees to ensure a non aggressive stance.

'It's a rough and ready translation,' I said to Mark, 'But it is confirmation of the previous email.'

'Okay, we'll get an official translation from the Americans later but that's good enough for me. Two sides of the triangulation, I'd love a third, maybe somebody will come up with something overnight, even if it's less tenuous than this, However I'm prepared to run with what we've got.'

'What about the line "Future projects will ensure America also becomes a puppet state"'

'No idea, but it proves the importance of bringing the current Chinese government down. If they go there won't be any future projects. As always Jonathan, you've done a superb job, now go and get some sleep.'

I didn't argue, my head was spinning. I went to my room, threw my clothes onto the floor, climbed into bed and drifted off within seconds.

Chapter 20

I awoke to hear someone knocking at the door. It opened and an elderly looking stout lady wearing a white coat walked in holding a tray.

'Morning Jonathan,' she said in German with a thick Swiss accent, 'It's six thirty. Mark asks if you'll join him for breakfast at seven o'clock?'

'Do I have a choice?' I responded smiling.

She grinned in return. *Thirty years ago* I thought, *I bet she was a real beauty.*

'Coffee and orange juice' she said putting down the tray, 'to help you wake up.'

'But I'm an Englishman' I protested, 'We always have tea in the morning.'

She looked a bit nonplussed. 'Oh sorry, I will go and get some.'

'I'm joking, coffee is fine.'

She left chuckling to herself.

I climbed out of bed, my arm had stiffened again overnight and felt sore. I knew I really should rest but I did my ablutions and at ten to seven made my way downstairs. I went to Mark's office. He sat gazing at a computer screen looking ashen.

'Mark, I know you don't need much shut eye but looking at you I think sleep is the order of the day.'

'No it's not that,' he paused still gazing at the screen, 'Reports are coming in, there's been a second military coup in Zambola.'

I virtually collapsed into a chair, stunned at what I'd heard.

'Who?' I asked.

'Too early to tell, they came over the border with full military might, tanks, air support, fully equipped military, the lot. They've taken the capital with the indigenous army virtually wiped out, huge civilian losses and major structural damage. They're taking no captives, it's total carnage.'

'Have you heard from Imran?'

'No.'

'Fucking hell,' I said thinking about my friends, Father Steve, Yvette, Henri. Jacques, Sareb and all the kids at the school.

'It must be the Chinese,' said Mark, 'Nobody else in the region could muster such forces so quickly.'

'There's your triangulation,' I replied, 'if we can prove it. Imran's are only hope.

'He's not answering his satellite phone.'

'Let me try a few of my contacts.'

I phoned Imran, Jacques, Henri and Father Steve. The lines were all dead.

'I'm delaying this morning's meeting until we know what's what,' said Mark, 'I'll brief them and take it from there. Hopefully we'll have more information soon, my best guess is the Chinese have started their move through Africa. But we need proof damn it.' Mark rarely swore, I could tell he was deeply concerned.

'Can you fly me in?' I asked not relishing the thought of another long journey.

'If need be yes, but I need answers quickly.'

'With the information Caterina copied could we hack into the Chinese systems? We know their security is crap.'

'Like it.' said Mark immediately picking up his 'O' phone and pressing a series of buttons.

He was obviously talking to some sort of computer whizz and within a couple of minutes he'd gone through the complete scenario.

'So in a nutshell we need to know what the Chinese involvement is. Put as many teams on this as possible, it is number one priority bar none, code Kennedy and I jest not.'

'Code Kennedy?' I asked.

'Strong possibility of World War.' after a moment's silence he spoke again, 'If what we suspect is true you'll be on the first plane to Hong Kong not Zambola.'

I nodded, the thought of meeting Zan's family appalled me but I knew I had little option.

'Lets go and have some breakfast,' said Mark.

We walked into the dining room, ten tables of four were laid out and a couple of people from last night's meeting were just leaving as we entered. I ordered some scrambled eggs from the Swiss lady I'd seen earlier. Mark poured coffee.

Stirring his cup he said,' I realise the next few days are going to be difficult and it really sticks in the throat to be working with the Triads but I can't see another way forward. If it doesn't work, God help us all.'

'I'll need background info on Zan, who she really is and where she's from.

'I'll get it loaded onto your 'O' phone under *Zaninfo*. You can look at it on the flight over.

We sat in silence, Mark stared pensively ahead of him. His phone rang. He listened eventually turning to me.

'They believe they can hack into the Chinese system but its going to take several hours. In the meantime you're going to have to get out to Hong Kong. The sooner the better. Heinrich will organise flight tickets.' I nodded, feeling sick at the prospect.

Mark's phone rang again. He stood up quickly beckoning me to follow.

'It's Imran on satellite' he said walking briskly back to his office.

'I'm with Jonathan, you're on loudspeaker, tell us what you can.'

'It's a mess. They came into Kanina at dawn with tanks, air cover and hundreds of well armed troops shooting at will. The Alliance forces stood no chance. It's been total annihilation. I have the Imam tucked away, he's OK but there's no chance of fighting back.'

'What about civilians?' I asked.

'Anyone caught on the streets has been shot, buildings have been blown for no reason. It's a sick joke.'

'Who's behind this?' asked Mark, 'It can't be Kasenga, he hasn't got that level of military might tucked away.'

'We don't know, but I intend to find out. The one thing I can confirm is that the equipment is Chinese.'

Mark and I looked at each other.

''We're trying to hack into the Chinese systems now to see what we can find. I'll come back to you when I know something. In the meantime, take care of yourself.'

Mark killed the call and dialled again, 'Heinrich I need to get Jonathan on the earliest flight possible to Hong Kong,' He put the phone down and looked at me.

'I'm not sure if it's fair to let you handle this one on your own, it's bigger than any of us. I'm going to organise backup.'

I nodded, I wasn't feeling particularly brave at that point.

'Do we have resource in Hong Kong?'' I asked.

'A little, but not enough to take on the Chinese military, or the Triads for that matter.'

We sat in an uncomfortable silence for a few minutes not quite knowing what to do next. Eventually Heinrich walked in and broke the mood.

'You're on the 13.10 from Zurich to Moscow. I'm afraid I can't get you in business class but it's only a ninety minute flight. There's a fifty minute stopover and then a direct flight to

Hong Kong, that is business class. Just under fourteen hours in total. It's the best I can find. We'll have to leave soon to get across to Zurich. It's a three hour drive but that'll be quicker than flying or catching the train.

'Go' said Mark. I'll speak to you when I know something.'

'I'll have a bag packed, tickets and passport in ten minutes, see you at the front door.' Heinrich turned and left the room.

'Good luck,' said Mark, I just nodded and went up to my room. I rinsed my face, had a pee and went back downstairs to see Heinrich walking out of the front door with a small travel bag.

'You can take this on board' he said, 'it'll be quicker than checking in.'

The fresh morning air was invigorating as we walked across to Heinrich's car. I looked out at the mountain range, covered in snow and felt a sense of foreboding as I climbed into the car, I had no idea where this was leading, but knew that if we failed the carnage on the streets of Kanina would be multiplied across the world. I shivered involuntarily. I literally had the world's salvation in my hands. I felt well out of my comfort zone, scared and very unsure.

For the first part of the journey we drove in silence. I was deep in thought about what lay ahead, I believe Heinrich understood and stayed quiet. The road was busy but the traffic moved at a good speed. We were taking the most direct route crossing the flattest part of Switzerland through Bern and Solothurn. There was little or nothing in terms of scenery and after a while I became somewhat bored.

Heinrich handed me an envelope.

'In there you will find your passport, money, credit cards etc. There's a thousand Hong Kong Dollars and just over two hundred Euros to start you off. One of our men will be waiting for you outside customs in Hong Kong. You have been checked in online and I have printed the boarding pass.'

I looked at the passport, a British one with the name Peter John Summers and the photograph that was on my real passport. The date of birth was just over a year older than mine.

'Heinrich, where do these come from?

He smiled, 'We have a little man!'

'He must have a very sophisticated printing press.'

'You could say that' he replied airily.

I stuffed the money and cards into my wallet and the passport and flight ticket went into my jacket pocket. Handing my old cards to Heinrich he put them in the dashboard drawer. Mark had said he's had an interesting life, with time to kill I decided to find out a little more about him.

'So what's your background Heinrich?'

'Now there's a story,' he replied through a fixed grin.

'I'd love to hear it.'

He took a deep breath and started to speak.

'My Father was in the SS during the war. Quite high up and responsible for all sorts of nasty things. I'm not accountable for his deeds but it did have a direct bearing on my life. After the Nuremberg trials he spent ten years in prison before being released. He then lived in East Germany met and married my Mother while working for the Stasi, the East German secret police. They needed good operators and he needed a job. In the fifties it was a bit of a ramshackle operation and those who rose through the ranks of the Nazis unsurprisingly made good Stasi officers. However he was also working for the Americans. They'd 'arranged' for his release from prison and it was their contact who introduced him to the right people in the Stasi. Eventually an informer from the American side spilled the beans and my Father disappeared. I loved him, he was a decent man, despite the mistakes he'd made while working for the Nazis.

However to cut a long story short the Stasi insisted I should spy for them, it was their way of proving my loyalty to the country. Psychological blackmail truth be told. I didn't have much choice, they were mean and nasty degenerates. However through a contact of my Father's I was also asked to work for the Americans which made my work more than acceptable. I threw myself into the job and soon became very useful spying on friends and lecturers at university. I'd wire tap and bug people, and used what became known as 'Zersetzung' a form of mental harassment to gain information. As a group we would damage the reputation of dissidents, destroy relationships and generally make life impossible for people. I qualified as a nurse and spied on colleagues in hospitals, doctors, nurses, administrators even patients. It was a crazy time, we were all spying on each other and there was information overload, with the authorities not knowing what to do with it all or how to make use of it. I rose through the ranks and helped create an administration system which started to make sense of everything we had on file. This was in the early days of computers and microfiche. We pieced together info creating a web which tracked people's lives. It was raw and unsophisticated compared with modern day systems but with money and people we were surprisingly effective. I then went to work in places like Egypt, Ethiopia, Libya and Cuba helping to set up administration controls for their secret police operations. I got involved in all sorts of things that I'd rather not talk about but all the time I was feeding information back to the US. It couldn't go on forever and eventually, like my Father I was caught or should I say I was imprisoned due to being suspected of being a spy. They were paranoid and I would have disappeared but I was lucky. The forerunner to The Organisation got me out of jail, mainly due to a certain individual who showed incredible loyalty towards me.'

'Mark?' I enquired.

He nodded, 'Mark was my contact, confidante, mentor and friend. I've worked for him ever since. He's the best man I've ever known.'

'Quite a story.'

I got the impression that he didn't want to say anymore so I started looking at the headlines on my 'O' phone. There was a small paragraph about the Zambolan counter coup in both The Times and The Telegraph but the rest of the English press printed nothing. Le Figaro in France had basically the same article. Zambola to the world was an irrelevance; I wondered how it would go down in history.

We kept to the north of Zurich travelling up the A1 and then turned onto to the A51 for the last few miles following the signposts to the airport, only stopping to pay tolls. We'd been travelling a little over three hours as we approached the main concourse. Heinrich handled the traffic with ease.

'I'll drop you off at the terminal but you'll have to shoot off straight away. You're only allowed to stop for a couple of minutes.'

'That's fine' I replied.

As we pulled in I shook Heinrich by the hand. We'd become quite close and I felt I could trust him implicitly.

'Good luck,' he said, 'Hope to see you soon.'

Chapter 21

Heinrich had already checked me in so I made my way through security which was surprisingly efficient. I past the myriad of shops selling supposed duty free products which I knew I could buy cheaper online. Looking at the monitor I realised the flight had already been called. We had cut things rather fine so I walked briskly to the gate where there was the usual sea of humanity waiting to board the plane.

I wasn't looking forward to flying with a Russian airline as my experiences in the past had been pretty dismal, with tired old Ilyushin jets, miserable staff and dreadful food. However I was pleasantly surprised to find myself boarding an Airbus 320 and even in economy there was plenty of leg room. The flight stewardess was somewhat starchy but started to thaw when I spoke in her own language. I was on the aisle and there was a rough looking Russian hunched in the window seat. Lunch was pleasant enough, soup and beef stroganoff with a small bottle of drinkable red wine. I felt like asking for a second but decided it was probably better to keep my wits about me for the time being.

I explained to the stewardess that I only had a fifty minute stopover before my flight to Hong Kong. She grimaced, 'It will be a thirty minute walk through the terminal. You had better come and sit near the front to get off quickly.' She beckoned and I followed like a lapdog. Good service, I thought, it was easy to knock.

Sitting down on the front row I opened my 'O' phone. Zan's information had been loaded and the thought of looking at it made me feel sick in the pit of my stomach. I was about to learn who the love of my life really was. The girl to whom I'd become engaged, the girl who I'd loved more dearly than anyone I'd ever known, the girl who'd been killed in front of me. I'd been so busy in recent weeks the pain of her loss had become more bearable. Now it was suddenly back, with vengeance.

I turned my head not wanting to read the information but I knew I had to. Eventually I forced myself to look at the screen. There was her picture, I'd never had one and this was the first time I'd seen her in nearly a year. That smile, I could never forget that smile, the twin feelings of love and despair swept over me simultaneously. I rubbed my eyes to hide the tears which started to flow freely. I still loved her and I knew I would never get over her.

'*Sod i*t' I thought, '*I can do this later.*' With that I put the phone in my pocket and ordered a whisky. '*To hell with the world.*'

I drank two miniature bottles and then dozed a little until we touched down at Sheremetyevo Airport in Moscow. To be fair to the Russians efficiency had improved dramatically over the years and within minutes I was off the plane and walking past dozens of duty free shops. All of them were selling designer gear and none had any customers. There must have been more shops than passengers. I had to go through a couple of security checks which was particularly irritating as I was only in transit and it slowed me down. The guards were typically Russian, rude and aggressive. The fact that I spoke their language helped little.

Eventually after what seemed like walking forever I arrived at the gate a little breathless and limping again. I'd noticed in recent weeks that my limp had all but disappeared unless I did heavy exercise. I made a mental note to get into a training regime so that I could lose it completely and sort my arm at the same time. Passengers were already boarding so I took my place in the queue. There were many who appeared to be Chinese businessmen. Although relationships were never great between Moscow and Beijing obviously the business community saw things in another light. I idly wondered how they would feel if China took control of Africa and the Middle East.

Once on the plane I sat down in a middle seat with no one on either side. This pleased me as I wasn't in the mood for conversation. I ordered some orange juice after take off knowing the task I had to perform and dreading it. Eventually I took out my 'O' phone and started reading about Zan. For the first time I discovered her real name:-

Yingtai Leung
Single
28

Education
Hong Kong Academy, top grade International Baccalaureate Diploma (45 points), Christ's College Cambridge BA Economics First Class Honours, MBA Harvard Business School.

Languages
Cantonese, Mandarin, English and French.

Employment
Graduate trainee at Deloittes Hong Kong, qualified as a Chartered Accountant before joining Hong Kong Security Bureau. Seconded to The Organisation after two years

Background
Daughter of Hong Kong industrialist Kan Leung. Second generation Hong Kong entrepreneur. Turned Leung Industries from a small but successful trading company into a multi national operation with interests in shipping, hotels, motor dealerships and haulage.

Mother Bo Leun. Several family members work for Leung Industries including older sister Meihui Leung, 32. Powerful and cunning, PA to her Father. Brother Donghai Leung Head of Security. Known not to be bright, in a position arranged by Kan Leung to keep his son out of trouble. Previous drug and alcohol abuse.

Interests
Third Dan Black Belt-Jujitsu
Piano Grade 8
Swimming - offered a training position with Chinese Swimming Association at fourteen but declined to focus on academia
Dance
Netball

I read the report a couple of times. Strangely it didn't bring me closer to Zan, it was almost as if I was reading about a total stranger. Somehow I was hoping for more colour but realised that was personal. For the job in hand there was enough for me to go on. My first port of call had to be Kan Leung, Zan's Father. If I couldn't get close to him perhaps Meihui her sister was the key.

I ordered a glass of white wine and sat staring into space. I could have watched one of dozens of films on the in-flight system, most of which looked rank and the rest I'd already seen. I dozed and chatted to the steward occasionally, eating the food when it arrived and drifted through the interminable journey just wanting it to be over.

We were due to arrive at 10.05 in the morning local time, 3am in Geneva and 4am in Zambola. My body clock would be all over the place but I'd travelled enough to know I could get through the day. With an early night I'd be fine the following morning.

195

Eventually I heard the words I'd been waiting for, 'Doors to manual,' I smiled as always thinking, *one day I really will find out what that means.* We touched down at Hong Kong International, ten minutes early and managed to get off the plane without too many traumas.

Terminal One was bright, modern and spotlessly clean. It had an air of efficiency and grandeur. The walk through to passport control wasn't too long for a major airport where the young officer smiled as he scanned my passport and waved me through. As I only had hand luggage I was able to cut the baggage belt and walked straight through to the main concourse.

As is always the case a sea of people stood jostling for position waiting for passengers. I saw the name *Peter Summers* on a sign being held by a small Chinese man in his early forties. I nodded and he beamed as he came across and shook my hand. *How many times have I been through this?* I asked myself.

'Mr Summers it is a pleasure to meet you,' he said in almost perfect English. 'I am Donald Tse, most people call me Don. My car is just a short distance from here.'

We walked across the concourse with its vast array of designer shops but unlike Moscow these were busy with customers spending money. Chatting amiably about the flight and the weather we approached car park one and the lights flashed on a Mercedes C Class, it was spotlessly clean. Don took my bag and put in the boot.

'You are booked into the Inter Continental,' he said as we climbed in. It has a wonderful Chinese restaurant with two Michelin stars.'

'That should do nicely.'

'We'll be there in about 40 minutes depending on the traffic.' Don eased the car into the ensuing traffic jam.

I wondered how much he knew and it was as if he'd read my thoughts.

'I am the Head of Operations for China,' he said. 'We are not presently a big function as China has pulled away from The Organisation. Nowadays we are somewhat clandestine because officially we don't exist here. I've been with the company for twelve years and worked mainly across Asia-Pacific. I've known Mark as you call him and we've worked closely for most of that time. We have complete trust in each other. Accordingly he has brought me up to speed with developments and to say it is scary is an understatement.'

'Do you think Kan Leung will help?'

'Don't know. I can't find any connection either with The Triads. He's as clean as a whistle. He was obviously checked thoroughly when Yingtai joined The Organisation. As were the rest of the family. Apart from her brother's drink and drug problems there is nothing to suggest anything untoward.'

'Yet we know Yingtai was involved with The Triads.'

'And that is what puzzles me. I can't find any connection. I have a pal in ICAC, the Independent Commission Against Corruption here in Hong Kong. These guys are good and if there was the slightest whiff of corruption or scandal they would know about it, and they don't. It just doesn't ring true.'

I sat looking at the traffic as we wound our way into the city.

'I'll phone Kan Leung's office this afternoon and try to make an appointment to see him.'

'Good luck with that. Apparently he rarely talks to anyone outside his inner sanctum.'

The airport was on Lantau Island and we travelled along Highway 8 looking out onto the Zhujian estuary. Traffic was heavy but flowing. As we approached the Tsing Ma Suspension Bridge, linking Lantau with Ma Wan and Tsing Yi islands the traffic came to a complete halt.

'Often the case' said Don with a rueful smile.

I could see enormous tower blocks which looked hideous.

197

'Park Island housing development.'

'Appalling' I exclaimed.

'Land is in short supply, people need to live somewhere.'

Crossing over onto Tsing Yi island I noticed the central peak and surrounding area hadn't been built on. It looked quite incongruous.

'Green belt' said Don.

We crossed over water again heading into Kowloon and route three was bumper to bumper. Crawling at a snails pace we eventually inched off the highway and came down to the waterfront. Don pulled up outside the hotel.

'Get your bearings,' he said, 'we'll talk later.'

We shook hands as a doorman opened the car door. He took my bag from the boot and ushered me into the foyer. Check in was incredibly efficient and a porter took me straight to my room. I handed him a one hundred Hong Kong bill which didn't seem to impress him. Ten quid in my language was more than he deserved for carrying a small bag. The room had a delightful view of the harbour but I wasn't in the mood for playing tourist.

I went online and found a number for Leung Industries.

Dialling, the response was almost immediate.

Without thinking I spoke in English 'Mr Kan Leung's office please.'

'I'm sorry Mr Leung is not available.'

'His PA will do.'

'Whose speaking please?'

'My name is Peter Summers. I was a very good friend of Mr Leung's daughter Yingtai, I would like to pay my respects to Mr Leung.'

A silence followed and then the interminable muzak. After a couple of minutes a new voice came on.

'Mr Leung's office can I help you?' It sounded like a middle aged woman, deep and husky.

I repeated the statement adding 'Perhaps I could make an appointment to see Mr Leung.'

'I'm afraid that will not be possible.'

'You must understand,' I said, 'Yingtai was my fiancée before she died.'

Again there was a silence, and then, 'One moment please.'

A good three minutes must have passed as I listened to a Viennese Waltz. Eventually the music came to an abrupt halt and the same voice spoke, 'Where are you staying?'

I gave her the details.

'We'll be in touch.' with that the line went dead.

Chapter 22

I paced up and down not quite knowing what to do next. The view across the harbour was to die for but I just couldn't focus on its splendour. I kept asking myself, 'If that woman doesn't come back, how the hell can I get hold of Zan's Father.'

Sitting on the bed a feeling of exhaustion came over me. This was all getting a bit much. I lay down and closed my eyes.

The next thing I knew I heard hammering on the door. I'd been in a deep sleep and was totally disorientated. I sat up and shook my head.

'Who is it?' I shouted.

'We are from ICAC, the Independent Commission Against Corruption. Please let us in.'

I opened the door and four burly men in tight fitting suits pushed through. They looked like thugs rather than policemen and didn't give me the opportunity to argue.

One of them, younger than the others and incredibly overweight spoke in good English. 'Your passport is fake, you are under arrest for illegal entry. You do not have to say anything but anything you do say will be taken down and given in evidence. Come with us.'

I was immediately grabbed by both arms, frog marched out of my room, down the corridor and into a lift. The four of them spoke in Mandarin obviously assuming I didn't speak the language. I stayed quiet thinking I may learn something.

'That was easy' said the one holding my left arm.

'Pretty boy isn't he' said another fondling my arse, 'I could have him.' He looked like a complete pervert with died blond hair, an earring and shaven eyebrows. He kept leering at me. I desperately wanted to hit him and hoped I would get the opportunity.

'Be a good boy and you may have your chance.' said the guy who'd spoken to me. I assumed he was the leader, as he spoke he had a sick grin on his face.

The first one smiled back and flushed. I kept a nondescript expression on my face.

The lift door opened and I was paraded through reception and outside to an unmarked Toyota Celica. I was aware of people staring at us, we must have made a pretty sight. It was dark outside and they manhandled me into the back of the car with one thug climbing in either side. The other two sat in the front. Given that there was nowhere to go they released my arms and I sat rubbing them as if to get the circulation going. Carefully I rubbed my wrists around the watch I'd been given all those weeks ago and without making it obvious pressed the knob to activate the tracker. At least, I hoped it would.

'Where are we going?' I asked in English.

'Quiet' screamed the leader.

I shut up and stared out at the Hong Kong traffic. After about five minutes the car turned into an underground car park. We went down five floors before pulling up by a lift.

The leader got out and pressed a button. When the doors opened I was again grabbed forcibly and dragged from the car.

'Alright,' I screamed in English., 'there's no need to be so bloody rough, I'm not going anywhere.'

One of the thugs smacked my face knocking me to the floor.

'Do not tell us what to do' said the leader as I was dragged back up and pushed into the lift. I was a bit dazed and confused. We all stood in silence as the lift descended to God knows where.

The doors opened to reveal a concrete corridor dimly lit. I was frogmarched to a grey metal door and pushed inside. The room was small, dingy and smelt of urine. It was so hot I broke out into an immediate sweat.

'Strip him' the leader screamed.

My clothes were ripped off with the pervert stroking my balls and fingering my arse. Another one held me tight while squeezing my nipples. I tried to push him away when the leader screamed in Mandarin.

'Sit him down and take off that fucking watch.'

The pervert ripped it off my wrist while forcibly pushing me into a wooden chair with my back to the door. He handed the watch to his leader who screamed 'Out' and they all left the room. There was silence, I blinked a couple of times trying to make sense of what was happening. There wasn't much to look at, in front of me there was a small desk behind which were two other chairs.

After a few seconds the light was switched off and I sat in total darkness, naked and scared. I tried to think through exactly what had happened. These people said they were from the Independent Commission Against Corruption. Why would they arrest me over a fake passport? Surely that was an Immigration Department issue. Another thing worried me, I didn't believe for one minute that The Organisation would be issuing dodgy passports, so why had I been arrested? Why was I in a dingy room without any formal charges being made?. Surely I would be questioned by immigration officials at an Immigration Office.

I was confused, hot, thirsty and frightened. Something wasn't quite right and I couldn't put my finger on it.

After an hour or so the light went back on and the leader came into the room with the pervert.

The two sat down behind the desk and stared at me for several seconds. Eventually the leader spoke.

'We know you are a spy working for The Organisation. We have your watch with their tracker. What are you doing here? Being caught spying In China carries the death sentence. You'd better start telling the truth.'

I said nothing. Eventually the pervert stood up, came round and started kissing my neck. It was revolting. His hand stroked my chest and started moving down towards my penis.

'I'll tell you all I know as long as you get this pervert off me.' I said quietly.

'Sit down' said the leader in Mandarin. The pervert scowled but made no attempt to argue.

I spoke quietly but in an assured manner. 'I am the fiancé of Kan Leung's daughter Yingtai. She died tragically last year. I have come to pay my respects to Kan Leung.'

The leader translated for the pervert. The two of them looked at me. I got the impression they didn't quite know what to do next.

After a minute or so the leader said, 'Tell me about The Organisation.'

I stared back at him, 'I have nothing to say.'

'You are an enemy of the Peoples Republic of China, unless you tell us you will be put on trial and almost certainly be given a death sentence.'

I just sat, staring at them.

The two stood up without saying a word and left the room. The lights went out again several seconds later. I lost track of time, three or four hours must have passed before they came back.

The leader walked in with two of his henchman following. He sat down opposite me saying nothing, just staring. I looked at his eyes, they were dilated, it was obvious he was on something. The pervert kissed me on the lips, he reeked of whisky, they'd clearly been drinking and looking at the state of the leader using drugs as well.

Cogs started turning in my brain, it was becoming apparent who these people were. Now wasn't the time to show my hand. Being drunk and stoned they could be dangerous. *Just play the game* I thought.

The leader laughed as I struggled to free myself from the perverts grip.

'Enough' he said.

The pervert pulled away sulkily and stood by my side.

'Tell me about The Organisation.'

I repeated my earlier statement, ''I am the fiancé of Kan Leung's daughter Yingtai. She died tragically last year. I have come to pay my respects to Kan Leung.'

'We want to know about The Organisation. Tell us or life will become very painful for you.'

I again sat in silence staring at the wall.

The leader stood up, 'Do what you want, but I want him alive.'

With that he stood up and left the room. The pervert approached me and I saw an opportunity. I punched him in the face and as he recoiled the other one came at me from the side. I was ready for him and using a move Zan taught me during training I clenched my fist and hit him in the throat. He collapsed immediately. The pervert came back at me but I was far too quick and kneed him in the balls. As he fell to the floor I again hit him full on in the face. His head went back and hit the wall. Unconscious he fell to the floor.

If these guys were from the ICAC I was in the shit. It seemed obvious they weren't. The passport wasn't fake, there was no way The Organisation would balls up on that, ICAC would not have known about my involvement with The Organisation. An official law enforcement body would have taken me to a proper office and charged me. These guys weren't professional, in any way.

As the two lay moaning on the floor the door opened. The leader and the third henchman were both holding guns pointing at me. I was in the shit and knew it.

'Sit down' said the leader in English. 'Handcuff him' he said in Mandarin. By now his speech was slurred and I was secured to the chair. Behind me there was a knock on the door. I tried to turn round to see what was going on but the third henchman pushed my head tight into my lap. It hurt like hell.

I heard a woman's voice.

'What's going on?' she asked sharply in Mandarin.

'I have this piece of shit from The Organisation. I am going to find out exactly what they are up to and how this will affect us. Yingtai failed where I will succeed. Our Father will find out that she wasn't the golden girl but I am the golden boy.' He laughed hysterically.

Now it was my turn to show my hand. Despite having my head held down at my knees I spoke as clearly as I could in Mandarin.

'Meihui, my name is Peter Summers, I was the fiancé of your sister Yingtai. I loved her with all my heart and all my soul. I grieve for her every day as I'm sure you do. I have come here on Organisation business. Important business that could have a dramatic effect on Leung Industries and all the people of China. I cannot stress the seriousness of the situation. Let me talk to you and your Father.'

'You tell me., screamed her brother Donghai, the leader of the motley little crew that had 'arrested' me, the supposed Head of Security at Leung Industries.

'I wouldn't piss on you.' I retorted. 'Now please Meihui, I know you are a very successful and intelligent person. Get this thug off me and let me talk to you and your Father. I can't stress the importance of what I have to say.'

'No' screamed Donghai, 'You are mine, I want the credit, I want the recognition, you are nothing to do with this Meihui.' By now he was almost hysterical.

'Let him go and get him dressed,' said Meihui quietly but with complete control. 'Go and sober up Donghai otherwise I'll be telling Father about this incident and he'll see you in the state you are currently in. You've abused Father's trust once again, this is the last time I'll cover for you. Now go. I'll wait outside for you Mr Summers while you get dressed.'

By now the henchman had released his grip and was undoing the handcuffs. I gathered my clothes which were scattered across the floor and dressed. My shirt was badly ripped but apart from that I was in reasonably good shape. The two thugs I'd decked were stirring. The pervert looked at me and smiled. As I left the room I kicked him hard in the small of his back. He moaned as I stepped over him.

'Little shit,' I whispered in Mandarin.

I walked into the corridor and got the shock of my life. Zan stood in front of me, although it wasn't Zan, the woman's eyes were small and mean and her lips were tight. Zan's eyes were large and loving, her lips were full. There was warmth in Zan's smile, I doubt Meihui had smiled in many a year, she looked cold, calculating and sad.

'I'm sorry,' I said staring at her, 'You are so like Yingtai, I'm sure you've been told that a thousand times. It came as a shock.'

'As teenagers we would play games with boys, even though she was much younger than me with makeup people couldn't tell the difference. We had such fun,' She nearly smiled at the memory, and when she smiled I was looking at Zan. 'Come to my office, I'll get you a new shirt and then we can talk to Father.'

'Thank you.'

'I apologise for my brother's actions. He means well.'

I looked at him, he stood quivering, obviously terrified of both his sister and Father.

'He's a liability.'

She nodded as we walked towards the lift.

'You can shower in my office before our meeting.' The doors slid open and she pressed the button for the twenty third floor. 'I'd rather you didn't mention my brother's little indiscretion,' she said as we started to move.

'Why do you stick up for him?'

'I understand him and since Yingtai died he's all I have left.'

Our eyes met and the love we both had for Zan somehow created a bond. I hoped I was going to be able to work with Meihui.

'When Yingtai was brought home, she had a ring on her finger, was that yours?'

'I bought it at Singapore Airport and put it on her finger in Sydney. We had seven idyllic days together on a Fijian island and then your thugs blew her away.' I could feel the bitterness well up inside me as I spoke and felt angry for opening up.

'I understand how you feel, believe me, I loved my sister more than you'll ever know.' The lift doors opened and our conversation came to a close.

'Follow me,' she said. The corridor was very different to what I had seen in the basement. We walked along a thick green carpet, I knew this to be a lucky colour in Chinese culture, symbolising money. *Very apt* I thought.

Tasteful pictures adorned the walls, these weren't copies either. We walked past several workstations where PAs were either typing feverishly or talking on the phone. Office doors stood open, inside meetings were going on with anything from two to a dozen people in attendance. This was a big operation, I had no idea how much of it was legal.

Meihui's office was at the end of the corridor, richly furnished with dark oak panelling and the same deep rich carpet as in the corridor. A huge desk stood adjacent to the window behind which a panoramic view of the Hong Kong harbour would normally have been seen but today it was obscured by mist.

'The shower is through there,' she said pointing at an internal door.

'Could I ask you to find my phone and watch?

She nodded and I made my way to the bathroom. To describe it as sheer opulence would be an understatement, onyx surfaces, gold taps, sumptuously thick towels soft lighting, large mirrors and a beautiful collection of soaps and toiletries. After luxuriating under a hot shower for a couple of minutes I felt alive again even though I hadn't slept all night. There was a knock on the door and a young girl brought in a new shirt, toothbrush, razor and comb. I quickly shaved and walking out saw Meihui sitting at her desk.

'You look better,' she said, ' I can almost see what Yingtai saw in you.' She half smiled and again looked so like Zan. It was incredibly unsettling.

'Only almost?' I joked.

The smile disappeared, 'Here's your phone,' she said stiffly, 'I'm afraid the watch is broken beyond repair. We will replace it.'

'Not a problem, it was company issue.'

'Father will see us in an hour, I'll leave you here as I have a meeting to attend. Coffee and breakfast will be brought in. I imagine you need it.'

'Thank you.'

She hesitated slightly, 'Perhaps we can have dinner tonight, I would like to talk about Yingtai.' I saw a softer side to Meihui, she was actually letting her guard down a little. *'Perhaps there is a little bit of Zan in her'* I thought.

'I'd like that' I said, 'I'd like that very much.'

She nodded, turned and walked out of her office expressionless. I wandered how much of an act the persona of the hard business woman was.

Picking up my phone I rang Don.

'Hello,' he answered in a non committal manner.

'Don, I'm fine. Had a little fracas late last night but that's sorted. I'm having a meeting with Kan Leung and his daughter in an hour. I'll phone you again after that.'

'Thank God' he responded, 'We tracked you to the Leung Industries Head Office and then nothing. I've been trying to work out what to do next.'

'I'm phoning Mark now.'

I re dialled. It was 9am in Hong Kong, 2am in Switzerland. I wasn't surprised when he picked up.

'Are you okay?' he asked. I repeated what I had said to Don. 'How are Caterina and Tanja.'

'They're going to be fine, probably released in a couple of days, you did a great job Jonathan.'

'Tell me about Zambola.'

'Firstly we found a way into the Chinese computer system. It confirms what we suspected, China organised the counter coup. It transpires they've been training militia in various centres across Africa. To them this was just a military exercise to see how well the troops react in a live situation. Sadly I have to report they did very well. We haven't got a hope of putting the Alliance back in control so we have to work on the bigger picture. Kasenga is back as a figurehead but very much in the pocket of the Chinese. I will shortly have ten nuclear devices at

209

my disposal but I need manpower to place them across China. We've designated remote areas to keep casualties to a minimum. However if need be we want three placing in cities. I hope before we detonate them the Chinese will come to their senses.

'How do we get the devices into China?'

'I'm rather hoping Leung Industries will fly them in from the States. A major part of their business is "import export". The thought is they could land in an industrialised area where officialdom won't take much notice. It will be just another consignment for Leung Industries, something that happens every day.'

'What happens if we deliver the bombs and they use them for their own purposes?'

'The bombs have trackers built into them, if they placed them in the middle of Bejing we'd know. If they try to dismantle them we can neutralise them. Only we can control them and that's by satellite technology. If they do anything stupid the bombs become a useless piece of garbage.'

It all sounded simple and logical, almost too simple. All I had to do was convince Kan Leung. *No pressure then*, I thought.

'Send me the proposed locations.'

'No probs.'

'Have you got anything I can use as backup?'

'I'll let you have a copy of our proposal for the UN. It covers everything in fine detail. I've just got the final draft.'

'Good, I'll call later.'

A young man wearing a white shirt and black bow tie walked in carrying a tray. He put it down on Meihui's desk. I could see fried eggs, ham, pancakes, orange juice, coffee and water. I drank the orange juice immediately followed by the water. I hadn't realised how dehydrated I'd become. The food tasted good and I was just finishing my second cup of coffee when Meihui returned.

'How are you feeling?' she asked.

'I'll be fine, how's your brother?'

'We've had to sedate him.'

'And then what?'

She sighed and shook her head. 'He'll have to leave the company, we're going to put him in rehab for starters. It's not a long term solution, we've tried before and failed. But at least he can dry out there.' She paused, 'It would appear two of his friends are in hospital.'

'They're lucky not to be in the mortuary.'

Again I could almost see a smile. *Christ this girl needs to loosen up a bit,* I thought.

'I hope what you have to say is worthwhile. I'm not used to making an idiot of myself in front of my Father.'

'Your brother more than compensates.'

I could tell she was uncomfortable and didn't really want to make small talk. Neither did I truth be told, so I decided to put her out of her misery.

'Can I borrow a room while we wait for your Father? I have a couple of calls I need to make.'

'Of course, follow me.'

I was taken back up the corridor and she showed me into an office about four doors away. I spent the next twenty minutes reading the placement details for the nuclear bombs and was just getting into the UN report when there was a knock on the door. Meihui walked in.

'Father will see us now.'

I got up and followed her back to the lift. We went up a couple of floors and as the doors opened I saw a mature woman sitting at a desk.

'Good morning Miss Leung' she rasped in Mandarin, your Father is ready for you.'

Meihui nodded and walked towards double mahogany doors, she knocked and went in. I followed and saw an enormous office again richly furnished. Kan Leung sat behind a large mahogany writing desk. As he stood I saw a slight man with thick white hair combed back. He was wearing tortoiseshell glasses, an immaculate pin striped navy blue suit, white shirt and a deep red tie. This I knew to be a very positive colour in Chinese culture, associated with money, fertility, and good luck.

'Mr Summers,' he said with a very English accent, 'It is a pleasure to meet you. I trust my daughter has been looking after you.'

We shook hands, I kept eye contact, an expression of sincerity in China.

'Can I offer you tea?'

'That would be kind thank you.'

'As an Englishman I'm sure you would prefer Indian, with milk?'

I smiled, I was prepared to do the niceties before we got down to business.

'Very thoughtful, thank you.'

We chatted about the weather in England, rugby and jet lag before it became obvious that now was the time to get down to business. Meihui remained silent throughout the conversation. I took a deep breath and began.

'Mr Leung, I knew your daughter Yingtai extremely well. You are aware that she joined The Organisation. We met on a training course and fell in love. We then worked on a project together to destroy the Ndrangheta in Italy, an organisation similar to the Mafia who were involved in global drug running and money laundering. We were successful in closing a major part of that operation down. Sadly and tragically Yingtai was murdered on the direct orders of senior personnel in that organisation. I too should have been killed, but I was lucky.'

I knew Leung would know all this bearing in mind the Triads had taken control of the Ndrangheta. I wanted him to know that I knew he was directly responsible for his daughter's death.

'Before Yingtai was murdered we had agreed to get married, she was wearing my engagement ring at the time of her death. I loved your daughter with all my heart and all my soul. I will never recover from her death and have spent many months mourning while hiding away from the world trying to make sense of it all. Friends from The Organisation have helped me find a way forward and given me a sense of purpose.'

Leung looked at me and said nothing. The word inscrutable came to mind. I continued and he just stared at me.

'A few weeks ago a colleague went missing while working on a project in Zambola, a small country in central Africa. I was asked to go out there and see if I could find her. To cut a long story short I did find her, languishing in a prison. She was desperately ill but we were able to get her out. She is now in a hospital in Geneva and hopefully will make a full recovery.

While in Africa I discovered a plot by the current Chinese government to invade and take control of African and the Middle Eastern countries. You will be aware they have been investing heavily in that continent over recent years. This has been part of a plan to gain control of resources across that area to keep them out of Western hands. It transpires they set up the Arab Spring and the Islamic State to destabilise Northern Africa with the direct aim of taking control. All this is documented and I will let you have a copy of the report that is about to be sent to key members of the United Nations. If China does take control many economies around the world will be either severely weakened or destroyed. International trading houses such as Leung Industries will be forced out of business. I'm not being dramatic, this is reality. The Western world as we know it will be severely damaged and may not recover.'

I paused, Leung looked at me critically. His eyes narrowed.

'Why are you telling me this,' he asked quietly, 'even if it's true, which I sincerely doubt, what can I do about it?'

'It is true, the evidence is irrefutable as you will see when you read the report.' I gave him a couple of seconds to let the news sink in. 'I'm sure like me you have no love of the current Chinese regime. We have to make it collapse from within. A plan has been devised which will create a situation where the current leaders will lose face and oblige China to retreat. They will be forced to resign and hopefully a more pragmatic government can be put in place.'

Leung was impossible to read, I took a sip of tea and continued paraphrasing the plan I outlined in Geneva.

''We intend to confront China at the UN, tell them we know what they're doing. Explain that unless they pull back from Africa there will be severe consequences and then leave it. We will then monitor troop and arms movements closely. This will give us time to plant small nuclear devices in far reached places across China. These will be well away from populated areas. If they ignore us we will set them off, one by one with each one closer to a major conurbation. There will come a point when they will be forced into submission.

To stop them retaliating we need to put the bombs in place first. As we'd be talking hours between detonations, they won't have time to retaliate. In theory they could send missiles across to the western seaboard of the US or Australia. But they'll be told if they do, both Beijing and Shanghai will be blown immediately. At the same time another bomb will be exploded in an outlying region to show we mean business. The hope is they won't dare send missiles, it would be tantamount to suicide.

This is where you come in.' Again I took a breath. Leung stared at me, I believed he was totally focussed on what I was saying but I wasn't sure. His expression was unreadable and his daughter sat impassively.

'We haven't got the manpower to plant bombs across China. Getting troops in and out as well as bombs and equipment would be a logistical nightmare. It would take too long and we would be too late. With your business contacts we believe you can help. You have the logistics and manpower to fly the devices into China from the USA and plant them across the country. This will help overthrow an unsavoury government and avert a real possibility of World War Three. By helping us you will help put in place a Chinese government more in tune with Western ideology which can only be good for Leung Industries.

Kan Leung kept staring at me. After a good minute he started shouting, he was furious.

'This is ridiculous. I've never heard so much garbage in my life. A plot made up by Western governments to destroy my brothers across China. And you expect me to help you? It is preposterous. Get out.'

I was amazed, Chinese people rarely showed their feelings or emotion. It was as if Leung had lost all sense of Chinese sensibility.

'Why should anyone make up such a preposterous story?'

'I'm not going to argue,' He screamed at me, his face purple with rage. He'd got himself into an apocalyptic fit and couldn't speak. He just waved his hands in anger shooing me away.

'Can I just leave the report for you to look at?'

Turning his back he gazed out of the window still waving his hands, incandescent with rage and saying nothing.

'Come' said Meihui beckoning me out of the room.

I followed and in silence we made our way back to her office. She sat behind her desk and pointed to the chair in front. I sat and looked at her.

'Meihui, this is not bullshit. The report comes from the highest authority. Please read it, I beg of you, for the sake of mankind.'

She stared, her face stern, devoid of emotion.

'I do believe you loved my dear sister Yingtai as I loved her. I realise it could not have been easy for you to come here following her death, Therefore I have to accept that your motives are true. I will read the report and join you for dinner tonight. We will talk further then.'

'Thank you,' I said breathing a sigh of relief. If I could get Meihui onside at least there was hope. 'Give me your email address and I will send it straight over.'

Chapter 23

I caught a cab back to the hotel and explained to a pretty young receptionist that I'd lost my key. She smiled gave me another and I went up to my room. I touched base with Mark and Don, lay on the bed and slept for several hours. I awoke to the phone ringing, it was a Hong Kong number.

'I have read the report and will meet you at six in the Lobby Lounge for a drink.' Meihui sounded brisk and business like.

'Shall I book a restaurant?'

'Already done, I'll see you at six.'

The line went dead, I looked at the time on my phone, it was five past three. I pondered what to do for the next couple of hours. I vaguely thought about sightseeing but couldn't really be bothered. Looking at the hotel blurb I decided to have a massage.

One thing about working for The Organisation was that I never had to worry about paying for such things. I expected an attractive lady and felt very disappointed when an effeminate man started pummelling away. I can't say I enjoyed the experience but it killed time and after I'd showered and changed it was nearly time to meet Meihui.

I arrived at the bar and sat down. A waiter came across as she walked in.

'A better meeting place than last night,' I quipped kissing her on the cheek. She was skinnier that Zan, I could feel her bones as I held her. Again she nearly smiled.

'A drink for you ma'am?' asked the waiter in English.

'Vodka tonic,' she responded tartly.

I really wasn't in the mood for booze, I needed all my wits around me.

'Orange juice please.'

Meihui looked at me. 'It's been a pretty difficult couple of days.' I said. 'If I have a drink I'm frightened I'll fall asleep.'

'We will talk later about the political situation,' she said taking control, 'But first of all I would like to give you something.'

She took a small box out of her handbag, beautifully wrapped with a paper rose adorning it.

'Please,' she said handing it to me, 'As an apology for my brother.'

I unwrapped the box carefully and opening it could hardly believe my eyes. Inside was a beautiful Rolex watch with a black face and what I guessed to be a white gold strap. This wasn't a cheap Chinese fake either but the real McCoy. Off the top of my head I reckoned it must have cost about twenty thousand sterling.

'I can't accept this, it's far too generous.'

'Do not insult me, take it as a gift from one person who loved Yingtai to another.'

'Thank you,' I said simply slipping it on my wrist, 'Thank you very much indeed.'

I took her hand and squeezed it. She didn't pull away and holding my stare tears came to her eyes.

'No one will ever know how much I miss Yingtai,' she said, 'What Father engineered was obscene, and it cost her life. For that I can never forgive him.'

'Her joining The Organisation you mean.'

She nodded, 'And putting that fool in charge of what was left of the Ndrangheta. The man knew about her but he let those bastards track her down and kill her. The stupid thing was, we didn't even need to know what The Organisation was up to,' she sounded bitter, 'You could never get close to us even if you tried. Not close enough to do any damage. Truth be told, I'm sure you know that.'

I was amazed at how honest and open she was.

'Tell me about Yingtai,' she said, 'Tell me everything, from the moment you met, so that for a few minutes I can bring her back to life, at least in my mind.'

I called the waiter and ordered another round, except this time I joined her with a vodka. With all this emotion I needed something. I was still holding her hand but pulled away as I started to speak. I told her how Yingtai and I met on a training course in Kenya, about a wonderful evening we spent together in an African safari park, how we worked together finding out about the Ndrangheta, how she helped save my life, how our friends were murdered, how we finally destroyed a major part of the Ndrangheta and how we went off to Australia and Fiji in the hope of spending the rest of our lives together. Finally I gave her a complete account of how Yingtai was murdered. By the time I stopped speaking tears were rolling down Meihui's cheeks and I was pretty choked up as well. This supposedly hard woman was still grieving and I felt guilty thinking maybe I could use this to help our cause.

'I think we should eat.' I said.

'We're booked into the Yan Toh Heen in the hotel. It's supposed to be very good but I've not eaten there.'

We made our way to the restaurant saying little. Once again the views were immaculate, looking out across the harbour towards Victoria Island. We were seated and the menus handed to us.

'What would you like?' asked Meihui, again taking control.

'You order,' I said, 'You're the local.

The young waitress scribbled furiously as Meihui spoke.

'Duck, suckling pig, crispy chicken, glazed cod and wagu beef.

'A bit much for two of us?' I suggested.

'They are half dishes and we don't have to eat it all,' came the cool response, 'White or red wine?'

'I'm easy.' She ordered a Chablis, I doubted it was a special offer from the local supermarket.

I thought back to a similar meal I'd had with Zan in Shanghai. I told Meihui about it. She liked the story and smiled. We talked more about Zan, her early life, school and we laughed together at the memories. The food was magnificent and the wine loosened both our tongues. I actually felt myself warming towards Meihui.

After a while we went silent and I knew it was the time to change the subject.

'You've read the report, what are your thoughts?'

She looked at me quizzically.

'I am scared, I cannot believe the Chinese government could be so stupid. There can be no winners.'

'Will your Father help us?'

Again there was silence for more than a few seconds. Meihui ate and looked down at her food. Eventually our eyes met and she spoke.

'I will be honest with you. My Father is not the man he was, sadly he was recently diagnosed with early onset Alzheimer's. In truth I control Leung Industries, he is now very much a figurehead. His memory is not what it was and he has made some bad decisions in recent times, one of which cost Yingtai her life. He comes to Board Meetings and I tell him as much as he needs to know about the company, including forward planning, monthly sales and profitability figures etc. I listen to him and sometimes act on what he says. As a sounding board he can be useful. Sadly, and too regularly it's as if his mind cannot focus on current events and he gets angry and upset. You saw this today, it was as if it was all too much for him to comprehend.'

'My Grandmother had a similar problem,' I said, 'I do understand, it is sad pathetic and incredibly frustrating watching those you have loved lose their mind.'

By now I was holding her hand again, I'm not even sure why but it just seemed the right thing to do.

'Now about your little problem,' she said, 'I will help you, I have no choice. It's not that I care about the world, but I do care about Leung Industries. I care about what my Father has built and what I intend to build on. There is only one thing, I will have your bombs placed in outlying regions. However, I will not place your bombs near any city or town. I will not be responsible for the deaths of thousands. If you want to deal on that basis consider it done. If not, then you are on your own.'

'It's a deal, I said. 'Many many thanks, I could kiss you.'

'I would like that.' She squeezed my hands and for once was really smiling and looking deep into my eyes. She looked more like Zan than ever.

'Come with me' I said, almost croaking.

We went up to my room without saying a word. I opened the door and as we walked in we kissed passionately. Within seconds we were on the bed ripping at each others clothes. She was wonderful, wild, passionate and loving. I woke several hours later and she was crying, I held her close. *God knows where this is going* I thought but for that moment I didn't give a damn.

We made love again and again and then she got up.

'I don't normally do one night stands' she said, 'And I'm not sure why I did. It's all the emotions of Yingtai, my Father, my brother and now the world on the edge of collapse as we know it. Don't hate me, but I don't think I can see you again like this, I'm sorry. From now on it's business.'

I tried to grab her but she pulled away and started to dress. I lay there not knowing what the hell to do next.

'I'll phone you when I have the infrastructure in place to carry out this task. Give me a couple of days. With that she walked out of the room. I slept fitfully, not feeling very good about anything at all.

The following morning I updated Mark and asked Don to join me for coffee.

When he arrived I showed him my new watch.

'Wow,' he said they don't come cheap.

'Can you get it checked quickly for bugs and trackers? I need it back asap.

'Leave it with me.'

With little to do I spent a couple of hours in the gym My fitness levels were nothing like where they had been the previous year and I knew I needed to do a lot of work to bring myself back up to speed. I reckoned it would take a good couple of months and made a mental note to exercise daily, wherever possible.

I called Meihui but went it straight to answerphone, I thanked her for last night. It sounded rather stuffy after what had happened so I phoned back and left another message.

'I really meant what I said, I did enjoy last night, I enjoyed your company and just being with you. I hope we can meet again, if only for dinner.'

For the first time in many a day I had little to do. To kill time, a receptionist told me about a bus tour around the city. I walked down to the bus stop and would have had an enjoyable few hours had I been in the mood for it. I went on the 'Peak Tram' which took me to the top of Hong Kong island, back across to Kowloon on the ferry, on a sampan ride in Aberdeen and to the maritime museum. Stanley was the highlight, very different to Hong Kong itself with its bars and restaurants along the promenade and a Chinese temple dedicated to Tin Hau, the Goddess of Seafarers.

Don rang and asked where I was.

'Don't move' he said, 'I'll be with you in twenty minutes. I sat playing with a cup of coffee looking out across the water. It was warm and I felt relatively relaxed. Eventually Don appeared walking up the promenade. We shook hands and he handed back the watch.

'Your hunch was right, there's a tracker and a listening device built in. They've been disabled. Here's another one, but it's company issue.' I smiled putting it around my wrist but feeling sick. The Rolex went in my pocket.

I got a cab back to the hotel having had enough of mad cap bus drivers barking orders at forlorn tourists.

Lying on my bed I wondered how long I'd be marooned in Hong Kong. I felt bored and needed something to happen. I pondered my future and realised if I didn't sort out this mess I wouldn't have one. There was a knock on the door, after the last occurrence I was a little anxious as to who may be waiting for me. Through the pinhole I saw Meihui.

'I hoped you'd be here' she said walking straight past me.

'Didn't your tracker tell you where I'd be.' I said throwing the Rolex at her.

She looked at me, totally non committal, the guard was down again.

'I thought for this escapade we were on the same side.'

'We are' she said, 'but I have to be sure.'

'Of what?'

'Of you, this could all have been a part of a deliberate hoax to destroy us.'

'And?'

'And now I know it isn't. You're not the only ones who can get information out of Chinese intelligence.'

'What have you found?'

'Confirmation of your story, that's all you need to know. We have a meeting tomorrow morning.'

'Who with?'

'Friends who will help us without asking questions. I'll send a car to pick you up at 7.30am.'

'It's on then,' I said almost in disbelief.

'I always deliver,' she replied grabbing hold of me and kissing me passionately.

Pulling away she said 'This can lead to nothing, we both know that.'

Several hours later we were sitting on the bed eating room service pizza together with a bottle of white wine.

'Am I as good as Yingtai?' she asked.

'Don't ever go there' I barked quite viscously. I think she was stunned by my vehemence. 'I learnt a long time ago never to do comparisons. You are your own person and I like you for what you are.' She threw her arms around me and we kissed again for a long time.

'I'm sorry' she said softly 'I shouldn't have asked.'

I knew I was lying, she could never live up to Zan, she wasn't even close. However, I was prepared to go with the flow, I needed her and truth be told, she needed me. Neither of us had a real choice.

Chapter 24

She left in the early hours without saying a word. I slept and woke to my phone ringing, it was 6.30am.

'Hope I didn't disturb you,' said Mark.

'You should try sleeping' I quipped, 'they say it's good for you.'

'What news?'

I told him about the meeting that had been arranged.

'Good man. Now things have moved on over here. The Chinese computer system has revealed over fifty sites that are being used across middle and northern Africa to train indigenous troops. It's a huge operation. We've decided that as the first thermo nuclear device goes off in China one of those sites will be destroyed in a similar manner. As the second one goes off in China another will be blown in Africa. The same with the third etc. We will bury as many bombs as possible adjacent to the sites across the continent and they will be triggered using the same satellite technology as in China. This is all dependent upon how long it takes you to organise the placing of bombs across China. I doubt we'll have the times to plant fifty bombs but we can do severe damage. If we only take out half a dozen in Africa together with what is planned for China I feel certain we will severely weaken Chinese resolve.'

'Brilliant' I said thinking the plan through, 'What time scales are you looking at?'

'That is very much down to you, but if you can work on a fourteen day implementation programme that should give us more than enough time.'

'You mentioned ten nuclear devices for China, can you get hold of another fifty?'

'Maybe not fifty, but procurement is one of my strengths.' I could almost hear Mark smiling as he spoke.

'What about backup should the Chinese respond?'

'We'll have nuclear subs in the Pacific to knock out anything they send over.'

'Good plan, I'll be in touch after the meeting.'

At seven twenty five I walked out of the hotel. A taxi driver shouted, 'Mr Summers you come with me.'

I climbed into the back of the cab and he pulled out into the Hong Kong traffic. We drove up Salisbury Road and into the Cross Harbour Tunnel. Yet again the traffic was "bumper to bumper" and we crawled along at a snails pace with regular stops.

'Very busy' said the driver in broken English.

'As if I hadn't noticed' I thought.

We eventually came out onto the Gloucester Road with enormous skyscrapers towering above us. We made our way down to the Port of Hong Kong where dozens of ships were either loading or unloading hundreds of containers that lay on the dockside. We drove down to a non nondescript building about ten stories high.

Pulling up the car door was opened by a man in his mid twenties wearing sunglasses, a smart dark suit, shirt and tie. I looked at my watch, we'd travelled all of five miles but it had taken nearly fifty minutes.

'Follow me please' he said. I climbed out and we walked into the building through double doors passing a security man who glared at me.

I followed the man into an open lift, the doors closed and we started to move upwards. *At least I'm not going to have another night in a cellar* I thought.

'May I have your phone for security?' he said. There was no point in arguing, a shame in a way as I'd planned on recording the meeting.

The doors opened to reveal a cavernous space with a boardroom table in the middle. Furnishings were at best shabby and sparse. I counted eleven men of various ages sitting around the table. All wore suits. I felt dramatically underdressed for the occasion wearing only jeans and an open shirt.

Meihui sat at the top and nodded as she saw me. She beckoned me to sit next to her and started talking in Mandarin.

'We do not do introductions here. Suffice to say I trust these gentlemen implicitly. Perhaps you can start by giving us some background as to why you need our help.'

I looked around and could see everyone staring at me, they were paying avid attention. I basically repeated what I had said to Kan Leung two days previously. The inscrutable Chinese gave nothing away and as I stopped speaking there was silence.

'Are there any questions?' asked Meihui.

Silence.

'Have you all seen the report which is being presented to the UN?' I asked.

Four of them nodded.

'We are currently translating it and everyone will have a copy before we leave here.' said a bright looking young man sitting at the far end.

Crikey I thought to myself. Here I am talking to The Triads in Hong Kong and it could be any legitimate business in any land.

'How do you intend getting the equipment into China?' asked a middle aged man with grey greasy hair and thick set glasses.

I paraphrased Mark. 'We hope that through one of your import export operations we can fly the equipment from the USA without creating any alarm. I am sure you will advise which airport to bring the merchandise in. The thought is that the plane could land in an area where officialdom won't take too much notice.

In other words, an area under your control.

'It will be just another consignment for Leung Industries or whoever, something that happens every day. Should anything go wrong and officialdom do try to dismantle the bombs the internal mechanisms will automatically blow making them useless.'

So try to fuck us and you'll be left with nothing. Every man around the table nodded, they knew exactly what I was saying. These guys would be the ones responsible for planting the bombs, they knew what they had to do, I really was at the sharp end. I knew that one slip from me and I'd never be seen again.

'What size are these devices?'

'They are the size of a large rucksack. Their power is about five kilotons. We estimate that if one of them was detonated in a city at least five hundred thousand people would be killed. The devices are known as suitcase nukes, more than powerful enough to create upset and alarm.'

'How do we set them?'

'All you need to do is bury them at the designated places. We will control everything else via satellite.'

'When will this happen?'

'Yesterday would be good,' there were no smiles, 'In all seriousness we await to hear from you. Let us know when you can organise transport from the US and we will arrange delivery. We would hope the devices could be in situ within seven days.'

I noticed a couple of them looking at each other. I wasn't sure what to read into that, maybe we were asking too much.

'Anymore questions?' there was silence and Meihui looked at me.

'Thank you, we'll be in touch. Your driver will take you back to your hotel.'

I stood 'Good luck and thank you for your support.'

With no reaction I walked to the lift. The same taxi was waiting outside. Twenty minutes later I was standing outside the hotel.

What the hell do I do now? I asked myself.

I rang Don and we agreed to meet for dinner that night. Not really in the mood for Asian food I asked if he knew a good steakhouse.

'Morton's' he said, 'It's about half a mile from your hotel. Probably easiest if we meet there.'

'Eight o'clock?'

I phoned Mark and gave him an update. The conversation wasn't long as there wasn't that much to say.

'How did you find The Triad people?' He asked.

'Ridiculous as it may sound I could have been in any business meeting in any city in the world.'

'No I could believe it because that is what they are, businessmen and women. The fact that we don't like their business is almost irrelevant. The basic rules are the same.'

I went to the gym and half heartedly did some exercise. I felt down and couldn't shake it off. I'd had two great nights of sex but I think Meihui was the problem. She was too close to Zan and I couldn't forget that. There was a feeling of guilt and I knew it was stupid. I couldn't be a monk for the rest of my life but to have an affair with the sister of the girl I loved was just stupid, even though the love of my life was dead. What's more, Meihui was cold and calculating, truth be told, I didn't trust her.

I started to get angry with myself. I knew I had to find a way forward but this wasn't it. I wanted out of Hong Kong as soon as possible.

Lying on my bed I tried to make sense of it all. I was half dozing when Meihui rang.

'Hi,' I said trying to raise a bit of enthusiasm.

'Are you okay?'

'Probably a bit tired after last night's exertions.'

There was no reaction and that really pissed me off. Most girls would have at least giggled. Zan certainly would have and come back with an excellent retort. With Meihui nothing. Cool and detached she spoke.

'You did well this morning, my people are on board.'

I should have been elated and I tried to sound enthusiastic.

'That's great,' I said wanting to slap her.

'Where do we go from here?'

'We have a cargo flight leaving San Francisco Airport in two days time at 2pm flying to Wuhan in Central China. This works well as there are good transport links. It is a busy airport and with our infrastructure no questions will be asked. We would ask that you organise the shipment directly to the plane at San Francisco. We do not want to get involved with export paperwork in the US. That will be down to you. Your people will be responsible for loading the merchandise. We will take responsibility from the moment we are out of US airspace. There is a lot of trust here. However if we are let down and our people are abused in any way there will be consequences. I trust I make myself clear.'

'Perfectly.'

Internally I shuddered, this woman could be nasty.

'I will call again when the shipment arrives.'

There was a difficult silence 'Will I see you again?' I asked.

'Probably not, there is no need, we can handle things from here, I'll be in touch.'

I'd been dumped and although I felt relieved I also felt a little sad. I knew she wasn't for me and I really didn't want anymore memories churned up. However in many ways she made me feel closer to Zan than I'd been since her death. However Zan had a very special place in my heart and I knew Meihui was little more than a conniving bitch. She was a sad soulless woman and in that respect, the total opposite to her sister.

'I'll await your call.'

'Goodbye' she said and the phone went dead.

I rang Mark and gave him the news.

'Lets hope we can trust them,' he said.

'What can they do?' I asked, 'The bombs have trackers built in, if they placed them in the middle of Bejing we'd know. If they tried to dismantle them they'd blow. They need us as much as we need them.'

'True.'

'I might as well come back to Switzerland, my work is done here.'

'Stay a couple of days, at least until the merchandise arrives.'

'Why,' I replied feeling a bit fed up as I wanted out, 'I'm not sure what I can do, Wuhan is nearly six hundred miles from here.'

'I'd just feel more comfortable knowing you were in the vicinity.'

I knew where Mark was coming from and couldn't really argue. The hotel was decent enough and I could kill a couple of days sightseeing.

I decided to stroll to the restaurant as it was only a few hundred yards away. However, rain was lashing down as I walked out of the hotel so I hailed a cab.

'Morton's Steak House at The Sheraton please.'

I climbed in and as the driver pulled out I said.

'Put your meter on.'

He tutted pressed a couple of buttons and started back towards the airport.

Usual bloody taxi driver I thought.

'No' I said in Mandarin, 'The Sheraton, Nathan Road.'

Eventually we arrived. I threw thirty dollars at him. 'Don't take the piss' I said as he scowled.

It would have been quicker to walk. Don was waiting under a canopy. We shook hands and I followed him up to the restaurant. I was getting used to the spectacular views of the harbour by this stage and although Don tried and failed to get a window seat I really wasn't bothered.

'You must have the fish cakes as a starter' he said, 'they are to die for.'

I took his advice and also ordered a sirloin steak and salad.

Don was very genial and good enough company.

'This place has won several awards as the best steakhouse in Asia.' He said beaming.

'Let's hope it lives up to expectations.'

Conversation was polite but a little strained. He wasn't a sportsman and we had little in common. The food was as good as I could have asked for but I wasn't sorry when I got in a cab to go back to my hotel.

I was getting a bit fed up bouncing around the world and what would seem like a very glamorous lifestyle to many was becoming increasingly wearisome. On the short ride I realised this job was not really for me. I had a flashback to just over a year before when Zan and I had agreed the same thing. I knew I had to finish the operation but after that I vowed to move onto pastures new.

I went straight to bed and was just dropping off when my phone rang.

232

'Mr Simpson,' said the voice in English with a very definite Chinese intonation. 'My name is Jo Lin, I was at the meeting this morning.' I recognised his voice, he was the bright looking young man who had talked about translating the UN report. 'I am Ms Leung's PA,' he went on with a sense of urgency. 'She's been kidnapped, it is our belief the kidnappers are on their way to you now. If you are in your hotel room I suggest you get out quickly. Phone me back on this number when you have the opportunity. Don't ask questions, just do it now please.'

Why did I believe him? God knows, there was something in his voice that gave the call credibility, a sense of fear perhaps. I dived out of bed, opened the door and peeked out. There was nobody. Wearing only boxer shorts and a t-shirt I ran down the corridor in the opposite direction to the lift shaft. I ducked round the corner and listened out for I'm not too sure what.

I vaguely wondered how I would explain my current attire if a security man walked past. That however wasn't my biggest concern. There was a fire exit at the end of the corridor and my initial impulse was to head for it. I was mulling over what to do when I heard the ping of the lift and then people running. They banged on a door quite forcibly.

'Open up,' I heard in English, 'This is the police.' I didn't dare peek around the corner for fear of being seen, I just stood still, my heart beating again at twenty to the dozen.

'He's not there' I heard in Mandarin.

'Break it down' said another. I heard some heavy crashing and then for a second nothing.

'Fuck it he's gone, some bastard's tipped him off.'

'Shit' said another, 'Now we're in for it. You stay here, if he comes back, kill him.'

I heard more running and mumbling. I assumed they were waiting by the lift. Again I heard the ping and it went silent. I weighed up the situation.

Someone had kidnapped Meihui and wanted me. It was impossible at that stage to work out who. The only clue I had was the person currently in my room. Hopefully I could make him or her talk.

The easy option was to head for the fire exit. I realised that would not tell me anything. Gingerly I made my way back down the corridor. I knocked on the broken door loudly and stood against the wall so I couldn't be seen through the peephole.

'Security,' I said in Mandarin, 'What has happened?'

'Go away,' came the response.

'You have damaged hotel property, I am therefore at liberty to enter your room.'

The door swung open and before he had time to turn I pushed his head hard against the joist. He immediately collapsed onto the floor unconscious or dead. *So much for interrogation* I thought. However, I wasn't too bothered having looked at him. In another situation I would have laughed, it was the pervert who'd kidnapped me last time, Donghai's man. I just looked at him, *what was going on*?

I didn't have the time or inclination to work it out. I just knew I had to disappear quickly. I dressed at breakneck speed grabbed my passport, wallet and phone and made my way to the fire exit.

My fears were firstly real security coming to see what was going on and secondly somebody may have been left as a lookout in the reception area. I wasn't therefore about to go through the main entrance.

I ran back up the corridor and down the emergency stairs to what I assumed to be the ground floor. Hitting the bar on the fire exit door I heard the alarm go off as the door sprung open. I ran outside where the streets were still thronging with people and lost myself in the crowd. I slowed down to walking pace but kept moving. As I walked I rang Don. It took about five rings before he picked up. The wait was awful.

'You want a bedtime story?' he asked jokingly.

I told him what had happened.

'Get a cab to the Harbour Grand Hotel, it's only a couple of miles but far enough away from trouble.'

I hailed a taxi and couldn't have given a damn whether he had the meter running or not. I jumped in and sank back on the seat relaxing for a second. I was stressed out, my heart rate hadn't slowed, I could feel myself shaking. *Get a grip* I thought.

'You want nice girl?' asked the driver.

'No' I replied acerbically.

'I find you nice boy.'

'Be quiet', he shut up.

Chapter 25

I was about to call Joe Lin, Meihui's PA when Don phoned back. 'I've booked a room in your name, I'll meet you there.'

I phoned Joe Lin, 'They came but I got out in time. I'm alright, I'll phone back in about ten minutes when I'm in a position to do so.

'Okay', he responded.

Walking into reception I said in English, 'I have a room booked in the name of Summers.'

'Your passport please and a credit card for extras.'

She typed furiously and smiled at me. Bells rang in my head.

'Here is your room key, a porter will show you the way, enjoy your stay.'

A burly looking man in a smart uniform came across.

'Your luggage' he enquired.

'Somewhere between Singapore and here,' I responded.

He nodded, obviously having had this conversation many times before.

We went to the room where he wanted to show me how the TV worked. Working his tip was fine but I wasn't in the mood. I gave him one hundred Hong Kong dollars. 'That's fine' I said and as he left I rang Don and gave him the room number.

I then rang Mark and outlined what had happened. Don arrived, I put Mark on loudspeaker so we could have a three way conversation.

'I can't stay here,' I said, 'It's quite likely that in the very near future a body will be found in my room at the Inter Continental. As soon as the police type in my passport details I'll be tracked here. I need a safe house and a new identity.'

'You can stay with me' said Don, at least until your new ID arrives.'

'No' said Mark, 'that could lead to contagion, we need another way.'

Don spoke again 'I'll book a hotel using one of my aliases, I'll check in and pass the room key onto you, stay there quietly until the new ID arrives.'

'Fine,' said Mark, 'Now the two of you get the hell out of there, use different exits, Don stay a while so that you won't be linked quickly by surveillance cameras. It's bad enough you'll be seen going into the room but hopefully that won't be discovered for a couple of days. Phone me when you're both in a safe place, now go.' With that the line went dead.

'I'll go to the Waterfront Bar,' said Don, 'And arrange for a colleague to join me. With luck they'll be showing some football on TV. It's as close to foolproof as I can come up with.'

I went straight down to reception, walked out of the hotel and kept on walking. It was 1.30 in the morning but the night air was still warm and at least the rain had stopped. As I walked I rang Joe Lin.

'What the hell's going on?'

'We were working late in Miss Leung's office, that's not unusual. I was making coffee in the kitchen when I heard loud voices. "You come with us," someone shouted. ''Who are you?'' asked Miss Leung sounding very calm and collected. "You do not ask questions otherwise we shoot you." Then I heard shuffling and the door close. I looked into her office and she'd gone. Immediately I phoned a couple of Miss Leung's associates who were at the meeting today. They categorically deny any involvement. And why should they be involved? Miss Leung has done nothing but good for their businesses. She is highly admired. We don't know who carried out this task but believe it has to be something to do with today's meeting. It is too much of a coincidence, that's why we assumed they would be after you. We were correct in that assumption.'

'Are we on the same side at the moment?' I asked.

'I can give full authority for that.'

'How?'

'The people I've spoken to have empowered me.'

I took a deep breath and hoped he wasn't bullshitting. I knew this to be a pivotal moment. If he was playing it straight there was a possibility we could salvage the plan. If he wasn't the whole world could go up in flames. After a second of anguish I told him about the body in my room.

'This is down to Miss Leung's brother Donghai.' I said.

'It can't be, he's in rehab.'

'I think you'll find he's got out. The body is one of his henchmen, I recognised him. It has to be Donghai. Pick him up and we may find out where she is, and possibly save her life. Have you got the resource?'

I could almost hear Joe Lin's brain assimilating everything. 'I'll get back to you.'

I found a late night coffee bar and sat staring at an Americano. None of this really made any sense. Why would Donghai want to kidnap his sister? How did he get out of rehab? What was he trying to achieve? He didn't know anything about the Chinese operation in Africa, he knew nothing about our plans to bring down the Chinese government. Only Kan Leung knew and he was away with the fairies. Or was he? My mind was working overtime. I ordered a second Americano. Early stages of Alzheimer's didn't mean he was totally doolally. Meihui said he'd made some bad mistakes. I knew planning and communication were early signs. I thought back to his outburst when we met and the way he just waved us away, unable to speak. I assumed at the time it was temper but I realised later he was losing his communication skills. Maybe however he had enough to outwit or bully lower ranked employees. If nothing else, Alzheimer sufferers retain much of their intelligence. Maybe Donghai went running to him and started telling stories about Meihui and me. May be Kan reacted with another bad decision. May be, may be, may be. I was beginning to feel tired and my brain was fogging up. I couldn't face another Americano and I was just about to start tramping the streets again when I got a text.

'I am booked into the Regal Airport Hotel. Once I have checked in I'll send the room number.' Smart I thought, another faceless hotel well away from Kowloon. The chances of being picked up would be minimal. I left the coffee bar and walked down the street. There was still a buzz to the city, I was just another faceless person in the crowd. I found myself on Temple Street and realised I was in a red light district. Beautiful Asian girls were coming up to me and offering their services. *The perfect cover* I thought half smiling, probably much better than The Regal, and maybe more enjoyable. Then again, I didn't really fancy a dose of the clap.

Eventually Don text the room number and I hailed a cab. Rather than go straight to the hotel I asked the driver to take me to the airport. By now the roads were reasonably clear and twenty minutes later we arrived. I paid and gave a tip with no argument. I didn't want to be remembered. I then walked around the concourse before getting another taxi to the hotel. I was probably being paranoid but I wanted to make the trail as complex as possible in the hope that I couldn't be traced.

I walked straight past reception and nobody even looked up. I knew I'd be on a security camera but by the time that would be looked at I'd be long gone. I went straight up to the room and Don let me in. The mini bar was well stocked so I had a large Scotch and ginger. Don poured himself a beer. I told him about my conversation with Joe Lin.

'With The Triads on your side I would imagine Donghai will be picked up very quickly. He's a junky and a coward so hopefully he'll start talking quickly. The Triads have ways of producing quick results.' He half smiled as he spoke.

'There's little we can do now' I said, 'I suggest we call it a night and get some sleep.'

Don nodded and rose to leave. We shook hands promising to touch base first thing.

I slept well much to my surprise and woke at about 7.30 feeling reasonably fresh. I showered but cursed as I didn't have a shaver. Thinking back to the months I'd spent in Amsterdam I laughed at myself, I hadn't worried about such things then. *A days growth won't do any harm.*

I ordered room service breakfast and Mark rang.

'I'm worried,' he said, 'You're in dangerous territory. One slip and you're done for.'

'I'll be fine.' I said feeling anything but.

'A lady called Rika is flying in from Tokyo with your new ID. She'll be landing at about 12.30 your time. Stay in the room until then.'

I rang Joe, 'Any news?'

'Two henchmen went to the clinic and forcibly removed Donghai. He hasn't been seen since.'

'My best guess is that he's hold up at the Leung Industries Head Office.' I told him about my little escapade. 'I can't tell you what floor we were on, it was down in the bowels.'

'We'll get it checked out.'

I sat watching CNN and BBC World News for about half an hour but couldn't concentrate. My mind was in overdrive.

Where the hell was Donghai? Was it Donghai that kidnapped Meihui? If not him then who? How far could I trust these Triad people? What were the chances of being picked up by the authorities in Hong Kong? Was it worth talking to Kan Leung again? Could I play the guilt card, he was directly responsible for the death of Zan and now maybe his other daughter as well. Who else could we talk to, if his Triad cohorts were having no luck then what chance I? There must be somebody who could help.

Then it clicked, Leung's wife, Zan's Mother. It would be difficult, I knew the Chinese *thrice-obeying* rule - comply with fathers in youth, husbands in marriage, and sons when widowed. However her husband was sick and her son a junky, With Meihui in trouble she may just be the key.

At about eleven Joe rang again, 'Kan Leung has contacted one of his compatriots who was at the meeting yesterday,' I assumed he meant a fellow Triad, 'He's said Leung Industries would not be involved in any activity that could damage the infrastructure of China. In other words, your plan is dead.'

'Donghai has got to him.'

'We think so.'

'Where is Meihui?'

'We don't know, nor have we found Donghai. Meihui's mobile just goes to answerphone and there is no trace of him.'

'What about his mobile?'

'The number we have is dead, he must have switched it.'

Fat lot of use you are I thought.

'How could he have found out about this?' I asked.

'Kan Leung knew your plan, Donghai knew you and your relationship with Meihui. Two and two have been added and that is where we are. Donghai has used his Father's illness to gain power.'

'How can Kan Leung convince others if he's got Alzheimer's?'

'He has early onset Alzheimer's. Therefore he has periods of clarity which can last for hours, even days. During these times he seems perfectly rational and could fool anybody into thinking he is his old self. Don't forget even with Alzheimer's he still has his intelligence and cunning. He can and does make supposed logical decisions. Sadly these are becoming less rational and less often. Meihui has become adept at using him as a front man but tempering his extremes.'

'We need to speak to Meihui's Mother Bo Leun.' I said. 'She's the key to this.'

'Not in Chinese society'.

'She's lost one daughter,' I replied, 'She's about to lose another, her husband's ill and her sons a junky. Unless you've got any better ideas I can't see another way forward. If we don't move soon Meihui will also be dead and you'll be out of a job.'

There was a silence for a couple of seconds.

'Let me talk to my people.'

'Make it quick.'

By now I was becoming very frustrated, the phone rang, it was Don.

'The plane will land on time. We need to lose all trace of your current identity. Do you have sunglasses?'

'No.'

'Leave immediately and buy some on the way out of the hotel. Get a taxi to the Sham Shui Po district, it's a very poor area where I've hired a room. I'll text you the address. We'll meet Rika there and change your ID.'

I left the room, bought some shades in the hotel shop together with a flat cap before jumping into a taxi. Again, I headed to the airport, got out and walked around the concourse trying to ensure any trail would be lost. I then got another cab to Sham Shui Po. As we approached I put on the shades and hat.

I was startled by the obvious poverty, so different to the obscene wealth on show elsewhere in Hong Kong. Groups of old people sat on cardboard boxes outside slum dwellings with dozens of refuse bags and rubbish dumped outside the buildings. No doubt rats were having a field day. Unsavoury gangs of teenagers stood at street corners and run down electronic stores did little to enhance the area. I wondered how the hell they could make a living in such an environment. The scene reminded me of a 1930s film shot in Brooklyn with the unemployed milling around like lost souls. I climbed out of the taxi by a shop selling computer accessories. The text said I should go through a door to the right and up to the first floor. The acrid smell of cheap Chinese food wafted over me as I climbed the rickety stairs. Another door stood half ajar and I saw Don standing by the window grinning. He handed me a takeaway coffee.

'Delightful.' I said.

'Useful' came the reply, 'We will never be tracked here.'

I brought him up to speed.

'Can you find out where Meihui's Mother lives?' I asked.

'Shouldn't be a problem, but better if one of Kan Leung's associates accompanies you. You'll be more readily accepted.'

'They'd better get a move on, the merchandise is supposed to be flown over tomorrow.'

For a few minutes we made polite conversation until an oriental women walked in. She was in her early thirties, good looking, petite and smartly dressed. Looking totally out of place in the current surrounding she smiled.

'Hi, I'm Rika, it's good to meet you both.'

We all shook hands and she went on.

'I have your new passport credit cards and a simple disguise just as a precaution. Sit down please as I need to cut your hair and dye it.'

I sat at on a plastic chair and Rika got out an electric razor.

'I prefer scissors,' she said, 'but this is easier to get through airport security.'

After a few minutes she took a tube of what looked like toothpaste out of her bag.

'We're going for a dark look,' she said smiling, 'Very popular in these parts.'

After a couple of minutes she was combing what was left of my hair. I normally wore it reasonably long, now it was cropped short and instead of mouse brown, it was jet black.

'Now she said, these are coloured contact lenses just to add to the disguise. She popped them into my eyes and much to my surprise I was hardly aware of them being there.

'Finally,' she went on, 'Glasses with clear lenses.'

I put them on and looked at myself in a mirror. The transformation was quite remarkable. Even I didn't recognise myself.

She handed me a passport, it was French. I was astounded, my passport picture had been touched up to show dark hair, glasses and deep blue eyes.

'Very clever,' I said.

'The passport was used by another courier to enter Hong Kong, therefore the visa is valid. It is an old one so there will be no problem with biometrics.'

'How's he going to get out? I asked.

'He'll have local ID.'

Don't ask too many questions I thought as I was handed three credit cards. I was now Emile Giroud and very unlikely to be picked up while in Hong Kong.

'To make doubly sure,' said Don, 'Rather than the authorities cross checking passports at hotels, we've hired an apartment using a local alias. The chances of that being matched are minimal.' He handed me a key and the address.

'Thanks people.'

'Right, you go,' said Don, 'Lose yourself then take a taxi to the International Finance Centre. Get out, lose yourself again before getting another taxi to the apartment. With luck, by then the trail will be stone cold. I'll come round later with a change of clothes.'

Chapter 26

We all shook hands and I made my way downstairs to the street. I walked for about half a mile idly looking at the junk in the electronic stores while being pestered by store keepers. I just smiled and walked on.

As instructed I got a couple of cabs and found myself close to Soho on the other side of the harbour to the Inter Continental. The apartment was charming, one bedroom a living room with upmarket modern furniture and a kitchenette.

There was no food which was a shame because I was hungry. There were however tea making facilities so I sat down with a cup pondering where I should go from here.

Don arrived about and hour and a half later with a suitcase and a couple of sandwiches. As we were eating my phone rang, it was Joe Lin.

'I am instructed to give you the address of Kan Leung. I will meet you along with one of my associates outside at five o'clock this evening. We have arranged a meeting with Kan Leung. Hopefully and informally you will be able to talk to Meihui's mother. Good luck.'

'Make or break,' I said to Don as I finished my sandwich.

The address was in Jardine's Lookout.

'It's an exclusive residential area above Happy Valley.' Don informed me. I phoned Mark with an update after which Don got up to go.

'Let me know if you need anything, and good luck.' We shook hands again. With time to kill I went for a swim in the apartment complex. It felt good to do some positive exercise and by the time I had showered and dressed I felt as ready as I could be for whatever lay ahead.

Checking my new passport and credit cards I debated whether I should leave them in the apartment. I decided that if for whatever reason I was picked up they could help me bluff my way through. I put them into the inside pocket of the jacket Don provided, put on the glasses, left the building and hailed a cab. The driver put his meter on immediately. I smiled, not really understanding why I got so uptight about such irrelevancies.

We climbed into the hills above Hong Kong passing some beautiful property. There was obviously serious money in this part of the city. I idly wondered how much of it was clean. We drove up to a magnificent colonial style mansion looking down onto the metropolis and across the harbour. There was little in the way of a front garden but tall trees screened the house to passers by. A long wheelbase Lexus with tinted windows was parked outside.

As the taxi came to a halt the back door of the Lexus opened and a large looking mean man in his late fifties stepped out, I remembered him from the meeting at the docks. Joe Lin got out from the other side.

'Mr Summers,' Joe said in Mandarin, 'It is good to see you again.'

We shook hands, but there was no introduction to the large man. Nevertheless I shook his hand. He glared at me and said nothing. It all felt so surreal, only a few months ago I'd been fighting people like this, now we were working together.

Joe walked towards the house and pressed a button on the wrought iron gate.

'Joe Lin and guests to see Mr Leung.'

A buzzer could be heard and Joe opened the gate. We followed and walked up the path to an entrance porch. The door was opened by a young Polynesian maid dressed in a traditional Victorian black and white uniform. She smiled and ushered us into an imposing entrance hall with furniture as far removed from Ikea as you can imagine. Beautiful pictures adorned the walls, a delightful French regency display cabinet was filled with traditional Chinese ornaments, a Queen Ann table stood to one side next to a deep rich red chaise longue.

'Follow me please' said the maid and we were taken to a large airy living room where the furniture was even. Kan Leung was sitting on a four seater settee with his wife beside him. Afternoon tea had been laid out on an onyx table in front of them. Leung again was immaculately dressed in a Western suit and tie, Bo Leun wore a high collared Chinese floral dress. She was small and dumpy and much as I tried I could see nothing of Zan in her. They rose and Joe Lin introduced me but not my compatriot.

We shook hands and I bowed slightly trying to remember Chinese etiquette.

'Please,' said Kan Leung and ushered us to sit on a settee facing him.

'Tea,' Bo Leun said as she poured for the three of us.

'Have you been in Hong Kong long?' asked Kan Leung obviously having no idea who I was.

I pondered, was my disguise that good or was it the effect of Alzheimer's?

I decided to basically repeat the conversation I'd had with him previously to see if that drew anything.

'Mr and Mrs Leung, I knew your daughter Yingtai extremely well. We worked together closely for many months and fell in love.'

Bo Leun grabbed her husband's hand as I mentioned Zan, I had her complete attention.

'We were on a project to destroy an organisation similar to the Mafia. We were successful but sadly and tragically Yingtai was killed in the line of duty. I too should have been, but I was lucky.'

Bo Leun looked at me with a stony face, Kan Leung seemed distracted.

'Before Yingtai died we had agreed to get married, she was wearing my engagement ring at the time of her death. I loved your daughter with all my heart and all my soul. I will never get over her and have spent many months mourning while hiding away from the world. Friends have helped me find a way forward and given me a sense of purpose. Life can be strange and to cut a long story short I contacted Meihui to help me on a project I was working on to avert a major world catastrophe. She agreed to assist along with the gentlemen seated here and some of his colleagues. Sadly Meihui was kidnapped last night from her office. Your son Donghai has also disappeared. We have no idea why or where they are. We were wondering if you could help us?'

Bo Leun looked at me and then her husband.

'I have lost one daughter,' she said bitterly, I could see tears welling up in her eyes. 'From what you are saying I may have lost all three of my children.' She turned to Kan Leung and with real hatred in her eyes spoke. 'My husband, do you know anything of this?' Her voice was controlled but I could hear the menace in her tone.

His expression was one of shock. 'No, nothing,' he said. He was either a great actor or our previous meeting was a complete blank.

She glared at him and then turned to me, 'What can we do?'

'We are not sure what is happening, we have tried contacting both Meihui and Donghai but can find no trace. The number we have for Donghai is dead, Meihui's phone was left in her office. We wondered if you have a number for Donghai? Their captors may talk to you or allow your children to speak, My phone has a tracking device built in, if I put your sim card into it we may find them. It's a long shot but worth a try.'

My heart was pounding, Mark, Don and I had concocted this plan earlier. We hoped Donghai would talk to his Father. Everything depended on the severity of the Alzheimer's, how much Kan Leung was in control and how much he remembered.

'Give Mr Summers your phone,' Bo Leun demanded. Chinese women often exerted influence through their husband, it was their way. They weren't however normally this open in public. She sounded desperate. I wondered just how much control Bo Leun actually had.

Kan Leung looked confused and uncomfortable.

His wife held him by both hands, 'For the sake of your family, give Mr Summers your phone, please.' Her voice trembled, I could tell she was frightened.

'I do not understand what is happening,' said Kan Leung.

'It doesn't matter,' replied his wife kindly,' Do this for me, for Meihui, for Donghai, before its too late.'

He looked at her and then me. Putting his hand in his pocket, he pulled out his mobile and handed it to me. He looked ashen, a beaten and confused man. In another place I would have felt sorry for him. He was no longer strong enough to fight, he was sick. I took out the sim and put it in my own phone.

'Okay.' I said, 'Let's call Donghai, if he picks up I'd be grateful if you could speak to him Sir in general terms, just ask how he is and let the tracker do its work.'

I scrolled down to Donghai's number, switched on the tracker together with the loud speaker. I dialled and handed the phone to Kan Leung. The answer was almost immediate.

'Father how are you?' Donghai's speech was slurred, he was either drunk or stoned.

His Mother shook her head forlornly, Kan Leung spoke softly but he sounded assured.

'I am well my son and how are you?'

'I am fine thank you.'

'Where are you?'

'I am with some clients Father.'

''Do you know where Meihui is?'

'I have her sir, do you not remember, she betrayed us and you asked me to look after her.'

Bo Leun's eyes looked wild, she was about to say something but I raised my hand to stop her. The look she gave could have killed. However she accepted my gesture and stayed quiet.

'Is she safe? Kan Leung asked.

'She is my Father, I will look after her, don't worry.'

I signalled to Kan Leung to kill the call.

'You are a good son, thank you.'

'Goodbye Father.'

The phone was handed back to me. I pressed a couple of buttons and a map came up on the screen.

'He's at Tai Tam Road, Hong Kong Island, we've got him.' I could feel the excitement in my voice.

'Send me the coordinates,' instructed Joe, I pressed the relevant buttons and the unnamed man picked up his mobile to relay the information.

'We will have the place surrounded within the hour,' he said.

251

I turned to Joe Lin, 'Can you take me?'

'Of course.'

Bo Leun spoke, 'Save my children, please.' Tears streamed down her face, Kan Leung stared into space looking totally vacant.

I nodded, 'We'll try our best.' Joe Lin and the unnamed man followed me to the door. By now it was dark and Joe led me to a Toyota Corolla parked fifty yards down the road.

'A car like this doesn't create any interest,' he said as we climbed in.

I sent a text to Mark updating him and copied in Don. I felt a little scared and apprehensive. I was isolated from my world working with a deadly bunch of degenerates known as The Triads. So far everything we had done was on trust and I had no idea if this would hold. At any moment something could go wrong and there was nobody to help me.

'How long?' I asked.

'Fifteen, twenty minutes depending on traffic, it's on the other side of Tai Tam Country Park.'

I nodded not having a real clue where he was talking about. We set off, and within minutes hit heavy traffic. I followed our route on my tracker and as we made our way onto the Island Eastern Corridor three lanes crawled along the North Shore of Hong Kong Island. At least we were moving albeit slowly and eventually we pulled off with the park on the right and made our way onto the Tai Tam Road. Conversation was limited, I think Joe was more anxious than me.

'I reckon we're about half a mile from them' I said. Joe pulled in and made a call.

'We're to wait here,' he said 'until our people are in place.'

Apartment blocks were intertwined with opulent houses. In the dark this again looked a very upmarket area. After five minutes of silence Joe's phone rang. He listened for a few seconds and pointed at two Toyota Hiace vans which drove past and pulled up a couple of hundred yards ahead.

'Our people' he said starting the engine and moving forward. We parked behind the vans where about fifteen men in dark clothing were disembarking. One stood by the roadside and spoke as we got out.

'You two follow me' he said in Mandarin. In the dark I couldn't see his features so it was impossible to say whether he had been at the meeting I attended. The house stood behind grand wrought iron gates and as he spoke they opened quietly.

I looked quizzically at Joe. 'Two men have gone in already,' he said with half a smile, 'Disabled the security system and opened the gates.'

Men piled in and we followed. Some circled round to the back of the house while two with a battering ram ran up to the front door. Within seconds the door sprung open and six men ran in. It was only then I realised these guys were armed with machine guns and pistols. I was actually quite impressed with the efficiency of the operation.

It soon transpired we needn't have made such a fuss. Donghai lay on a sofa, tied up, naked and comatose. The guy who spoke to us kicked him. 'Where's Meihui?' he screamed.

Donghai moaned, he was out cold, stoned almost to the point of oblivion.

'Shit' said the man, 'He's obviously been having his sexual treats, look at the wanker.' He kicked him again and then shouted, 'Search this place, top to bottom.'

We could hear people running from room to room. Donghai's eyes opened, his pupils dilated, he looked wild and deranged. Focussing on me he said, 'You,' and slumped back.

At that point a loud voice boomed out from a tannoy system.

'This is ICAC the house is surrounded, come out one by one with your arms held high.'

For a split second there was silence as I realised The Independent Commission Against Corruption had somehow got involved. Someone had informed them. Suddenly all hell was let loose. Machine gun fire could be heard from the garden and then bullets flew into the room. Glass shattered and wood splintered as we all fell to the floor. A couple of men were hit and I could see they wouldn't be getting up again. The shooting continued outside and then an explosion was heard. I was unarmed and in the middle of a fight on the wrong side of the law. *How the hell did I get into this I* thought. I wriggled behind a sofa to give myself some protection from a hail of bullets streaming in through the windows. For a full five minutes the shooting continued, the room so recently a centre of opulence had become a scene from hell. Bodies lay on the floor with blood oozing, expensive furniture had been torn apart, pictures crashed to the floor covered in bullet holes. A sea of glass shards covered the deep carpets. Then we were plunged into darkness, I had no idea if someone had pulled the plug or what, I just became aware that the shooting had stopped and I didn't have a clue as to what to do next.

Men with torches ran into the room, 'Come on, we need to get out quickly.' I heard.

'What's happened?' Joe croaked.

Another voice cut in 'They didn't expect our backup force, we had men in the garden and behind them on the road, they stood no chance but we need to get out, now.'

'Meihui,' said Joe, 'We have to find her, if she's found to be involved there will be severe consequences for us all.'

A voice shouted from elsewhere in the house 'She's here, tied up I think she's dead.'

'Fuck' said the leader, 'Get out, now' he was screaming.

'But we can't leave Meihui.' Joe said almost in tears.

The leader turned 'She's dead and the rest of us will be if we don't get out now, just go.'

I ran out of the house virtually dragging Joe as we passed a dozen bodies. We sprinted through the garden to his car now with two police vans behind it. The blue lights were still flashing but both vehicles lay empty. We climbed in and I could see Joe shaking.

'Start the car' I said firmly. He pushed a key into the ignition and the engine turned over. He sat there, staring at the steering wheel.

'Go' I screamed, 'Fucking go.' He looked at me with a blank expression. I rammed the gear lever into drive twisted the wheel and we started moving. Joe shook himself and started to drive. Blue flashing lights could be seen coming the other way. We passed half a dozen police cars screaming down the road. They didn't stop for us and we got onto the main highway losing ourselves in the traffic.

'We need to dump this car,' I said taking control, 'How far to the airport?'

There was silence, Joe was still in a state of shock. I turned and shook him 'How far to the fucking airport?' I bellowed.

'Thirty miles.'

'Too far, find a metro station.' He thought for a couple of seconds.

'Heng Fa Cheun is not far away we can park at Paradise Mall.'

'Fine, let's go, is the car in your name?'

'No, we use aliases.'

'Park it' I said, 'and then lose yourself for half an hour.'

'There is a supermarket.'

'Good. I'll go straight to the metro, we don't want to be seen together.'

'Where will you go?'

'No idea' I said lying through my teeth. As we spoke I was texting Mark – *in the shit need a flight ticket anywhere asap, should be at the airport within 60 minutes.*

We drove into a multi storey car park, went up a couple of floors and Joe pulled in. He looked at me, his face ashen, he was still in shock.

'Well done,' I said putting my hand on his shoulder. 'Stay here for ten minutes, get a taxi to another station, catch a train and change twice. Then get a taxi home. Hopefully any trail will be lost along with any connection between us.'

His looked as if he was away with the fairies.

'Are you listening?' I said shaking his arm.

'Yes, I understand, sorry.'

'The shipment from the US is tomorrow, make it happen'.

Joe looked at me blankly.

'This is what Meihui wanted,' I screamed, 'You know that. Can you make it happen?'

I was holding his tie with our faces inches from each other. I knew I was threatening, I needed to shock him back into reality.

He looked at me, I could see the terror in his eyes.

'Can you make it happen?'

'I'll try,' he said his voice breaking, 'because I loved Meihui. She was so much more to me than my boss.' He began to sob. I put my hand on his shoulder.

'Take care,' I said opening the car door, 'I'll phone later.'

I walked through the faceless mall with its parade of shops, sandwich bars and the inevitable McDonalds. I may as well have been in Luton as Hong Kong with its sterile atmosphere cold marble floors and international brand names. There was nothing in the way of local culture that began to attract me. I just walked at a pace not too fast or too slow following the signs to the metro station. Although I knew I'd be on CCTV I wanted to attract as little attention as possible.

256

I caught the metro and changed at Admiralty station and then Prince Edward before getting off at Kowloon Tong. I walked through yet another shopping mall and then got a taxi from a rank just outside.

'Airport.' I said.

'You want nice girl?'

'Fuck off.'

We drove in silence. I checked my phone.

You're booked on the 23.45 British Airways flight to London – phone when you can. A mobile boarding pass was attached.

Automatically I put my hand inside my jacket pocket and felt for my passport. *Thank God I didn't leave it in the apartment* I thought. I put on the glasses and said a silent prayer hoping I could get out of the country without too many complications.

The traffic was relatively quiet and forty five minutes later we were at the airport.

'Two twenty' said the driver in pigeon English.

I gave him two hundred and fifty, a reasonable tip, not too big or small so that hopefully he wouldn't remember me in detail. I knew I was becoming paranoid but details at this stage were paramount when it came to survival. We'd had this drummed into us at our training school in Kenya. It seemed obvious at the time and I got bored hearing about it. Now I realised why so much attention had been put into this aspect of survival.

As I walked through the airport I bought a travel bag, a few clothes shoes and toiletries. In the loo I took them out of their packaging and stuffed everything into the bag. I realised it would look strange going through security without baggage. I was making sure no alarm bells could be raised.

I headed to security, thank God it was quiet, I really wasn't in the mood for making polite conversation with tourists, businessmen and cretins. I passed through waiving my phone at the scanner and the bag went through without creating any attention. Breathing a quiet sigh of relief I carried on walking, the guards hardly looked at me.

The flight hadn't been called so I found a bar and ordered a beer. I had this fixation that I was going to be pounced upon any second by airport security, but I just sat as quietly as possible, sipping on my drink waiting, and praying for the gate to appear on the screen. I pondered why I hadn't been put on a flight to Zurich leaving at the same time. Then looking at the screen I smiled, that flight was Cathay Pacific, a Hong Kong based company. In theory it could be called back by the Hong Kong Authorities at any time, not so with British Airways. Whoever had booked the ticket was being as careful as me.

I thought about phoning both Mark and Joe but decided against it. I had no idea who was around me and I didn't want any overheard conversations being picked up by the wrong people. I was making sure, bloody sure.

I'd done everything I'd been asked to do and more. I'd found Caterina, discovered what the Chinese were up to and set up a delivery channel for the nuclear bombs. I'd achieved at the highest level in my opinion and there was nothing else for me to do. I'd catch up on what else had happened when I arrived in London. I just wanted out, and quickly

The departure gate appeared on the screen and I made my way to the pier. I was nervous and inwardly shaking. I tried my best not to show any concern. I knew this was the final hurdle, if I could get through the last security check at the gate I should be safe, as long as the plane took off quickly. I sat for a good ten minutes while the airport staff faffed about. I realised what was meant when people say 'it was the longest ten minutes of my life'. Sitting on an uncomfortable seat expecting to be arrested at any moment I was going through hell. It was one of the most agonising times of my life.

Eventually I heard the announcement I'd been longing for.

'Flight number BA 028 British Airways to London is now ready for boarding. Have your passports and flight tickets ………..

I didn't need to hear the rest. I sat for a second as others jumped up then deliberately, not too fast and not too slow made my way to the queue. The ground stewardess checked my passport and scanned my phone. *Please,* I thought, *just let me through.*

She smiled as she handed back my passport, I walked down the bridge and onto the plane breathing a huge sigh of relief. They'd booked me first class so I was escorted to my seat where I put my bag in the overhead bin. Sitting down, I put my seat belt on and closed my eyes. I was exhausted, the last few hours had really taken it out of me.

'Can I offer you a drink sir?'

'Once we've taken off,' I said, *belt and braces,* I wanted to make sure I was out of Chinese airspace, before I relaxed.

I sat feeling tense, very tense *'For Christ's sake move'* I screamed silently. A few minutes later the plane pulled back and we started to taxi towards the runway. After an uncomfortable wait the engines revved, I felt the g-force as we accelerated and then we were airborne. I was physically shaking but I'd got away, the sense of relief was beyond description.

The air stewardess walked down the aisle.

'I'll have a scotch please,' I said, 'a bloody big one.'

Chapter 27

I had to endure another twelve hours of boredom. After the scotch a stewardess brought a tray of food, lobster ravioli and tenderloin of beef. I ate quickly, my nerves still jangling and drank two half bottles of red wine in quick succession. By now I was half pissed but my mind was still racing. I kept going through the events of the last couple of days. One thing didn't make sense, who tipped off ICAC and what if anything did they know about our operation? They'd followed us into the house within minutes, why? None of it tied up. We could be screwed and not realise it. There was no way of knowing and there was little I could do thirty thousand feet up in the air.

I slept for several hours and woke with a hangover. The stewardess gave me some water, I played with the in flight entertainment and tried to sleep again. It was impossible. I really needed to burn off some of some of the nervous tension. I played solitaire and other stupid games on my phone just to kill time. The hours drifted by, I had a full English breakfast at one point, not because I was hungry it was more for something to do. I strolled up and down the aircraft a couple of times to get the circulation going. The flight was about half full, everybody else seemed to be asleep, the stewardess gave me a copy of the previous day's Daily Telegraph which at least gave me something to focus on for half an hour or so. I watched us cross the continents on a monitor and at last after what seemed like an eternity I could feel the aircraft begin to descend.

I switched on my phone before we landed. It immediately started peeping so I killed the sound. I had text messages from Mark, Joe and Don.

I opened Mark's first, *'You are booked on the 06.50 BA 724 to Geneva from Terminal 5. Phone when you get to Heathrow.'*

Joe, *'Thank you for helping me, she's alive and in hospital, not in a good way, phone when you can.'* It was guarded, understandable given the circumstances.

Don just said, 'Phone *when you can.'*

I looked up to see the stewardess grinning at me and shaking her head.

'Sorry,' I mouthed putting the phone back in my pocket as we touched down.

Once off the plane I phoned Mark.

'How are you?' he asked.

'Okay now, I'll give you the full details when we meet but it was a bit hairy.'

'I've been scanning the Hong Kong papers, the headline story is about a Triad attack on ICAC with a dozen officers killed. According to the story the Triads had kidnapped Donghai and Meihui Leung, ICAC were tipped off and tried to rescue them There followed a shootout and Donghai was killed in the crossfire. Meihui was found alive tied to a bed. She'd been heavily drugged, and is critically ill. It looks to me as if she won't make it. Apparently she'd been raped several times and beaten badly.'

I went sick as Mark spoke.

'She's in hospital and the family have put out a statement thanking ICAC for trying to save Meihui and Donghai with all

261

the usual platitudes. Don's trying to find out what's what from his contact at ICAC. He's got to go careful though.'

'Oh my God.' I said as everything clicked into place.

'Go on' said Mark.

'This is all down to Donghai, it was obviously all part of some deranged plan. He kidnaps Meihui and lets on to ICAC that the two have been taken by The Triads.'

'Why the hell would he do that?'

'His plan was probably to kill Meihui with drugs. He gets stoned himself as cover and his cohorts tie him up to make it look like a genuine kidnapping. The cohorts do what the hell they want with Meihui while he's comatose. I know from personal experience that he knocks around with sexual deviants. No doubt the dose of drugs he took was nothing like as heavy as the one given to Meihui. He comes out the hero and takes control of Leung Industries and probably a major part of The Triad movement as well.'

'Surely The Triads would get to him if he pulled a stunt like that.'

'We're talking many different factions, he blames one and blows them away. In its twisted way it's brilliant. The trouble was we got to the house before ICAC and believe me The Triad fighters don't mess about. I'll phone Meihui's PA and get back to you.'

'You're brilliant.'

'I wish.'

By now I'd arrived at transit security. Again my passport was checked together with the bag. I walked straight through, grabbed an Americano and phoned Joe. He picked up immediately.

'How is she,' I asked getting straight to the point.

'Very ill, it is touch and go as to whether she will live. The doctors have induced vomiting, washed her stomach out and activated a charger to bind the drugs. She's now having haemodialysis treatment to replace her blood.' He paused, 'We are also trying to establish why we were attacked.'

I told him my theory. There was silence at the other end as he thought it through.

'I'll tell my people.'

'Meanwhile the transportation has to continue.'

'I'll try.'

'This was Meihui's wish and command.'

'I know, I'll get back to you as soon as possible.'

I then phoned Don and filled him in.

'I guess that's me finished with this mission and Hong Kong.' He said.

'Never say never as Mr Bond would say.'

He laughed, 'Keep me in touch and good luck.'

I read the headlines on the BBC website and half an hour later got on the plane to Geneva. By now I was feeling more relaxed, I was tired but my job was done. The rest was up to others, talking to the Chinese at the UN, placing the bombs across China and Africa, and then who knows?

The flight was uneventful. It arrived on time and I sailed through immigration. The doors opened onto the main concourse and suddenly my heart soared. There stood a beautiful Latino girl with a grin as wide as her face.

'Caterina,' I shouted and everybody looked round. *To hell with them*' I thought.

I ran and grabbed her, we just held each other not wanting to let go. I pulled back, looked at her and we kissed. Not a social embrace, but a kiss of lovers, long and hard and passionate.

Eventually she pulled away, we were both crying our eyes out, I held her, tight.

'Jonathan I've longed for this moment.'

'You and me both,' I said looking at her. Truth be told, she looked far from well, she'd lost a hell of a lot of weight and her eyes were sunken with dark circles around them.

She looked at me, 'What have you done to your hair?' she said laughing.'

'Long story.'

She laughed again, 'We have to go, Heinrich is waiting.'

I put my arm around her waist, she was flesh and bones, nothing more.

'How are you?' I asked, 'and don't just say fine, tell me the truth.'

After a moment's silence she said, 'I am still weak and it will take time to build up my strength. I have to take many pills but I should make a full recovery.'

'Thank God,' I said squeezing her, 'Thank God.'

Heinrich's welcome was just as fervent when we got to the car.

'My friend,' he said shaking my hand vehemently, 'It is so good to see you again.'

He threw my bag into the boot and ushered us both into the back. We held hands and grinned like silly school children as Heinrich drove us out of the airport complex.

'When did you get out of hospital?' I asked, realising that less than a week had passed since I had left Switzerland. In many ways, it seemed like a lifetime.

'Only yesterday.'

'She's supposed to be in bed resting.' piped up Heinrich.

'I wasn't going to miss this,' she said squeezing my hand again, 'not for the world.'

'How's Tanja.' I was trying to get a grip on reality. So much had happened over the last few days I felt as if I'd become cocooned in an alien environment. It felt so good to be back in Switzerland with a wonderful girl holding my hand. I felt safe with a real sense of belonging. Something I hadn't felt for a long time.

'She's okay, but very frustrated and worried. There is still little communication with Zambola and she hasn't heard a word from Henri. She's back in Germany at the moment trying to get out there.'

'*God it all seems so long ago*' I thought.

As we approached the villa my phone rang, it was Joe.

'My people are prepared to carry out your plan. The plane will be waiting at San Francisco airport as arranged by Meihui, the rest is up to you.'

We drove up to the house, the door opened and out stepped Mark beaming. The handshake seemed to go on forever and I broke it by giving him Joe's news.

'You're a marvel,' he said, 'Grab yourselves some coffee I need to make a couple of calls.'

It had all been a bit too much for Caterina, as I held her she slumped.

'We'd better get you to bed,' I said lifting her in both arms.

'Follow me,' replied Henri. By the time we got to the room I was on the verge of dropping her. She may have lost weight but after a flight of stairs I felt knackered laying her on the bed. She opened her eyes, 'I'll be fine now you are here'.

'Have a rest,' I said bending down and kissing her on the forehead, 'I'll come and see you later.'

She smiled and closed her eyes again.

'How is she really?' I asked Mark as I walked into his office.

'Very weak, malaria, dengue fever, starvation and syphilis. It's going to take a long time before she's fit again. She shouldn't have gone to the airport today but try stopping her.' He half smiled, 'She's one feisty lady.'

'But she will recover?'

Mark nodded, 'Everything being equal.'

I left him and went into the drawing room. I was tired but felt determined to get through the day and shake off any jet lag. A young girl brought in a tray of coffee and biscuits. I sat nibbling unsure of what to do next. I flicked through the news channels killing time until Mark came in.

'The consignment will be loaded later today as agreed. Ask your friends to plant the merchandise within seven days of arrival, that's what I'm working on in Africa. If it's ten so be it but the sooner we move this forward the better.'

I relayed the information on to Joe, there was no change in Meihui's condition.

Caterina was fast asleep so I went for a walk in the grounds, it was a warm spring day and the sun on my back felt good. I remembered the last time I was in this garden I'd rung Caroline. Feeling a little guilty that I hadn't spoken to her for quite a while I phoned again.

'Well well,' she said, 'I was beginning to wonder of I'd ever hear from you.'

We chatted amicably but there was something slightly distant in Caroline's voice.

'Are you alright?' I asked with genuine concern.

'I'm fine,' she said hesitantly.

'But,' I responded.

'You know me too well.'

'Go on'

'Well, you've been away a long time and er...'

'You've met someone.' I said.

''Well er yes er,' she was covered in confusion.

'Caroline,' I said firmly, 'We've been friends for quite a while and I like you very much indeed. We're good for each other, as friends. I dug you out of the proverbial and then you dug me out. And that's great, but I don't think you and I could ever have taken it any further. We both know that and I for one am thrilled that you've found someone. I mean that.'

After a moment's silence she spoke, 'Thanks Dean, Jonathan, whoever you are. I've been dreading telling you. You're the most decent man I've ever known and I love you, but like a brother. I hope you find happiness.'

'Who is he then?' I quipped.

'He's an accountant, not as glamorous a lifestyle as yours but I like him.'

'That's great, will you stay with The Organisation?'

'Golly yes, this is my rock, the one stable thing I have in my life.'

'Along with me, as a friend, I'll always be here for you.'

I could hear her crying, 'No tears' I said.

'Oh bloody hell,' she sobbed, 'Why do you have to be such a decent bloke?'

'Keep in touch,' I said, 'I mean that, especially if you find yourself in the proverbial again.'

'And you.'

Killing the call I started to walk back towards the house. In a way I felt saddened as I genuinely liked Caroline. In my heart I was happy as I wanted her happiness and if I'm honest, I'd found Caterina. My life had been in turmoil since Zan had died but now I felt I had a sense of direction. I had no idea where Caterina and I were going but the thought of the journey excited me.

My phone rang again, it was Joe.

'I'm afraid Meihui didn't make it Mr Summers, she died just over an hour ago.'

I felt as if my world had collapsed. Again I felt sick and dizzy. I fell to the ground, vaguely aware of the soft grass under me.

'Oh my God,' I said, 'I am so sorry.'

267

There was silence at the other end.

'Poor Bo Lin, she has lost everything.'

'Business continues,' said Joe quietly, 'I will phone you when the shipment arrives.'

I looked up Mark was hovering over me.

'Are you okay?' he asked.

I shook my head and told him what had happened. He sat down beside me and put his arm on my shoulder.

'Words are scarcely adequate at a time like this Jonathan' he said, 'You've been to hell and back since joining The Organisation. Nobody deserves what you've been through. Take some time off, go away somewhere I can handle things from here.'

I looked at him, I felt numb.

'I tried that last year' I said, 'For all the good it did me. Just leave me alone for a while Mark, I'll be okay.'

Mark patted me on the shoulder, got up and made his way back to the house. I lay on the grass and closed my eyes. Yet again I felt like a lost soul. It was as if my isolation in Amsterdam had returned. I felt angry and confused.

I became aware of someone shaking me, I'd dozed off.

Opening my eyes I saw Caterina staring at me, she looked upset and I could see concern in her eyes.

'Jonathan, she said taking my hand, 'I am here for you. I am not sure if I can help you through this and if you want me to go away I understand. But I feel your hurt, your having lost Zan and now her sister. But you are not responsible, you must accept that.'

'Oh but I am,' I said bitterly, 'And for their brother, thanks to me all three are dead.'

'How can that be?'

'Because if I hadn't blurted out in Australia where Zan and I were going she would still be alive. Therefore I wouldn't have concocted this stupid plan to save the world. Thus I wouldn't have gone to Hong Kong and Meihui and Donghai would still be alive.'

She sat down beside me and put her arm around my shoulder.

'And I'd be dead along with millions of others, you can't blame yourself.'

I held her, 'I know you're right.' I said, 'But it's all so bloody unfair.'

'You have done an incredible job Jonathan, you can't blame yourself.'

I started to cry, the emotion of the moment took hold of me.

'I don't know what to do Caterina,' I said sobbing my heart out, 'I don't know what to do.'

She held me for a long time. Eventually I was able to pull myself together and we kissed passionately on the lawn.

'Thank God you're here' I whispered.

'I'll always be here for you Jonathan, I promise.'

'Mark said I should take a holiday, but not yet, it wouldn't be fair on the people we've lost. I've got to see this through and then perhaps we could go away together.'

'I can think of nothing better,' she said squeezing me tight.

In another world that moment would have been delightful, the sun beat down on us and the panoramic views of the Swiss mountains were wonderful. Sadly the numbness continued. I wanted to feel close to Caterina but I felt detached from the world.

We lay on the grass for a couple of hours talking and holding each other. It was an incredibly cathartic experience and although I felt a deep sorrow for Meihui I began to come to my senses. She, her Father and Zan had been involved in a despicable criminal organisation and the end result was almost inevitable. I felt desperately sorry for her Mother but she had lived well from immoral earnings and I couldn't carry the can for that.

'Lets go and find some tea.' I said.

Caterina smiled but I could tell she was far from well.

'And then I'm taking you to bed.'

Her eyes opened wide and she looked worried.

'To sleep, the other bit can happen whenever.'

She smiled, 'And it will happen Jonathan I promise you, but I need time, I'm sorry.'

'We're both a bit screwed up aren't we.,' I said. 'Time we have, as long as we can sort out those grotty Chinese.' I helped her up off the grass and we walked back to the house, arm in arm.

Heinrich stood by the double doors that lead into the drawing room.

'Are you okay?' he asked.

'Yeah, I'll survive, I'm just a bit shaken up that's all, can you organise a cup of tea?'

'You're sure you don't want a whisky or something?'

We both remembered the time we first met, when I'd lost friends in a massacre, when Caterina had nearly been killed and I drank too much whisky to escape the reality.

'Not this time Heinrich,' I responded, 'Tea will be fine.'

Chapter 28

I took Caterina back to her room and asked Heinrich to take some soup up for her. It was obvious she needed complete bed rest without the distractions of The Organisation. Later that evening I went to see Mark in his office.

'Shouldn't she be in a hospice or something?' I asked, 'She's so weak.'

'Probably, but try telling her that. The doctor is coming tomorrow, I suggest we take it from there.'

'I want to see this through,' I said, 'before I take a break. I've come this far, it would be wrong to pull away now.'

'Good,' replied Mark, 'For information the plane with our cargo is on its way to Wuhan. Let's hope your boys can do the job.'

'What about Africa and the subs?'

'Four subs will be in place across the Pacific within three days, two American, one British and one Japanese. I reckon five days for the bombs to be planted in Africa, the sooner your boys in China can do their job the sooner we can get this show on the road. It's really down to them from here on in. Once everything is in place I'll be heading for New York to present to some big wigs. I'd like you to be there if you don't mind. With what you have been through I feel certain you could add a little colour to the presentation.'

'Not another bloody aeroplane' I thought as I nodded amicably.

'Just a thought' I said, 'If we talk to the Chinese in New York we're effectively tipping them off. They could marshal their troops in Africa immediately and by the time we press the button the camps could be evacuated'

'We have satellites watching all the bases 24/7. if that happens we'll hit the button immediately.'

Swinging a PC screen around he revealed a PowerPoint presentation, 'Let me show you what I've put together so far, I would welcome your feedback.'

The heading was 'Operation Confucius.'

'What's in a name?' Mark said.

He'd given a resume of Caterina's disappearance, my exploits in Zambola and a full translation of the email Caterina found. He outlined China's involvement in the Zambolan revolution, the training camps and the plan to set off the bombs in Africa and China. He then went on to outline several possible outcomes:-

1. *Chinese reprisal.*
2. *Our response to reprisal.*
3. *Chinese acceptance of the status quo .*
4. *Collapse of Chinese government.*
5. *Possible names to head up a new government.*
6. *Fallout in Africa.*

He finished with an immediate action plan and timings.

'No mention of Triad involvement.' I said.

'That's on a need to know basis,' came the response. I remembered having this conversation way back.

The two of us spent half an hour tidying up the presentation and filling in timings at which point Mark said.

'Call it a day, we can look at it again tomorrow. I'm happy to go out for dinner but looking at you I would suggest an early night.'

'Good advice boss.' Jet lag was kicking in and I needed sleep.

'See you tomorrow morning.' I headed up to Caterina's room, as I walked in her eyes opened. She smiled and I lay down beside her. Once again we kissed, again she started to cry.

'Hey come on.' I said, there's no need for tears, not now.

She held me tight.

'I want to make love,' she said, 'But I can't, I'm not well enough.'

I kissed her again, 'There's no hurry, as Louis Armstrong sang "We've got all the time in the world."

'And we know what happened in that film,' she said squeezing me.

'Oh I know,' I said bitterly, 'I've got the t-shirt'.

We held each other and I dozed off waking with a jolt to see Caterina looking terrified.

'I'm sorry' she said 'It's just that what they did to me was horrible, despicable, revolting, it may take a long time to get over it.'

'We've both been through hell' I replied, 'Me mentally with Zan and you physically in Zambola. Neither of us deserved what we got but now we have each other and a lifetime to get over it. I thank God for that.'

We kissed again, *life could be worse*' I thought, '*a hell of a lot worse.*'

I stayed with Caterina that night sleeping fitfully. As dawn broke I was wide awake, after half an hour or so I got up.

'What time is it?' she asked.

'Six o'clock,' I kissed her on the cheek, 'Go back to sleep.' She snuggled back into bed, a text was waiting for me from Joe Lin.

'*Merchandise arrived safely and is now being distributed. I'll be in touch.*'

273

I forwarded it on to Mark and idly wondered what the hell I was going to do for the next few days.

I showered and went for a jog. The mountain air felt good and I felt quite invigorated after running for a couple of miles. I knew I was through the jet lag and felt fidgety wanting something to do. I explained as much to Mark over breakfast.

'Help Caterina,' he said, 'it may not be action packed but probably the most important job you'll do this year.'

I knew he was right but I felt distinctly uncomfortable with the world on a knife and me acting as nursemaid. I told him so.

'Everything is in place,' he replied, 'You've done a great job. Now relax and build yourself up for the next episode. This campaign is far from over and I want you to be healthy and ready for the next chapter. Get yourself into a fitness regime over the next few days, use the gym, use the pool. If you like I'll get a personal trainer.'

I nodded, 'Yes that's good, thanks very much.'

He smiled and got up to leave the table.

'You have to learn to pace yourself Jonathan, you'll be a much better person for it.'

For the next few days I got into a routine of getting up at 7am and immediately having a workout with the personal trainer. This went on for a couple of hours. He was a nice guy and quickly increased my fitness levels although I felt as if he was putting me through hell. He organised a masseur for my foot and arm, both of which had started to play up as the exercise levels increased.

After showering each day I took breakfast up to Caterina and normally had a chat with the doctor who visited every morning. A nurse came to check her early evening and it became obvious that she was beginning to recover. She started to eat well and her complexion became less pallid. She would get up mid morning and following coffee we'd go for a walk in the

274

grounds. These became longer each day and after a few days we started to explore the countryside. Her impish sense of humour returned and I could see she was gaining strength. I was actually beginning to enjoy the relaxed way of life and didn't feel in a hurry to get back to the real world.

I spoke to Joe Lin each day who kept me up to date with progress in China. He informed me that Mehui and Donghai had been cremated. Bo Leun attended the service but not Kan Leung, she was helped through the day by her sister. Apparently there was a lot of crying and wailing at the ceremony which is the Chinese way. Interestingly Bo Lyn stood stoically not showing any emotion. It was as if she didn't want to get involved with the traditional Chinese 'show.' It was her way of handling her grief.

I felt a pang of guilt. 'I should have attended.' I said.

'What good would it have done,' replied Caterina, always the pragmatist. 'Besides being caught in Hong Kong would not be a good idea.' She was right of course but I still felt bad about the whole scenario.

After eight days I got the call I'd been waiting for. Caterina and I were sitting in the garden on a hot sunny afternoon.

'The merchandise has been distributed,' said Joe Lin. 'The rest is up to you.'

'We're on,' I shouted running towards the house, Mark was in his office on the phone.

He looked at me and cut the call quickly.

'All the bombs are in place, we're ready.'

'Okay, said Mark, 'We're off to New York in the morning. The flights at 09.20 from Geneva so we need to be away from here at 07.30. We'll have a few meetings to attend.' He was slipping back into army mode and smiling wryly.

I went to break the news to Caterina.

'Mark wants me to go to New York with him, I should be back in a couple of days.'

'I don't want you to go, why does he need you?' She said kissing me.

'It'll do you good to rest, then we can go and find some sunshine.' I felt a stab in my heart as I remembered a similar scene with Zan. It seemed like yesterday. Again I felt full of guilt and remorse, I couldn't shake it.

'Don't be sad,' said Caterina.

'Thank God you're here,' I replied kissing her again.

Just before dinner I went to my room. A full set of clothes hung in the wardrobe and a scruffy travel bag lay on the bed. Yet another passport sat next to it along with credit cards and five hundred US dollars in cash.

I looked at the passport to see who I was this time. It reminded me of the old British TV game show: '*Tonight Matthew you're going to be,..*' I was again British with the alias John Pilton. I wondered for a second who came up with these names.

That night Caterina and I had a quiet meal together not saying much. We were both anxious for what lay ahead.

'I wish I was coming with you,' she said.

'Soon my darling soon.'

We had an early night and for the first time became quite intimate. She wasn't ready yet for a full relationship but this was the closest we'd been and it felt good. I realised that are bond was far more than just a physical attraction and we ended up holding each other incredibly tight.

I slept well and slipped out of bed early the following morning trying not to disturb her.

I showered shaved and dressed and as I was about to leave I bent down and kissed her, 'See you in a few days,' I whispered.

'You said two' she replied sleepily.

'I hope so,' I said, 'I hope so.'

Mark was already seated in the dining room and as I walked over he poured a cup of coffee for me. I'd have preferred tea but couldn't be bothered to argue. I nibbled on a croissant and he brought me up to speed.

'A meeting has been arranged tonight in the UN at six o'clock Eastern Standard Time. The head of the Security Council will be there along with delegates from the U.S, Britain, France, Russia, Germany and Japan.'

'Do all these countries have to be involved?' I asked naively.

'This is not a Security Council meeting as Germany and Japan are not on the council and China is. However all these countries contribute to The Organisation and have implicit faith in us. The meeting will be held behind closed doors using what we call "Protocol March". It's rarely employed but means all delegates are sworn to secrecy as part of The Organisation convention.'

'And if they refuse to sanction the plan?'

'There is a precedent,' he paused, 'Iraq. We still went ahead with those that disagreed sabre rattling in public but little more. It's possible Russia will baulk but with the evidence we're going to show them which is irrefutable they should come on board.'

'They may take the money on offer from China to shut them up.'

'What money?' asked Mark, 'They haven't been offered any.' He winked at me. 'This is high stakes poker. Winner takes all my friend, winner takes all.'

Heinrich appeared, 'The car's outside gentlemen.'

Another bloody aeroplane. I groaned silently.

We drove to the airport in silence. At one point Mark was tapping away furiously into his 'O' phone.

'Is there a problem?' I asked.

'No, it's another project I'm involved in.'

'Not more world domination?'

He smiled, 'No but it's interesting, we're looking at a couple of charities and trying to ascertain where all the money is going. It's certainly not arriving where it should be.'

'How many projects are you involved with?'

'Don't ask, suffice to say it takes a fair amount of juggling to keep all the plates spinning, and the mixed metaphor just about sums up my life.'

I'd got to the stage where I just drifted through airports without paying any attention and sitting waiting for the plane to be called I had to think hard as to which country I was in and where the hell I was flying to. On top of that I also had to remember who I was.

'Have a good flight Mr Pilton,' said the ground stewardess in English. I just about remembered in time, nodded and smiled. She was pretty and blond, much more interesting than the damned airport.

The nine hour flight was uneventful with Mark and I making polite conversation about anything other than The Organisation. Again I thought back to our training. *'In public never mention your projects or The Organisation even when off duty.'* I thought of that fateful dinner with Zan. Although we didn't mention who we were, our enemy was on the lookout for a Chinese girl with an English man. Our project had come to an end and we forgot the most basic of rules. We'd been spotted in a restaurant and even spoke about our plans. We told them where we were going and on the back of our stupidity Zan had been killed. I shuddered as I replayed the scene one more time in my mind.

'Are you okay?' asked Mark.

'Yeah sorry, I was miles away.'

I was very fond of Caterina, maybe I even loved her, but Zan was still there and I couldn't get rid of the feeling of guilt.

We flew into Newark and the queue for immigration was horrendous, snailing for about a hundred yards. Mark on an American passport slipped through but I had to stand in line with an officious security man walking up and down, snarling and being thoroughly objectionable. At one point my mobile rang. He glared at me and screamed.

'Son, if you wanna come into the United States I suggest you turn your god-damn cell phone off.'

Memories of Zambolan immigration flooded back. I smiled, wondering what the average American would think of their country being compared to a bankrupt African state. I felt like saying *'With prats like you old fella I'm really not that bothered, put me on the next flight back to civilisation.'*

Instead I just apologised and queued for nearly an hour before finally being allowed into the USA, centre of the Western World. At least, that's what they liked to believe.

Mark stood chatting to a guy in his mid forties, tall with short greying hair. He looked every inch the Wall Street banker wearing a sharp pin striped suit, white shirt, navy blue tie and shoes so shiny you could use them as a mirror. 'Welcome to America,' he said proffering his hand. 'I'm Tom Peters.'

'Tom is head of our New York desk,' said Mark. *Was he giving anything away?* I pondered. Probably not, Tom wouldn't be his real name and to any outsider what would New York desk mean?

'We'll get a taxi.' said Tom, 'it's much easier in New York than trying to drive and park.'

We walked to the rank where a steward signalled us to a New Jersey cab. I climbed into the back with Mark and Tom got in the front.

'I'm local,' Tom said brusquely to the driver, 'so don't bullshit me with double fairs for tolls. I use this route often so I know what I'm going to pay.'

'Okay boss' came the meek reply. Tom turned and winked, he liked to be in control.

The traffic was horrendous coming into New York and we crawled through the Lincoln tunnel and down West 40th Street making our way through Manhattan towards the UN building.

'You're staying at Millennium UN Plaza, it's not great but handy,' said Tom.

By now it was 2.45 in the afternoon New York time, 8.45 at night in Geneva and God knows what in Hong Kong. I didn't want to think about it in case my body clock rebelled. I knew I felt knackered even though I'd just sat on a plane all day.

'I suggest we check in and reconvene at 5pm,' said Mark, 'I could do with a power nap.'

'Amen to that,' I replied.

Check in wasn't exactly speedy with the usual palaver of passports and credit cards so after I was given my key I left the other two in the foyer and headed for the lift. My room although pretty faceless had a great view across Manhattan with the Chrysler building standing out like a beacon.

I set my phone alarm for 4.30 and put my head down. It felt like seconds later when the bleeper went off, by then I was in a deep sleep dreaming about Africa and Zan. I shook my head feeling groggy and confused. I showered and shaved to try and bring myself around. Dressing in grey trousers a navy blue jacket, white shirt and tie that had been packed for me in Geneva I felt a little annoyed For the UN I'd have preferred a suit but I had little choice in the matter.

Mark and Tom were sitting in the foyer as the lift doors opened. Fortunately Mark was also dressed relatively casually, I breathed a sigh of relief.

'Are you still here?' I asked.

They laughed, 'No an hours shut eye makes all the difference.' said Mark.

'I've been working in a small meeting room if you want to have a private chat' said Tom.

We went back into the lift and Tom lead us to a room with five tables and views over the East River and the UN building itself.

Tom poured coffee as Mark spoke.

'You've both seen the presentation I'm going to give. Hopefully we can have this wrapped up in a couple of hours. My only real concern is whether the Russians will play ball. An old friend of yours is part of their team,' Mark said looking at me, 'You know him as Alexei.'

I smiled at the memory, he'd been on my initial training course, a good guy and a great footballer.

'Hopefully you can use your personal relationship with him to help convince them.' I began to realise why Mark wanted me in New York. *What a wily old fox* I thought.

'Let me get this straight,' I said, 'This is clearly not an Organisation meeting, who exactly are we seeing?'

'Each country will have a mix of Organisation personnel together with government representatives. In total there will be twenty one of us, all security vetted to the highest level.

'I didn't know I was.'

Mark half smiled, 'Your job gentlemen is to talk to as many of the delegates as possible to ensure they are on side and fully appreciate the consequences if they were to try and pull this operation.' He paused, 'Any questions?'

Tom and I shook our heads.

'Lets go and put a stop to World War Three.'

Chapter 29

Mark walked towards the door with the two of us following. We trooped out of the building and walked the few hundred yards to the UN building. I'd been to New York a couple of times and seen the faceless fifties monolith before. It looked just like just another office block on the river bank. Security would tell us otherwise. I felt like pinching myself as I went through the third security check. I still saw myself as an ordinary bloke not that long out of university. Yet here I was at probably the most important political meeting of the twenty first century. '*How on earth did I get here?*' I asked myself.

We were taken by an officious looking woman in her mid forties to the main Secretariat Building, the one depicted in all news stories about the UN in New York. She pressed the button for the eleventh floor and guided us into what looked like a boardroom with a long table and twenty odd chairs around it.

Mark gave the woman a memory stick and after playing around with a laptop and tutting for a couple of minutes his presentation appeared on a screen.

She left the room and I poured coffee for the three of us. Within minutes the other delegates started to arrive. The Germans were the first followed by the French. We were introduced, the two Germans in their late thirties had blond hair and blue eyes, typically Teutonic. One of the French party was much more interesting, a gorgeous looking lady in her mid forties who spoke superb English. I was chatting to her when I felt a tap on the shoulder.

'Hello old friend' said Alexai giving me a bear hug.

'Can I introduce Francoise?'

'Trust you to be with the pretty girl,' he grinned taking the lady's hand and kissing it.

'So gallant,' she said looking a little embarrassed.

'I taught him all he knows about chivalry' I responded.

We all laughed, by now the room had filled up and Mark tapped the table.

'May we start the proceedings please.'

He ushered me to sit one side of him at the head of the table and introduced me to the Secretary General who sat on the other side.

I looked around, there were some incredibly big hitters and I felt well out of my depth. A thought struck me, the scene was so reminiscent of the meeting I'd had with the Triads. Two sides of the law operating in exactly the same manner. *The world is mad* I thought. I was glad not to be leading the conversation.

Mark stood holding the remote and the PowerPoint presentation began. Operation Confucius appeared on the screen.

'Good evening and thank you for joining us. What I am about to say will shock you and no doubt raise many questions. May I ask you to wait till the end of my presentation and then ask away.'

Mark spoke for about forty five minutes never stumbling, his audience totally captivated. The occasional gasp could be heard and regularly eyebrows were raised, especially when he talked through the forces the Chinese had created in Africa.

'Any questions?' he asked eventually. There was a stunned silence.

One of the Germans spoke, 'If you have this wrong then what?'

''I can assure you we haven't got this wrong.' Mark sounded a little exasperated. 'The Organisation is too detail conscious to make a mistake of this magnitude. We have checked and counter

283

checked. I am quite happy for your people to see the detailed information. I wouldn't be here now if I had the slightest doubt.'

'So if we agree what happens next?' asked the other German.

'I would request that we have your government's decision by tomorrow morning, if we delay proceedings anything could happen.'

'Like what?' asked Alexai's boss.

'Like the information from this meeting leaking and the Chinese taking Africa and the Middle East quickly. With the infrastructure they have in place they could make major inroads by the end of the week. We have to move before they do. If we don't, it's curtains for the world as we know it. Make no mistake, don't think for a minute any country will survive in its present format. You'll be starved out of existence if you don't play ball the Chinese way.' As he spoke Mark stared at the Russians.

'This may not happen, said one of the Japanese contingent, 'Perhaps you are being alarmist. Why not wait and see if the Chinese make a move and then act?'

'By acting now we can severely damage the Chinese infrastructure in Africa. If we leave it for them to act, to use a colloquial expression, the horse will have bolted, it will be too late. I repeat, the Chinese have built up a massive force in Africa, unless we destroy it or use political means to eject it the Chinese will have control of the world.'

I could see the delegates looking at each other uncomfortably. Following a moment's silence Mark spoke again.

'You need to speak to your governments, I can arrange detailed information packs for you but I would ask you all to return here by 9am tomorrow morning, hopefully with your blessing to proceed.' Again Mark paused. 'One more thing, by backing our plan there will be minimal casualties on both sides.

If we don't go ahead we face Armageddon, that is the reality. Thank you for your time.'

People stood saying very little, they were all in deep thought. Francoise shook her head, 'How can they be so stupid.' She said to me.

'The fight for world domination is nothing new.' I replied. As I spoke the Germans and Japanese walked past. They knew what I was saying.

'Can we go for a beer?' asked Alexai quietly.

'Good idea, are you bringing your boss?'

'No just you and me, it'll be better that way. We'll get a cab up to the Roof Bar just off Fifth Avenue, I like it there.'

'Been here a while?' I asked.

'Off and on', with that he winked and went to join his colleague.

'Alexai wants a one on one with me,' I said to Mark, 'Probably makes sense.'

Mark nodded, 'No problem, I'm having dinner with the Secretary General and a couple of others.'

'Anyone in particular?'

'Just a bit of networking,' *in other words, don't ask.*

I smiled and went to find Alexei.

Cabs were lined up plying their trade and the driver looked none too pleased that we were only going to Fifth Avenue.

'I suppose they all expect fares to the airport.' said Alexai.

'Life's a bitch.' I responded, he laughed.

We were dropped on Fifth and Alexei darted into an alleyway. I followed him into a lift which took us up to a rooftop garden. The doors opened to reveal a terrace covered in green baize. Wooden bench tables were spread out with large umbrellas and heaters. I was glad of these because the evening was turning chilly. A few people were seated close by but we went to the far end which was quiet. While admiring the views of Manhattan with the Empire State building dominating the horizon the waiter came over, we ordered two beers.

'Try the Ceviche' said Alexei, it's good.

Raw fish in chilli didn't really appeal but I went with the flow.

The waiter disappeared and Alexei spoke quietly.

'Give me the inside track.'

There was nobody in earshot but I still watched what I said.

'I don't have to, I helped Mark put his presentation together, I can assure you it's one hundred percent accurate. We've not only triangulated to ensure the reality, we've also had it confirmed through very unofficial sources.'

'Who?'

'I can't tell you, sorry.'

'You have to, I'm in The Organisation.' Alexei looked exasperated.

'Even Mark doesn't know who it is,' I said, 'But trust me, I implore you, it's all for real.'

I was lying, Mark knew Meihui had confirmed the story through her sources in The Triads. However I wasn't going to tell Alexei or anyone who we were involved with. If that got out it could scupper the whole operation. I was on dangerous ground.

'You know how it is Alexei, I am sure there are projects you've been involved in which you cannot tell me about. I respect that because I know and trust you. Please believe me and convince your government, this is for real. We have a way to combat the Chinese with minimal risk. The infrastructure is in place. With luck we could be sitting back here in two days time having a major celebration. Otherwise I shudder to think. We are on the brink my friend.'

The waiter brought the beers. 'Happy times.' I said raising my glass, 'Vashee zda ró vye,' came the response.

We ate and to be fair the food was good and very welcoming. Alexei had to get back to his people so after another beer we called it a night. As we shook hands I said, 'Get your lords and masters onside Alexei, I want to be able to do this again.'

He nodded, 'I'll do what I can.'

He took a cab while I walked back to the hotel texting Mark with an update. He responded with a request to meet for breakfast at 7am. Back in my room I got a text from Caterina. *Phone me when you can.* It was 2am her time so I was a little reticent. She picked up immediately sounding bright and perky. It made me feel better, I brought her up to speed.

'I should phone Alexei,' she said, 'maybe him hearing from another person within The Organisation will help.'

She was right but I was a little concerned. 'You're supposed to be resting.'

'I've been asleep most of the day, that's why I'm wide awake now. I'm bored and want to do something. I think I can manage a phone call, I'll call you back.'

While waiting I switched on the TV and ploughed through dozens of channels. I couldn't really focus on quiz shows and grotty soaps and smiled when BBC America came on showing a ten year old British comedy. *I wonder how many people in America are watching that?* I pondered.

Eventually Caterina phoned back. 'He's not a problem,' she said, 'the government personnel are a lot more reticent.'

'Understandable, let's hope he can convince them.'

I slept fitfully that night, but it wasn't real sleep. I was basically conscious with my eyes closed. At six o'clock I got up and went for a jog, down past the UN building, up 42nd Street and back to the hotel. The training had done me good and I felt alive by the time I got back to the hotel. I showered and changed then went to meet Mark in the hotel restaurant. Apart from a couple of businessmen at the far end we had the place to ourselves

Tom joined us and as always he was dressed immaculately. I wondered how much sleep they'd had.

'We seem to be winning,' said Mark. 'We've had many off the record conversations over the last few hours and the only ones prevaricating are the Germans. I think you flattered Francoise and I'm sure you could be her toy boy. Anyway the French are with us which is always a surprise. Alexei has done a good job with his people so thank you for that. We were with the British and Americans last night and needless to say they're on board. The Americans will ensure the Japanese fall into place. Don't ask, that's how it works.'

'So what about the Germans?' I enquired.

'Talks are ongoing at the highest level. Come 9am they'll be with us one way or another.' He smiled.

'Then what?'

'The Secretary General has asked for a meeting with the Chinese Ambassador to the UN at 10am. I'll be there and I'd like you to be present to ensure there are no language difficulties. He speaks English well enough but I want to make sure.'

I was shocked, suddenly everything was about to kick off, 'So World War Three could start today,' I said quietly.

'Yes, so after the meeting we'll be heading to our New York office to control operations. It's going to be an interesting day'

I ordered eggs sunny side up. I needed sustenance for what lay ahead.

We made our way back to the UN building and again went through all the security checks.

The meeting was in the same room as the day before and a few of the delegates were already drinking coffee as we walked in. Françoise came over and kissed me just a little too amorously on both cheeks. Alexei shook hands and winked as if to say everything is okay.

Two Englishmen approached me, we hadn't spoken although both were present at the meeting the day before. One was the Ambassador, his face vaguely familiar; I'd seen him pontificating on TV. The other didn't introduce himself but spoke.

'We haven't met formally but I gather you've done some incredible work. On behalf of her Majesty's government I thank you.'

I smiled feeling a little embarrassed not quite knowing what to say. Fortunately, Mark brought the meeting to order and we all sat down.

'Good Morning, ' he said, 'You've all spoken to your own people, unless you have anymore questions now is the time to vote. So I'm going to ask each country in turn. The first proposition is, "Are you in favour of the Secretary General calling the Chinese Ambassador to account for his country's military manoeuvres in Africa? The second proposition is, 'If we are not satisfied with the Chinese Ambassador's response are your countries in favour of us taking the actions outlined at yesterday's meeting? Please answer aye or no to both propositions.'

After a seconds silence Mark turned.

'America, how do you vote?'

'Aye and aye,' came the response.

'France, how do you vote?'

'Aye and aye.'

'Germany, how do you vote?'

There was a slight pause,

'Aye and aye.'

To say the man looked pissed off was an understatement. Obviously Mark had worked a little magic overnight. I breathed a sigh of relief. *Thank God for that* I thought.

'United Kingdom, how do you vote?'

'Aye and aye.'

'Japan, how do you vote?'

'Aye and aye'

'Russia, how do you vote?'

'Aye and aye'

Alexai winked at me.

Politics I thought, *what a load of bollocks. Here we are trying to save the world and we have to pussy foot around puffed up self important bureaucrats all playing the game. The trouble is, none of them know the rules.*

'We have a clear mandate,' Mark said smiling at the Germans. 'Thank you for your support. We will keep you updated throughout the next few hours and days. Let us pray World War Three can be averted.'

There was a scuffle of chairs as the delegates got up to leave. Mark, Tom, the Secretary General and I were left in the room.

'Such sad times said the Secretary General, sad times indeed.'

The Chinese delegation were due at 10 am, we made small talk to kill time although it was strained. We were willing the minutes to go. The coffee cups were collected and replaced and the room cleaned ready for our next meeting.

Just after 10am there was a knock on the door and the officious looking woman walked in followed by three Chinese men, one small, overweight and in his mid fifties. The other two also small but slim, one in his early forties the other mid thirties. I was surprised at how well dressed they all were. Obviously living in the West had rubbed off on them.

We shook hands, drinks were offered but declined. The Secretary General asked everyone to sit. Mark took immediate control.

The PowerPoint flickered into life and he started to speak.

'Gentlemen, what you are about to hear is going upset you. That is unfortunate, but you need to understand we have discovered that your government has put together a programme which is totally unsatisfactory.'

I looked at the three men, the word inscrutable came to mind.

'We have information confirming that your country has developed bases across Africa from which you intend to take control of both the African continent and the Middle East.'

There was no reaction, the three Chinese continued to look at the screen. Mark changed the PowerPoint page. A map of Africa appeared showing the manpower and arsenal at each site.

'Gentlemen, these facts are undeniable and not acceptable. Either your country agrees to pull out of Africa or we in the West will retaliate. You are forcing us to take pre-emptive measures. We have a clear understanding of what your plans are and we will not allow you to dominate the world in the manner you have chosen. You have until 13.00 hours Eastern Standard time to agree that you will pull back from Africa, otherwise a thermo nuclear bomb planted in China will be detonated. The first bomb is a warning. It is planted well away from any towns and cities so there will be minimal loss of life. The second bomb will be blown sixty minutes later. That will be closer to one of your cities but again loss of life will be minimal. The third bomb will again be blown sixty minutes later and be closer still. This will result in loss of life. We have many bombs planted across China and will use them unless you agree to our terms. China will effectively be destroyed. The choice is yours. That is all I have to say.'

The Chinese Ambassador looked at The Secretary General. For a moment he seemed lost for words. Eventually he spoke.

'This is preposterous and ridiculous' he said in almost perfect English. 'I cannot believe what I am hearing. Your so called proof is some kind of a sick joke.'

'This is no joke,' said the Secretary General. 'I implore you to pull back your troops and arms immediately. We have given you a warning. Unless you respond positively the loss of life in your country will be tragic. It is up to you and your government. I suggest you talk to your leaders now and come back with a proposal.'

The Chinese Ambassador shook his head, stood and walked out of the office in high dudgeon. His colleagues followed saying nothing.

'That went well' said Mark, 'Lets get to New York HQ, there's a car waiting.'

Chapter 30

'Where is HQ?' I asked.

'Fort Hamilton in Brooklyn. It's a US Army base and to the outside world it's used as a disaster relief centre, very apt considering.'

By now we were walking down the corridor. Mark was pressing buttons on his 'O' phone.

'Gentlemen, Operation Confucius is live' he said as the lift doors opened.

Outside the building an enormous Cadillac limousine stood waiting. Two soldiers saluted then opened the back doors. I got in one side, Mark shook hand with the Secretary General and climbed in the other followed by Tom. One soldier drove with his colleague in the passenger seat. Outside a cavalcade of outriders on big Harley Davidsons revved up and surrounded us as we manoeuvred out of the UN complex.

'One way to beat the New York traffic,' murmured Mark.

With lights flashing and sirens blaring we sped down FDR Drive passing through Manhattan at lightening speed. Traffic sprayed out across the road as we weaved through it.

Mark's phone rang. 'Okay,' he said turning to me while activating the loudspeaker. 'It's the President, let's see what she's got to say,' I shook my head, this was surreal.

'Good Morning,' came the unmistakable voice, a deep contralto sounding very much in control.

'Good Morning Ma'am,' said Mark.

'Just to confirm you have my full backing for this operation, your decisions are my decisions. This is my direct line if you need help in any way, be it with Army bigwigs playing politics,

293

be it equipment requirements, be it whatever you phone. Understood?'

'Yes Ma'am.'

'Good luck,' the line went dead.

By now we were on the Brooklyn Bridge heading across the East River. After about fifteen minutes we pulled into Fort Hamilton. We were waved through by the military personnel at the gate and driven up to a nondescript office block where the car doors were opened and we were ushered inside. Everything was happening so quickly I hardly had a chance to take in my surroundings. Up some steps across to a lift with open doors and immediately we descended into the depths of the building. An armed soldier stood by the control panel. Everyone remained silent.

The doors opened and a uniformed girl stood waiting.

'Good Morning Gentlemen,' she said briskly, 'Follow me please.'

We walked down a corridor and through a door into an enormous room which looked like a cross between Mission Control at NASA and a call centre.

At the far end the wall was covered by a huge electronic map of the world with lights flashing across northern Africa and China. You didn't have to be a genius to work out what they signified. Dozens of army personnel sat at workstations glued to their screens, some tapping on keyboards feverishly. There was a real air of calm, the mood was almost serene.

We were taken to a central area with comfortable leather settees surrounding a low table.

'Please gentlemen sit,' said the uniformed girl as a mug of coffee was handed to me.

'This could be a long day' said Tom, 'I think we'll need all the caffeine we can get and a lot more.'

A five star general came up to us.

'How are you old friend,' he said to Mark shaking his hand vehemently.

'I'll tell you later' said Mark, 'Where are we at?'

'Nothing yet, we have men monitoring satellite pictures of each camp in Africa. Any sudden movements and we'll blow them sky high.

'China?'

'The bombs are all live. On my command we're ready.'

Mark nodded, 'And now we wait, and that's the worst part.'

I looked at my watch, it was 11.10, we had nearly two hours to kill unless the Chinese caved in immediately. *Unlikely* I thought.

Most of the staff were sitting at their workstations staring at monitors. Some were writing notes, others on the phone. Nobody looked flustered, in many ways it was just another day at the office.

Real pros I thought.

I wiled away some time looking at the news online. It was a bit of a none news day with celebrity gossip and silly stories taking the headlines. *That'll soon change* I thought.

Following two cups of coffee to stem the boredom I was beginning to slip into a comatose state when a deep calm voice boomed across a tannoy system.

'We have movement at complex two. Image on screen.'

The world map on the wall shrank and a satellite image appeared with the words Complex 2 - Zinder, Niger written underneath.

It took me a couple of seconds to make sense of the image. Initially, I saw blocks which were obviously buildings. I could then make out dozens of trucks moving out of the complex and as I looked a dozen or so rocket launchers could be seen clearly pivoting out of the ground.

By now the Five Star General was sitting on one of the settees next to Mark, opposite Tom and me. Wearing a telephone headset he spoke calmly. 'Hit it'. His voice could be heard across the tannoy system.

He didn't have to repeat himself, within seconds the image disappeared to be replaced by a cloud of dust mushrooming upwards.

'Watch those other complexes, closely.' Another voice boomed over the tannoy.

An air of excitement and fear hung over the room. There was an eerie silence as people sat glued to their screens saying nothing.

After an excruciating five minutes of silence a third voice was heard.

'Movement at Complex Seven.'

Another image appeared on the wall, with the words Complex 7 – Al Fashir, Sudan.

Again, rocket launchers were being raised from horizontal to vertical.

The five star general spoke in a relaxed but clear tone, 'Hit it'.

Again the image disappeared to be replaced by a cloud of dust.

Mark pressed a button on his headset.

'Secretary General could I ask you to inform the Chinese Ambassador that two of his sites in Africa have been destroyed due to the actions they took, demonstrating that a state of war is now in place.'

'Do we hit China now?' I asked.

'Not yet,' replied Mark.

In the nest twenty minutes three more complexes were destroyed, Bangul in the Central African Republic, Josan in Zambola and Faya Largeau in Chad.

Each time Mark informed the Secretary General of the UN.

On the third occasion Mark looked grim. 'The Chinese are now refusing to accept calls from the Secretary General.' The Five Star General nodded.

Suddenly the room was pitched into blackness. A couple of stifled grimaces were heard.

Someone shouted 'Switching to auxiliary power, calm please.'

After a couple of seconds emergency lighting kicked in giving the room a creepy luminescent glow.

'Computer backup system,' someone shouted.

'Negative.'

The screens remained blank.

'Emergency procedure.'

'Negative.'

'Communication.'

'Negative, all systems down.'

I looked at Mark and the Five Star General.

'Oh my God,' said Mark and for the first time ever I heard fear in his voice.

'Go on,' said the General.

'I fear we have been hit by something we didn't take into account.'

'Cyber Warfare' The General spoke, it wasn't a question, it was a statement of fact.

Mark went on 'We know the Chinese have been working on this. They've been taking their brightest students from universities all over the country to create a centre of excellence. That is a front for Cyber Warfare studies. The ultimate weapon, take out all the computer systems in the world and everybody is left powerless. We know they've taken out power stations and banks as a test. We believe they also attacked NASA and the FBI but we didn't think they were this advanced. The US have spent billions in this area but they aren't even close to what has been achieved here.

'It was obviously a two tier approach,' said the General, 'take out Africa and the Middle East using traditional methods and then bring the rest of the world to its knees using Cyber Warfare.'

I looked at Mark, 'Future strategies will also ensure America becomes a puppet state,' I said, 'It was in the report the Japanese found.'

'A brilliant strategy,' replied Mark sounding resigned.

A uniformed man in his thirties marched quickly up to the General saluted and spoke.

'Sir, Major Goldberg, Communications-Electronics Command. Using non computer technology we've established that the lights are out across the US. All systems appear to be down, from stop lights in the streets, power, communication, TV, machinery, even cars. It's what some people were expecting back in 2000 with the millennium bug. Only this time it's actually happening. We've been hit by something big sir.'

'And the rest of the world?'

'We're trying to establish that sir.'

'Keep me updated.'

The soldier saluted again and went back to his post.

'What happens now?' I asked.

'We wait.' The General replied. Sooner or later we'll be contacted with their proposals. And then God help us all.

Mark spoke, 'I'm afraid within hours the fabric of society as we know it will begin to decay. It'll start with looting and degenerate from there. We can put the National Guard out, but this is too big. We're finished, they've won.

An uncomfortable silence ensued. I sat looking at the blank screen of my 'O' phone. Along with everybody else I didn't have a clue what to do. I couldn't believe this was the end of the world as we knew it, yet, there was no way out.

An hour went by, I sat next to Tom with the General opposite. I've no idea where Mark went. There was no conversation, we were all deep in our own thoughts. I felt helpless and frustrated. I wondered whether I'd be able to get back to Switzerland, would I ever see Caterina or my parents again?

Major Goldberg marched back up to the General.

'Sir, we have the President on a non secure landline. You'll have to come over to our section to talk to her.

'Lead on,' barked the General.

Mark appeared from nowhere and signalled for Tom and me to follow.

'Yes Ma'am understood,' was all we heard.

The General turned and in a loud voice said.

'The President has just conceded defeat to China. I'm afraid modern warfare is quick and brutal. It's over guys, I'm sorry.'

Chapter 31

Not knowing what to do I went back to where I'd been sitting. People were milling around looking at each other and saying very little.

A junior commander spoke, 'Guys if you want to go up and get some fresh air feel free, there's nothing we can do here.'

I decided to leave it for a while. I knew there would be a lot of stairs to climb with many people trying to get out at the same time. The lift was useless along with everything else.

Sitting feeling sorry for myself I felt bitter. Everything I had done in recent months had proved to be a complete waste of time. We'd achieved nothing and been out manoeuvred. The might of the West together with help from the Triads had failed and the world as we knew it would never be the same again. I could hardly believe it, I felt physically sick.

Suddenly the lights came back on. The world map flickered into life on the wall and as one everybody ran back to their workstations.

'We have full power.' the deep rich brown voice resonated across the tannoy, 'Gentlemen, we're back in business.'

The General appeared from God knows where, 'Nuke the bastards he screamed at the top of his voice as someone ran up to him with a headset.

'Retract that order,' he said calmly, 'hit all African complexes. I repeat hit all African complexes.

'Complex one destroyed.'

'Complex eight destroyed.'

'Complex eleven destroyed.'

Within a minute all the complexes in Africa had been hit.

'Okay.' said the General, blow the first nuke in China.'

He turned to Mark, 'Tell the Secretary General we've destroyed the bases in Africa, the bombs will be detonated every ten minutes in China getting closer and closer to major conurbations. Within two hours we'll blow six major cities unless they pull back from Africa and relinquish all nuclear weapons.'

Mark nodded, his 'O' phone was back in action. He dialled and spoke for just a few seconds.

A minute later his phone rang.

'Secretary General?' Listening intently a wry smile crossed his face. 'Thank you.'

He turned to us, 'This time the Chinese Ambassador picked up. He is relaying our message on to his government.'

My phone rang. It was Joe Lin.

''Hi Joe,' I said, 'Not a good time to talk right now.'

'Been having a few communication problems I hear,' he said laughing.

'Tell me more.'

'You remember Meihui confirmed through her own sources that the Chinese were to invade Africa.'

'Yes,' I replied guardedly.

'I'll be honest with you, we've known about Chinese plans with regard to Cyber warfare for many years. We realised we could use this technology as a business tool. We've had our own people working on their Cyber Warfare programme virtually since its inception. Most of our guys joined as smart graduate trainees straight out of universities from around the country. Meihui was able to confirm through these people exactly what China's plans were with regard to Africa. Their reports corresponded with yours.'

'Go on' I said.

'Unbeknown to the Chinese government we have built safeguards into the programming so that we could pull the plug at any time should they decide to do anything stupid. You're aware that Chinese systems aren't that secure and often programming is sloppy. It wasn't difficult to do this undetected. Today we were able to apply those safeguards. It's a good job we did otherwise by now the US President would be signing an armistice. Once confirmation reached my people that the Chinese had brought the Western World to its knees the order was given to destroy the programming. As we did the lights came back on in America. I think the English expression is "we saved your bacon".

'Why?' I asked.

'The approach of the current State Council of the Chinese Peoples Republic of China is not conducive to business. It's that simple.'

'I can't really understand why they didn't just knock out America before taking control of Africa.'

'They weren't ready. The programme used today had not been tested in any way. It was still very much in the development phase. Under normal circumstances there would have been many months of trials and assessments before they tried to use it. However you gave them little choice, they were desperate. It was I believe what you call a shit or bust scenario. Much to everybody's surprise the programme worked. My people were astonished but were able to take the appropriate action.'

'So now what?'

'You carry on with your bombing programme and within a few hours the current leaders will retire and a new pragmatic government will be formed. They will be more sympathetic to the Western way of life. That way you win, we win and so do the ordinary people of China.'

'Can you guarantee this?'

'It will happen.'

'And then?'

'Life goes on for you and for us. Hopefully our paths will not have to cross again.'

'I'm not sure if I should say thank you as I can't say I approve of the way you do business. However on a personal level I'm glad we met.'

'Likewise, and all the best for the future.'

The line went dead. The General, Mark and Tom were looking at me.

I relayed the conversation.

'My God,' said Mark, 'So the Triads saved the western world.'

'My enemy's enemy is my friend' I replied.

An hour later we got the call from the Secretary General of the UN. The Chinese government had fallen, the new leaders agreed to pull out of Africa and forget any plans for world domination.

'Peace in our time.' said the General sarcastically.

'It's as close as we are going to get' replied Mark, 'And the alternative doesn't bare thinking about.'

I phoned Caterina and updated her.

'We were that close,' I said.

'That is terrifying, and who knows it may happen again.'

'Hopefully next time we'll be ready rather than having to work with the Triads.'

'So now what?' she asked.

'I've been thinking about that,' I said, smiling for the first time that day. 'There's a little country in Africa that needs a bit of help and support. How about you and me lending a hand?'

I could hear her crying, they were tears of joy. After what seemed like an eternity she spoke. They were the words I'd longed for and prayed for:

'When's the next flight?'

ABOUT THE AUTHOR

Having survived the perils of the commercial world for 33 years Barrie started writing as a cathartic response to being put on the scrap heap by his employers. Realising that if writing was to become a second career he decided to learn about the craft and joined his local writers group. They have been inspirational in turning whatever talent he has into some semblance of order!

Barrie lives in Bedfordshire with his wife Suzanne and a scruffy mutt called Kate. His two children Luke and Rachel have supposedly flown the nest but reappear on a regular basis. Barrie needs to sell a lot of books to keep them all in the manner to which they'd like to become accustomed.

Due to lack of talent Barrie failed as a rock star but for nine years presented 'The 70s Album Show' on BBC local radio.

His first novel 'A Higher Authority' was published in 2014 and he is currently working on the third book in the series.

Made in the USA
Columbia, SC
05 October 2017